MAVERICK
LOVERS

FRIENDSHIP CHRONICLES 6

SHELLEY MUNRO

MUNRO PRESS

Maverick Lovers

Copyright © 2023 by Shelley Munro

Print ISBN: 978-1-99-106337-3
Digital ISBN: 978-0-473-50272-0

Editor: Evil Eye Editing

Cover: Kim Killion, The Killion Group, Inc.

Munro Press, New Zealand.

First Munro Press electronic publication January 2020

First Munro Press print publication October 2023

DEDICATION

For Paul, my partner in crime and fellow adventurer.

"Twenty years from now you will be more disappointed by
the things you didn't do than by the ones you did do.
So throw off the bowlines, sail away from the safe harbor.
Catch the trade winds in your sails.
Explore. Dream. Discover." – Mark Twain

INTRODUCTION

MAVERICK: [NOUN] AN INDEPENDENT person who has ideas or behavior that differs from the norm. Someone brave and impulsive who attacks life their way.

Finding and satisfying one lover is difficult...

Adding a second to the equation is an impossible challenge

Christina: her life is spiraling out of control. Her job, her friends, and her family relationships are slipping through her fingers, leaving her achingly alone and staring into the eyes of the black dog of depression. She claws her way free, and finally, a bright spot—she reconnects with a childhood friend. Not a boyfriend, but wow! That's the way her mind is marching now, straight to Mr. Sexy Pants.

Gabriel: he's seeing the success he's worked for after his parents kicked him from their home for something he didn't do. Christina's arrival makes him happy, makes him consider a future, a family, then Aidan arrives home. Off-balance because he has feelings for each of them, Gabriel screws up both relationships. Go him!

Aidan: Tired of traveling and clawing his way to the top, he's come home to claim Gabriel, the man he has always loved. The only problem—while Aidan was running away, Gabriel has moved on with his life. Prepared to fight, he can't hate the gorgeous yet troubled Christina as much as he wants.

Three lost lovers battle their way to a committed relationship that shouldn't be possible but has the potential to cement them into a solid and unconventional team.

1

A Hasty Trip to Waiheke Island

CHRISTINA SET HER WINEGLASS on the pub table and let memories wash over her. She, Maggie, Connor, Julia, and Susan used to meet here after work. Only two years ago, yet so much had changed. *So much*. Maggie and Connor had wed. Julia managed a successful burlesque club and had a famous musician husband, while Susan had met and married a farmer-turned-artist. Each of her friends lived in Auckland, but they had busy lives with young families. Getting together had become a logistical nightmare.

Christina understood.

She did.

She loved her friends, yet sometimes, she felt as if they'd left her behind.

Maggie, Connor, and Julia had canceled earlier in the day, but Susan was still coming.

On cue, her phone rang. "Hey, Susan. I—"

"Christina, I'm so sorry. The kids have been sick and off school this week, and I've caught their bugs." A loud sneeze punctuated her nasal words. "I'll have to cancel. I don't want to spread my germs."

Annoyance flashed through Christina, but she quickly quashed her uncharitable thoughts. Susan sounded miserable. "Don't be silly. You sound exhausted. Get yourself to bed. Next time, okay?"

"S-sorry." Susan sneezed again. She sniffed. "Say hi to the others for me."

"Will do." Christina forced her tone to remain even. "I'll ring you next week. Take care."

"Thanks." Susan hung up mid-sneeze.

Christina set her phone on the table beside her glass of wine. Tears stung her eyes, and she swallowed hard, her throat tight. *Self-pity*. A bad precedent. Her friends weren't trying to hurt her. Each had excellent reasons for canceling this reunion meeting. And it wasn't their fault her business wasn't going well because of an economic downturn. That was on her.

Her life.

Her problem to fix.

Yet none of her rational thoughts stemmed the traitorous tears that spilled free and ran down her cheeks.

She reached for her wine and took a huge sip. A sob escaped, and she set down the glass with a trembling hand. Alcohol wasn't the answer either. She was drinking too much. Acting sorry for herself, and falling into a crumbling, dark pit.

Christina swallowed hard, the blackness reaching for her. She needed to talk to someone—lay out her fears. Her problems. She'd counted on her friends...

A fresh surge of tears blurred her vision, and she fumbled in her handbag for a tissue.

"Boyfriend stood you up, sweet thing?"

Her head jerked up, and she bared her teeth at the smirking businessman. "Piss off!"

"Whoa, no need for attitude. I was trying to be nice. You know, you'd be pretty without the glasses." He leaned closer as if in concern, but he couldn't hide his smug confidence. "Revenge fucks are the best way to repair a broken heart."

Ew! Enraged, Christina surged to her feet, the force of her anger knocking over her glass. The wine splattered across the table and sprayed over the businessman. That killed his smirk.

He sprang away from her table, swiping at the wet patch on his thigh. "Bitch."

Christina didn't bother replying. She snatched up her handbag and stormed from the pub. Her determined steps took her along the waterfront and over the footbridge to the bars and restaurants at the Wynyard Quarter. She kept walking and walking, her pace brisk as she dodged between men and women ending their workday with a drink or an early dinner. Not yet six, the day hovered at dusk. Lights cast a sparkle over the city of Auckland, and the promise of spring filled the air.

Her steps slowed as her breathing settled to something resembling normal. Her phone rang again, and she stopped to answer. A glance at the screen told her it was her mother.

"Hi, Mum. All packed for the big trip?"

"I finished my packing last week. Your father, however, is still dithering over which shirts to take."

Her mother's exasperated tone lightened Christina's funk and pulled forth a faint smile. "That's Dad. Always doing things at the last moment."

"Yes." Her mother sniffed. "Why I rang—Bernice has the flu. I spoke to her a few days ago and promised to visit. Time got away on me. Could you check on her? I know you were meeting your friends tonight, but do you have time?"

"Sure," Christina said. "But that means I can't see you off at the airport tomorrow morning."

"You wished us a happy journey on Sunday when you came to lunch," her mother said. "It'd reduce my stress levels if you visited Bernice."

Maybe a trip to Waiheke Island and Bernice was the

thing to improve her mood. She'd been meaning to visit her godmother for ages. "I'll pack an overnight bag and catch a ferry over tonight."

Two hours later, Christina strode onto the Waiheke ferry. An assortment of other passengers boarded with her—workers heading home from the city, tourists, a family group with their dog, and men and women carrying shopping bags. After packing, Christina had stopped at her local supermarket and purchased fruit, vegetables, and a few other supplies, including a packet of biscuits for Toby, her godmother's dog.

Darkness had set in by the time she disembarked on Waiheke and caught the bus that would take her past her godmother's. She'd rung Bernice to let her know she was coming and left a message when she didn't get an answer.

Another twenty minutes passed, and Christina walked up the pathway leading to the front door of her godmother's cottage. The outside security light lit the garden, and Christina's brows drew together when she spotted the unkempt lawn and myriad weeds. Oh, well. Plenty to keep her busy. She wouldn't have time to mull and stay aboard the woe-is-me train.

She tapped on the door and turned the knob, not surprised to find it unlocked. Christina stepped inside to the bark of a dog.

"Toby," she called. "It's just me." A regular visitor during her teenage years, she'd often stayed with her godmother—a family friend—during her school holidays. Once she'd started working, the visits had become less frequent, but she still popped over at least three or four times a year. She set her overnight bag in the passage and dropped her bags of shopping onto the kitchen counter. "Bernice! Are you here?"

Christina walked toward Toby's barking and entered Bernice's bedroom. A sour smell filled the air—the stench of vomit—and a wash of unpleasant heat struck her as she stepped closer to the bed.

"Chris?" Her godmother's eyes fluttered open, her face pale and waxy in the moonlight.

"Bernice!" Christina darted across the remaining distance and placed her hand on her godmother's forehead. "You're burning up."

"It's the stupid flu."

"How long have you been sick?"

"Monday," Bernice's brow furrowed. "I think. It's Wednesday today, isn't it?"

It was Friday. "Let's get you cleaned up." Christina's brow creased as she cracked open a window. Her shoe skidded on something wet and suspicious. "Let me turn on the bedside lamp."

The increased illumination let her know the worst. Bernice had been too ill to get out of bed to let Toby, her Jack Russell outside. A scan of the dog's white ribs suggested she hadn't fed him either.

"I'll be back in a sec. Come, Toby." Christina snapped her fingers. In the kitchen, she filled Toby's water bowl and found a can of dog food in the pantry. She propped open the kitchen door that led outside, so Toby could wander in the garden when he was ready.

Next, she tackled her godmother. Christina gave her a glass of water and sat Bernice on a comfy chair positioned near the bay window while she stripped the bed, mopped up two Toby puddles, and removed and emptied a vomit bucket.

After giving her godmother a quick wash and changing her nightgown, she settled her back in bed. "Have you seen the doctor?"

"I've only been sick for two days," her godmother grumbled. "It's the flu. I'll be fine."

"It's Friday today."

"Friday?"

"Yes." *Doctor, tomorrow.* Thankfully, she'd met the local doctor several times, and he'd do a house call in these circumstances, even at the weekend. "Could you manage some soup?"

Bernice shuddered. "No."

"Symptoms? Do you have a headache? Aches and pains?"

"Yes."

"All right. I'll bring you painkillers."

"Thank you, dear."

But when Christina returned with the water, Bernice was asleep. Christina closed the window again, not wanting her godmother to wake up cold during the night. Toby followed Christina to the kitchen and nosed his bowl, his brown ears perking at her. She refilled his water bowl and opened the packet of dog biscuits she'd brought with her. Toby smelled as bad as the sickroom. Despite the late hour, she washed Toby and toweled him dry until his brown-and-white coat started to gleam. She settled him in his basket, checked on Bernice, and made up a bed in the spare room. Exhausted, she slid between the sheets and didn't wake until Toby nudged her with his wet nose.

"Toby?"

When Toby nudged her again, Christina glanced at her watch and bolted upright. Nine o'clock. She jumped out of bed and hustled to check on Bernice. She was asleep but still had a temperature. Christina rang the doctor.

"She needs to go to Auckland Hospital," the doctor stated, five minutes after his arrival. "She requires further treatment, more than we can give her here. A drip, for instance."

Christina checked her watch. Her parents would be in the air now.

"I'll call the helicopter to fly her to Auckland," the doctor said.

"Her illness is that serious?"

"Christina, don't make me go." Her godmother

sounded tearful. "I'd prefer to stay at home."

"Bernice, it will be okay. Doctor, she'll only be there for a couple of days, right?"

"Five days at the most. This bout of flu has done a number on you, Bernice. It will take time to regain your strength."

"What about Toby and the cottage?" Bernice fretted.

"I'm here," Christina said. "I'll look after both for you. Let me see if I can come to the hospital with you. I can catch the ferry back and stay until you're on the mend."

"Promise." Bernice grasped her hands, her grip surprisingly tight given the seriousness of her pneumonia. "Promise you'll stay and look after things for me."

"I promise," Christina said.

When it turned out there wasn't room for Christina on the helicopter since a pregnant woman needed transport too, she assured her godmother she'd be over to check on her in the afternoon.

As soon as the ambulance left to take her godmother to the helipad, Christina opened the windows to air the bedroom and took Toby for a walk.

The Fletchers were her godmother's nearest neighbors, and she walked in that direction, enjoying the solitude and the windless, sunny day after weeks of rain. Toby raced along the grass verge, sniffing and investigating the enticing smells.

A plaintive bleat grabbed her attention, and she grinned

at a goat and two tiny kids. The Fletchers had farmed cattle, but it appeared they'd diversified as many farmers had these days. Christina rambled aimlessly while she planned her day. She'd check on visiting hours at the hospital and catch an afternoon ferry. She could stay with her godmother for a few hours.

A whistle sounded, and Toby sprinted away. Alarmed, Christina hustled after the Jack Russell.

"Thought you were Bernice." The tall man with a broad chest, highlighted by his clinging and faded T-shirt, pulled a chord in her memory. A flannel shirt covered his arms, but she'd bet they were as sexy and muscled as the rest of him.

"Gabriel?" Christina asked in surprise, pushing her glasses up her nose to focus better. *Wow*. His jeans were faded in interesting places and did nothing to hide his powerful thighs and long legs.

The man scrutinized her then, his brown eyes sparkling in recognition. Messy brown hair, just past the cut-now stage curled low on his neck and over his ears while his jaw held the stubble of several days. "Christina! Are you here visiting Bernice?"

"Yes, except she's not well. The doctor sent her off to the hospital."

Gabriel straightened to his full height. He'd starred in her teenage dreams, and with maturity, he was even more attractive since he'd grown into his lanky limbs. His tan spoke of days working in the sun. Even his hair held glints of sun-kissed gold. His brow crinkled in concern. "She'll be okay?"

"I'll know more once I get to the hospital," Christina said.

"Should've checked on her," Gabriel said with regret. "Saw her last weekend, but I've been busy this week with the cows calving."

"Do your grandparents still have cattle?"

"These are my cows. I own the land bordering Bernice's cottage. Run a hundred head of cows and a herd of goats. I make cheese." He spoke with pride, his gaze attaching to hers in a faint challenge.

"That's so cool," Christina said. "Cheese-making is the perfect occupation, given there are so many vineyards on the island. Each time I visit, I'm surprised at the new businesses making gourmet food. I adore wandering the market and tasting the different produce."

"I have a stall there when I can manage it," Gabriel said. "One-man band. Can't always attend if another more important job crops up."

"I'll be here for a while because I promised Bernice I'd look after Toby and her cottage. Bernice will be home soon, and I'll be watching her to make sure she recuperates."

"What about your job?"

Christina recoiled, although she was certain Gabriel

hadn't meant the question as a dig at her. The pause lengthened, and she blurted out the truth. "I started a business, working as a personal shopper, and doing makeovers for school leavers and businesswomen. Things were going well until the turndown in the economy. Business is slow at present." She shrugged, stopping her explanation before she added another truth she hadn't yet faced. Business hadn't slowed to a trickle. It had dried up after another younger and more flamboyant woman had used her marketing smarts to annihilate Christina's business.

"Bernice said you were working in an accountant's office."

"I was, but I handed in my notice a year ago. My business exploded, so I took it full-time. In hindsight, I should've waited."

"I sell cheese at the gate. Have plenty of customers but can't give them my focus because of the cattle and goats, overseeing my cheese production, the other things in my day. Don't suppose you'd be willing to work in my shop for a few hours each day? Can't pay you much, but—"

Christina beamed and took half a step toward him, intending to squeeze him in a hug of gratitude before she reconsidered. Although they'd been best of friends as teenagers, and they'd shared a first kiss, she hesitated. "Are you married?" Christina gulped. *Great going!*

"No," he said. "Work long hours, and women hate that.

No girlfriend. No wife." A glint of humor flashed in his eyes. "You?"

She shook her head and sighed for good measure. "Nope. No entanglements."

"Why not?" Gabriel closed the distance between them and reached out to smooth a lock of hair behind her ear.

The casual gesture—an action from the past that brought a host of memories—had tears stinging her eyes.

"Aw, hell. I've upset you."

Christina gripped his shoulders, drawing him nearer and grabbing his full attention. "No, you haven't offended me. I've been down. Everything sets me off." She drew in a shuddering breath. "I haven't met a man to compare with you or with my friends' husbands. And on that note, I'd better hustle." She paused. "Depends on what happens with Bernice, but I might have to stay in the city tonight. If I can't get back, could you feed Toby for me and give him a run?"

"Why don't I take Toby with me now?" he suggested. "You can collect him when you get back tonight or tomorrow. Toby is used to my dogs. I've looked after him before for Bernice." He pulled out a cell phone. "What's your phone number?"

"That's a great idea. Thank you." Christina rattled off her number.

Gabriel input it, tapped a few more keys and slid his phone back into his pocket. "I've sent you a text, so you'll have my number too." He whistled, and two exuberant Border Collies bounded from the undergrowth. "If I don't answer the phone, leave a message, or text me. I'll make sure I check. I'm turning cheeses this afternoon, so I should hear my phone if you call."

"Thanks."

"Not necessary. Bernice has always spoiled me. This is the least I can do."

Christina understood this sentiment since Bernice had always been her champion too. She raised her right hand in farewell and turned for the cottage. Ten steps into her homeward journey, she gave in to the instinct to glance over her shoulder. She discovered he was staring. At her backside. Heat rushed into her cheeks when he winked. She gasped and turned back before she stumbled and made an ass out of herself. His soft chuckle carried on the wind, propelling her feet to greater speed.

The dark edges of her thoughts had faded while speaking with Gabriel, and it was with greater confidence that she marched to the cottage. Bernice was in good hands. A hospital stay would sort out her godmother and offer Christina time to make plans. Time to get her life back on track and to halt this slippery slide into wretchedness and misery before it became too late.

As she wiped her feet and entered the cottage, the landline phone started ringing.

"Hello," Christina said.

"Am I speaking to Christina Kingston?" a mature feminine voice asked.

"Yes, I'm Christina."

"Normally, we'd do this in person, but I understand you live on Waiheke Island."

A chill ran down Christina's spine. "Yes."

"I am head of ward six," the woman said. "My name is Muriel Teesdale. I'm afraid I have some bad news."

2

OLD FRIENDS, NEW PROBLEMS

GABRIEL FLETCHER WATCHED CHRISTINA'S departure with pleasure—the sway of her hips beneath the pair of tight black jeans. The bounce of her loose curls against her back. The faint jangle of her golden bracelets. She was much as he remembered. Physically, at least, although her curves were more defined in this adult version.

He whistled his dogs, pausing until Toby followed, and headed out to check on his cows and calves. Unwillingly, his thoughts slipped to the past.

Lost opportunities.

Things had changed once Christina attended university to study accountancy and marketing. Although Bernice had mentioned Christina visited several times a year or they saw each other when Bernice traveled to Auckland, he hadn't seen Christina since her eighteenth birthday.

His life was different. The big flare-up had occurred the following week that turned his world upside down. If it hadn't been for his grandparents...

He owed them so much.

Aidan too.

With an irritable huff, he turned his mind to cheese. After purchasing twenty more cows and paying for a vet when one of his cows had trouble calving, his budget was tight this month. Still, he knew from experience if he attended the market each week and opened his farm store for regular hours, the income would more than offset a part-time wage. Freeing up his time meant he could up his cheese production. Selfishly, he hoped Christina stayed for several months.

His phone announced a text. *Bernice's health has deteriorated. Will stay in Auckland overnight.*

Gabriel pushed out a sigh and fired off a text to his grandmother. She'd kick herself, as had he, for not checking on Bernice. His mind drifted back to Christina, and he wished he had time to visit the city to support her. Bloody mortgage. Still, he'd be with her in spirit and offer prayers for Bernice's steady recovery.

Then, as he always did, Gabriel buried himself in his work. His way of pushing aside weighty matters he didn't want to deal with. He knew what he was doing but continued marching along the same track. Routine and following a proven path had kept him sane when his world had imploded. No reason for the strategy to fail him now.

AROUND HALFWAY THROUGH THE forty-minute ferry ride to the city, Christina's phone rang. She scowled at the number.

"Christina speaking," she said.

"Good morning, Miss Kingston. I'm calling about your agreement with my rental company."

"Mr. Singh?" she asked.

"Yes, the building is old with a multitude of problems, and I have decided to demolish the entire block and replace it with more upscale apartments."

"When?" Christina's stomach did an alarming roil. Her apartment suited her, although the rent pushed the boundaries of her budget since she hadn't replaced Susan once her friend had moved in with Tyler.

"First of next month. I know this is short notice, but I intend to offer an incentive to my tenants. I will refund the rent you have paid in advance and your tenancy bond, plus I will give you a one-off payment of one thousand dollars if you agree to vacate by the first of October."

"But that's two weeks from now."

"Yes, I realize this, but I require your decision by the end of the week."

"And if I don't agree?" Christina asked in a faint voice.

"All my tenants pay their rent one week in advance, and my lawyers tell me, I can give you a week's notice to vacate. I am offering you two weeks plus an incentive. You will find the paperwork in your mailbox."

"But—" Tears once again blurred her vision, and her throat tightened. Nothing was going her way this year. *Today.* What with the hospital calling to tell her of the flu complications and her godmother's heart damage and now this bombshell.

"My decision is final," Mr. Singh stated, his tone implacable. "Good day, Miss Kingston."

The firm click sounded in her ear as the ferry backed into its mooring at the city wharf. Numb, Christina shoved her phone into her handbag. Another problem to solve. Finding accommodation in Auckland was bad enough. An apartment or flat to fit her budget would be nigh on impossible.

She caught the inner link bus to Auckland Hospital and found her way to her godmother's ward, after backtracking and asking once for directions. Bernice was asleep when she entered, appearing frail and old. A drip ran from her arm while her breathing was slow and raspy. A spike of fear shot through Christina. She'd never seen Bernice so vulnerable, and the even *beep-beep-beep* of the heart monitor underscored her fragility.

Christina crept to the visitor's chair next to the bed and sat. Usually, she toted around a portable handicraft project, but in her haste to catch the ferry, she'd left her half-made scarf sitting on the bedside table in her godmother's spare bedroom. She passed five minutes by studying her surroundings. Her aunt's chart at the end of the bed and the hand sanitizer unit on the wall. A box of disposable gloves. The small hand basin and the door leading to the patient bathroom.

Seeking further diversion, Christina rifled through her handbag, and she pulled out a notebook and a pen. No time like the present for soul-searching and considering her future, such as it was.

1. Find a new apartment.

2. Decide whether to continue with the business.

3. Find a job?

4. What do I want to do?

5. Contact Mum and Dad about Bernice.

She scowled at her list because not one of the numbered items held an easy answer. Even contacting her parents held pitfalls. Her mother had talked about this holiday for months. Her parents had scrimped and saved, and telling them of Bernice's illness would cause problems. She wanted her parents to enjoy this vacation.

"Christina?"

Her godmother's breathy voice had Christina jerking up her head and her pulse darting into a one-hundred-meter dash. "You scared me. How are you feeling?"

"Tired," Bernice said.

"A case of the flu will do that. Add in complications like pneumonia, and you end up in the hospital."

"Don't tell your parents I'm not well. Both June and Edward have planned their retirement trip for so long. Promise me." She spoiled her demand with a round of coughing, and Christina jumped up to hand her tissues.

"You're using your illness to make me behave," Christina said. "You have me minding your cottage and walking Toby, and now you're suggesting I fib to my parents."

Bernice coughed once more, her shoulders shuddering as she wheezed and spluttered. Once the spasms faded, she wiped her mouth. "Your parents returning home wouldn't make my illness fade. I want them to enjoy their time overseas and make memories."

"And if Mum asks how you are?"

"T-tell her, I'm recovering from the flu. Tell her you're looking after Toby and me. None of those things are lies."

"True." Christina could see arguing was distressing

Bernice. "My landlord rang me earlier. He's kicking the tenants out so he can demolish the apartment block and build luxury units."

"Stay with me at the cottage," Bernice croaked.

"I'm happy to stay while you recuperate, but after that, job hunting is my focus." Christina sighed, letting her unhappiness free in that brisk exhalation.

"What about your business? You were so excited and happy to be doing something you loved."

"I still love it, but my success drew others into the market. Now, with the economy the way it is, people aren't spending on luxuries. I met Gabriel this morning. He offered me a part-time job selling his cheese."

"Gabriel is a good boy. Work for him. Sell some of your handicrafts. You have boxes of scarves you've made and not worn. June complained about the space they're taking up in her spare room." Bernice coughed again and didn't speak for several minutes.

Her harsh breaths were unnerving and scary.

"I'm tiring you. The nurses will chase me away." Christina rose and neared the hospital bed. She brushed wisps of steel-gray hair off her godmother's forehead before bending to kiss her brow. "Is there anything you need? I didn't think to bring you clean nightgowns. I can bring one or two things for you tomorrow."

"Chris-tina." Bernice grabbed for her hands. "I-I..." She trailed off and gasped a breath. Her chest rattled, and it was long seconds before she attempted to speak. "I love you. Like a daughter."

Her words became a whisper, and Christina leaned forward to better hear.

"B-believe in you."

"Shush, no more talking. Sleep."

"W-wait. Cottage yours. Stay. Please." Bernice's face grew paler, the strain on her features betraying her agitation. The beep of the machine changed to erratic.

"Thank you," Christina murmured. "I'll stay for as long as you need me."

Bernice caught her gaze and held it. She clasped Christina's hands with a strength that belied her brittle appearance. "Promise."

"Cross my heart," Christina whispered, fighting not to cry in front of her godmother. She loved this woman so much. Bernice and her mother had attended boarding school together, been attendants at each other's weddings. Bernice had been alone since her soldier husband died in service, and she had never remarried. Never had children, but she'd showered Christina with love and taught her to knit and crochet and embroider. She'd taught her to sew and passed on her love of fashion and makeup. While other teenage girls had bemoaned their mothers, Christina had cherished the fact she had two standing in her corner.

A nurse appeared in the doorway, her gaze going to the monitor by the bed. "Time for a rest."

"I'll visit you tomorrow afternoon. You pay attention to the nurses and rest." Maintaining a cheerful persona tasked Christina when the truth bubbled in her mind. Damage to her godmother's heart. Recovery would take months and going forward, Bernice would never be as strong. She kissed her godmother's cheek. "I'll bring you some of your things tomorrow when I visit."

With her fake smile intact, Christina speed-walked from the hospital room before her tears started falling. She made it. Just. She marched past the busy nurses' station and pushed through the double-doors that defended the ward. Outside, the bland corridor turned blurry, and she almost plowed into a striding doctor. His stethoscope dug into her breasts as he gripped her forearms and saved them from falling.

"S-sorry," she gasped, her cheeks fiery hot. A pretty crier, she was not, and she hated to imagine her appearance.

"Are you all right?" He was young—younger than her—and he looked like the studly boy from next door. She'd bet he was popular with the nurses.

"I will be," Christina said. "I... Thank you."

He smiled at her, a blast of white teeth and dimples and sparkling blue eyes. "No problem."

Christina found her lips curling in response until she glimpsed an eye roll from the female doctor accompanying him. "Once again, I'm sorry. I'll let you get back to work." Sidestepping the pair of doctors, she continued down the corridor, eager to escape the sterile walls and the scent peculiar to hospitals. Disinfectant. A hint of hand sanitizer. A whiff of flowers. Body smells. Christina shuddered and thumped the call button for the elevator.

She loathed seeing her godmother this way. Part of her wanted to tell her parents, but Bernice was right. Christina hated to spoil their long-awaited vacation. She fumbled for a tissue and blotted her eyes.

She'd use her list to keep her focused and provide her with a sense of control when everything in her life ran off the rails and crashed. Her list offered her direction. She sucked in a deep breath, held it for four seconds, and pushed it out. After repeating her deep breathing five times, she formed a plan: collect the paperwork from her apartment. Really, when she thought about her apartment, she had one option, and that was to sign the papers, take the incentive and move on. The rent had drained her meager savings, and this decision mitigated the problem.

By the time Christina arrived at the harbor terminal, she walked taller because she'd made decisions and acted. She'd wrestled for control, and despite the hollow sensation in her chest, had pinned on a smile. Christina juggled her suitcase to her other hand, straightened her shoulders, and stalked onto the ferry. The depression crept after her, but she ignored the beast, satisfied to have a plan and a way forward through her messy life.

ACCORDING TO THE DOCTOR, her godmother passed away at 12:07. Her heart, he'd explained. Now, five days later, with the formalities taken care of, numbness had set in, sinking deep in her bones. She'd contacted her parents, told them Bernice had expected them to continue their holiday. Her mother had spoken of returning until Christina had told her not to be silly. Did she want Bernice to haunt her? Her mother had laughed then, wryly agreeing her friend was capable of this feat.

Now she sat in a lawyer's office in Oneroa, the largest town on Waiheke Island, waiting and so glad of the blissful silence. The constant stream of visitors and friends and neighbors had kept her busy, but now, she ached for solitude.

"Miss Kingston?" A tall, slender man with a receding hairline and a friendly smile stood before her.

Christina started. "Yes. Sorry, I was miles away."

"Understandable," he said. "I admired Bernice. She was a fine lady, and I'll miss meeting her at the various island functions we hold to amuse ourselves. Come into my office. Can I get you a cup of tea? I'm having one with chocolate biscuits."

"You wish," said the elderly receptionist.

The lawyer winked at her and ushered Christina to

his office. "She never lets me have chocolate biscuits. Says they're bad for my waistline." He patted his flat belly. The man didn't need a suit to hide the evidence of overindulgent business lunches.

"I'm Henry Wainscoat." He shook her hand and ushered her to one of the two upright chairs that sat before his desk.

The secretary bustled into the office, bearing a tray with a teapot, two cups, a jug of milk, and a tiny bowl of sugar lumps. Christina smiled at spotting the biscuits. Not chocolate ones, but shortbread. She poured a cup of tea to Christina's specifications and one for her boss before leaving and shutting the door after her.

"Now, I know you're curious, but we'll get the formalities over and done with first. Did you bring your ID with you?"

Christina handed over her passport and sipped her tea while she waited.

"Right. Bernice's will is straightforward. She has left her cottage and everything she owns to you. There are conditions you must fulfill, however. You must live in the cottage for the next six months. You must look after Bernice's dog, Toby. And the final condition, you must embrace life here on Waiheke Island." The lawyer paused.

Christina stared at him, nonplussed by the conditions, by all of this. She hadn't expected… "I thought Bernice would leave her cottage to her family. I know she has a niece and a nephew in Christchurch."

"She appreciated your regular visits and informed me you were the daughter of her heart."

Christina blinked hard. She'd done enough crying over the last few days. She sipped her tea and swallowed. "I'd already told Bernice I'd oversee Toby and look after the cottage."

"And I presume you'll continue to do that?"

"Of course," Christina murmured. At least it meant she'd have somewhere to live until she started work on that stubborn list of hers.

"The third condition that you must immerse yourself in Waiheke needn't be an onerous one. We have a thriving theater, art gallery exhibitions, concerts, and other civil events throughout the year, such as fun runs, movie nights, and fireworks displays. Our weekly market attracts visitors, and the various wineries are always holding different events. Pick several activities that interest you and take part."

"Why has Bernice made this a condition?"

"She didn't tell me, and I didn't ask for explanations."

"How will I know when I've achieved or failed?"

"Bernice appointed me to judge and decide if you meet the conditions of the will. She told me since I involved myself in the community, I'd be in the perfect position to determine if you followed instructions. With that in mind, and because I understand you haven't spent a lot of time here, I asked my secretary to collect information regarding upcoming events. She also passed along a tip, which I shall pass on to you. Bernice said Gabriel would be the perfect partner-in-crime, and you'd be doing him a favor if you dragged him out of his workaholic state." The lawyer's eyes twinkled as if he were enjoying a joke. "I understand you met Gabriel when you were both teenagers."

"Yes," Christina said, still dazed by this turn of events.

"Now that I've explained the conditions of Bernice's will, can you please sign here and here?" He indicated two spots on two different documents. "They're to confirm you're aware of the conditions and accept them. Once you sign this one, the clock starts ticking."

"Wait, you didn't tell me what would happen if I fail to meet my godmother's criteria to your satisfaction."

"In that case, I will sell the cottage, along with all of Bernice's possessions. I will split the money between you and Bernice's niece and nephew. Your share will be ten thousand dollars."

Christina scrunched her brow as she concentrated on reading the two documents. Her brain refused to focus, confusion, and doubt, and sadness fighting for supremacy. When the words turned into a blur, she scrawled her signature and repeated the action on the second legal document.

"Excellent. This folder contains details of activities and upcoming events on the island along with full particulars of everything I've told you today." He pushed a green folder across the desk. "Do you have questions?"

"No."

"Very well. If anything occurs to you later, please call. My business card is in the folder. No doubt, I'll see you around the island. On 1 April, next year, I'll contact you, and we will ascertain whether you've fulfilled your godmother's conditions."

"Thank you, Mr. Wainscoat." Christina picked up the green folder and rose.

"Call me, Henry, my dear. Don't forget, if you have any questions, do not hesitate to contact me." He ushered her from his office and greeted an elderly couple who sat waiting for him.

Dismissed and struggling to push away her desolation and the sense of overwhelm, Christina stumbled from the lawyer's office and made her way to the parking lot where she'd left her godmother's red Mazda hatchback. She returned to the cottage, unbelieving and still unable to make sense of the situation.

Once inside, she exchanged her best navy-blue business suit for comfortable jeans, a scoop-necked apricot-colored T-shirt, and her denim jacket. Henry had suggested she seek out Gabriel, and she decided this was an excellent suggestion. She'd interrogate her friend, and perhaps it was time to make good on her promise to sell cheese.

3

I'm Here To Sell Cheese

"Did you know the contents of Bernice's will?"

Gabriel started and jerked upward on hearing Christina's strident demand. He thumped his head on the stainless-steel bin, he was scrubbing. Rubbing the sore bit through the hairnet he wore, he extricated himself and rose to face Christina. Temper flashed in her brown eyes while two patches of rose colored her cheeks.

He grinned and grabbed her in a bear hug before she could react. She froze at his touch, then relaxed against him. With her sun-kissed hair and her high color, she made a pretty picture. A tempting package. He gave in to the impulse he'd harbored since he'd first seen her almost a week ago.

He kissed her. Not the slow, lingering lover's kiss he was tempted to lay on her, but a friendly peck that still shoved urgent need through his body. She frowned at him, and he tweaked her pert nose before stepping back.

"Bernice's will? I know nothing."

A car pulled up in the driveway, reminding Gabriel he'd put up the shop sign.

"I'm here to sell cheese," she announced. "Is everything priced, and do you have change?"

"Yes, and yes." It was Gabriel's turn to frown.

"You wanted me to help, so here I am. Is Toby okay?"

"He seems happy enough, hanging with my dogs."

"Excellent. Carry on. I'll sell cheese, and we can talk later tonight. I need your help."

Gabriel didn't hide his confusion. "Call if you have any problems. I'll be working in here, cleaning equipment."

Christina gave a curt nod and strode off. Two days ago, he'd given her a tour. He doubted he'd have queues of customers arriving to swamp his place due to his irregular opening hours. Hopefully, with Christina's help, he might turn that around.

Feminine voices sounded in the distance—too far away to decipher actual words. Gabriel debated leaving his task to check on Christina, then recalled her mood. *A high dudgeon*, his romance-reading grandmother would've said with an amused *tut-tut*. He grinned, his uncertainty easing at the thought of Gran. She was a wicked-wise woman, and he'd learned a lot about the female species from her. She and his grandfather were the constants in his life, and thanks to them and their support, he had a farm and a purpose.

The beautiful and intriguing Christina knew where to find him. His grin broadened, and a wave of lust tightened his muscles. *A wolfish smirk*. The description slipped into his brain, again courtesy of Gran.

His grandparents chided him for working so hard.

"Go out. Socialize. Meet a girl. I've just read a romance about a woman who arranged blind dates. I know lots of nice girls. If you want, I could do that for you," his grandmother had said.

"Now, Beth." His grandfather had winked at him. *"I heard you discussing that racy romance with him. One hundred colors or some such. I doubt any of the girls you know would like their bottoms spanked."*

Gabriel picked up his scrubbing brush and settled back to scouring his stainless-steel vat. He grinned as memories of the conversation about match-making and *Fifty Shades* poured through his mind. He loved the duo so much. They'd remember Christina because he'd asked his grandmother for kissing advice. Thanks to his grandmother's instructions, the kiss—his first attempt—had been an enormous success.

Yes, Christina's arrival would thrill his grandparents, and to tell the truth, he was a happy camper too.

Gabriel had implied the shop was quiet, but she served

a steady stream of customers. Gabriel produced two varieties of goat's cheese and a firm, cheddar-type cheese, although he'd told her he enjoyed experimenting and making other types on a smaller scale.

"You cannot fathom how ecstatic I am to see Gabriel's shop open," one woman declared, waving her bejeweled fingers above her head—a gesture of happiness. "I have a dinner party tonight and the goat's cheese is perfect. Just perfect."

Christina held her knife ready to cut off a wedge. "How much would you like?"

"I'll take the entire piece," the woman stated.

Christina wrapped the cheese in plain white paper and quoted a price. The woman didn't blink but handed over her credit card.

This interaction continued throughout the afternoon, varying slightly, but one thing was clear. Gabriel's cheese was popular, and he needed to stock more in his shop and do the sales thing at the local weekend market.

It was almost five, and she had one lone wedge of the hard cheese left. Christina wandered from the shop and up the short driveway to remove the *shop open* sign.

A couple pulled up in a black SUV. The woman, sitting in the passenger seat, opened her window. "Are we too late?"

"I have a wedge of the cheddar left."

"We'll take it," the woman said. "Gabriel's cheese is

exceptional. Gracie rang to tell me the shop was open, but we were at the kids' sports day. Do you know when you'll be open next?"

"Tomorrow," Christina said, crossing her fingers since she wasn't certain of Gabriel's stocks of cheese.

"Do you know which cheeses will be available?"

"No, I'm sorry I don't." Curious, she asked, "Which cheese were you wanting?"

"He has a divine blue cheese."

"If you don't mind waiting, I can ask him," Christina said.

"We'll wait," the woman's husband said.

"All right. Let me get the sign in. I'll be right there." Christina yanked on the sign, spotted the closed sign slotted behind it, and switched the two before trotting down the driveway to search for Gabriel.

"Gabriel!"

"Here," he said, making her jump.

She whirled, her hand pressed against her chest. "Stop doing that. Do you have any blue cheese available for sale?"

"Not today," he said. "I'll test a sample tomorrow, but my gut says it still needs more aging."

"All right." Christina was glad of an excuse to turn away from Gabriel. Inappropriate thoughts kept exploding in her mind like an emotional firework display. Her body stood at high alert, every part of her aware of him, and that had a knock-on effect with the fireworks. A stupid circle that highlighted her body's craving for sex and physical contact. She forced her mind back into the game. "I'll let the customer know."

"I'll swap the sign out," he said.

"Already done. This is my last customer." She retreated, but the heat at her back told her Gabriel was following. She entered the shop and found the woman waiting.

"It's a tiny wedge." The woman pouted.

"Julie," Gabriel said.

Christina turned to face him and caught the faint widening of his eyes when he noticed the empty refrigerated display.

"What do you need, Julie?" he asked. "I can get it for you from out the back."

Christina waited while the woman rattled off her order, and Gabriel disappeared. Everyone had raved about Gabriel's cheese, and the bare refrigerator underscored the popularity of his products. "How did everyone know to come for cheese today?" she asked.

"Waiheke grapevine." Julie wrinkled her long, narrow nose. "Gabriel needs to open his shop more often."

After Julie left with her cheese, Christina cleaned and wiped the surfaces.

"I can't believe you sold everything," Gabriel said after waving off Julie and her husband.

"Julie said it was the Waiheke grapevine. From what I learned this afternoon, your cheese is a hit, and the locals love it. You need regular hours for your store. Open on set days and hit the market each weekend to get the tourist and casual weekender trade. Do you still have cheese to sell?"

Amusement tugged at Gabriel's lips, and she barely withheld her sigh of appreciation. Although he was not classically handsome, his confident persona and magnetic smile sure made her pulse jump into a lustful tango. Those stupid fireworks in her brain exploded again.

"Have a decent stock of cheese, although now that the locals have their cheese fix, I doubt tomorrow will be as busy."

"Why haven't you hired someone to operate the store?"

"My budget hasn't run to paying a wage," he said. "Come to a stage where I have to sell my cheese because it's aged right. In the past, I'd open the store when I had cheese ready."

"Makes sense," Christina said. "I'd better get Toby and return to the cottage. Leave you in peace."

"Stay for dinner," Gabriel suggested. "You said you wanted to talk. Eat dinner with me and talk. One stone. Two birds."

"Can you cook? What's for dinner?"

"Gran taught me to cook. Tonight, I have a beef-and-red-wine stew Gran made for me. I thought mashed potatoes, broccoli, and carrots."

Christina's brows rose. "Dessert?"

"Carrot cake."

"Cream cheese frosting?"

"Yep."

"Sold," Christina said. "What can I do to help?"

Gabriel trespassed into her space and slipped his arm around her waist, drawing her against his side. "You can choose the wine and keep me company while I prepare the vegetables."

"I can do that." She inhaled his scent of soap and man and a pungent hint of cleaning solution. The man never used to act as touchy-feely, but she enjoyed the physical contact, so she didn't protest.

Gabriel shifted his hand to the small of her back and urged her from the shop. Outside, he shunted her to the left and along a narrow concrete path that led behind his cheese-making buildings.

"I don't remember this house being here," she said.

"It wasn't when you used to visit. My grandparents had it transported here."

Something in his tone urged her to think before she spoke. Hadn't Bernice mentioned his grandparents? "Are your grandparents still living in the same house?"

He grinned, giving her a flash of white teeth and the impression his momentary tension had eased. "Yes, they're not far away. A ten-minute walk. Grandad helps me with the cattle some days. He enjoys milking the goats. Says it gives a man time to think."

"And the rest of your family? Do they still live on

Waiheke?"

Gabriel's smile died. It was like a light switching off, and the change in his demeanor forced an icy surge down her spine. Ah. She wished Bernice was still here for her to ask questions since her godmother had known everyone and held many connections within the community. It was clear questions regarding Gabriel's family were out of bounds, and she wondered what had changed since they were teenagers. She racked her brain, trying to think of any clue her godmother might have let drop. While connected to the grapevine, Bernice had never gossiped, which left Christina none the wiser.

"They still live here." He toed off his rubber boots, and she stooped to remove her runners.

Gabriel opened the door and shunted her inside. "Welcome to my home. I'll give you a quick tour. This way." He led her down a passage, the aged wooden floorboards cool beneath her sock-clad feet.

"Cute socks," Gabriel said with a nod to her feet. "I have a friend who loves novelty socks. He has dozens of pairs. I've never seen a person who owns so many."

"My friend, Susan, gave me the tiger socks in last year's Secret Santa," Christina said.

"Bathroom, separate toilet, spare bedroom. Master bedroom." He paused at each doorway before urging her onward.

Christina gained a quick impression of the rooms. He'd

renovated some while others, like the spare room, were awaiting their turn, the bold seventies wallpaper screaming for a makeover. "Wow, that's a big bed."

His brown gaze sought hers. "Like my comfort." While his delivery was deadpan, there might've been a flash of humor in his eyes.

His reaction shifted so fast, confusion and doubt filled Christina. Had that been weird flirting, or had his words meant something else? Their paths hadn't crossed since they had been teens, not even during her visits to Bernice. His constant but friendly touching was messing with her brain, and she didn't trust herself to arrive at the correct conclusion. She could always ask, but that'd be weird. Right?

"Why don't you have a girlfriend?"

He shook his head and led her back down the passage. "Too busy. There was someone. Lounge. Kitchen. Would you like a glass of wine? Or you can have a beer."

"What have you got?" Christina wondered about the someone, but Gabriel's squared shoulders shouted his unwillingness to discuss the subject at greater length. She let it go.

"Red or white wine. The beer is from a local brewery."

"In the interests of broadening my horizons, I'll try the beer," Christina announced.

He chuckled. "That's my girl."

Christina's brows shot upward. What did he mean? She

frowned at his back, surprised by the disquiet filling her when they'd always had an easy friendship. As he opened the fridge and bent to survey the contents, her attention slipped to his backside and lingered. He straightened and turned, two bottles of beer in hand. For an instant, he froze, his gaze connecting with hers.

"Were you staring at my arse?"

"No!" Christina spluttered, trying to maintain eye contact. She failed. Also, the warmth in her cheeks told her she was blushing in champion-style.

"You're turning red," he informed her.

"A bad habit. I've tried to grow out of it, but the weakness returns to haunt me at the most inconvenient moments."

"I wouldn't call your blushing an inconvenience. It's cute. I find it charming." He set the two bottles on the counter and opened another cupboard to grab glasses. "Take a seat at the breakfast bar, and we can chat while I sort out dinner."

Charming? What should she do with that? "I can help."

"Sit." He whipped the caps off both beers. After pouring part of a bottle into one glass, he pushed the bottle and glass toward her. "You're lying. That blush reminds me of your discomfort after we kissed the first time and bumped noses before getting it right."

"N-no. You're mistaken."

"You're also stuttering," he added helpfully. "That's

another of your tells."

"You're very rude."

"Honest. I like honesty. You should remember that about me. Lies are unforgivable. I've learned this the hard way, and I refuse to inflict the same pain on anyone else." His voice grew harder, his jaw clenching and unclenching with his conviction.

Uncertain of what he meant, unable to read the emotional undercurrents that had sucked them under without warning, she remained trapped in his gaze. A tight sensation in her chest reminded her to breathe. Christina inhaled, held it for four seconds, and also exhaled on a count of four. The familiar coping method—a form of meditation—helped to ease her panic and allowed her to center herself.

If he wanted honesty, she'd fire it in his direction. "I like the way you look and enjoy studying your masculine form. So yes. You are correct. I was staring at your backside." The heat in her face increased, but this time, she owned her words and refused to hide her face behind her hands.

"For the record, I think you're gorgeous. Seeing you made my day. I'm glad you're here because some weeks I go for ages without meeting another person."

"Right. Okay, then."

Gabriel chuckled, and the burst of amusement startled her at first, then pulled an answering laugh from her.

"What do you think of the beer?"

She'd already tasted it, yet their conversation had rattled her, and she'd drunk without analyzing the beverage's nuances. She sipped it again. "I couldn't drink over one bottle in a sitting, but it has hints of honey and spice. It's pleasant." She checked the label. "A summer ale."

While she discussed beer, Gabriel pulled vegetables out of the fridge, along with a covered dish. He'd already switched on the oven, and he placed the casserole inside before turning back to the vegetables.

"What did you want to discuss?"

"I visited the lawyer this morning. Bernice left the cottage and Toby to me."

"That surprised you?"

"Yeah, I guess it did. There are conditions. I have to stay on Waiheke for six months, and I have to socialize. Throw myself into community life. I have to immerse myself in the Waiheke experience." The requirement still stunned her, bothered her a little. She fiddled with the label on the beer bottle, running a fingernail around the top until the edges lifted.

"Who decides if you've participated enough?"

Christina jumped, shot him a guilty look. "Henry Wainscoat. Bernice's lawyer."

"Are you staying?"

"I think so." She straightened. "Yes, I'm staying. The owner of the building where I lived gave the tenants notice. I'm homeless, so this has come at the right time. It's the requirement to embrace community I don't understand."

Gabriel grimaced. "My grandparents are always telling me I act like a hermit. My grandmother tsks and shakes her head, then she says, 'It's all very well working hard, Gabriel, but your workaholic ways mean the best parts of life are passing you by. Go out. Meet a girl. A boy.'" He cleared his throat after speaking in a higher feminine voice. He resumed talking in his usual tones. "The social circle is small on the island unless it's a function to attract tourists. It's difficult not to run into my family, so I avoid socializing."

A huge family blow-up then. Christina didn't question him since every time Gabriel mentioned them, his face blanked and his eyes turned dead. There was one other part that drew her interest, and she pursued that.

"Your grandmother told you to find a boy?"

He ran a vegetable peeler down the sides of a carrot, his big, callused hands competent and practiced. "Yeah." He lifted his gaze. "Turns out I enjoy kissing girls and boys. It's the person who attracts me rather than the sex. Does that bother you?"

Christina considered this for a few seconds. "No."

"No?"

His simple question held degrees of complication.

"No," she stated while her mind wandered to his parents. Was his sexuality the cause of the rift between them? "Your explanation makes sense. Besides, I was your first."

"First kiss." Gabriel barked out a laugh and sliced the carrots into battens. He washed chunks of potatoes he'd already peeled and placed them in a pot. The carrots dropped into a second pot. "That's done. I need to feed the dogs. Why don't you move to the lounge? Pick a movie or put on some music. Back in ten minutes." He wrinkled his nose. "Toby needs a bath. He's been playing in the mud with my two."

"No problem," Christina said. "I appreciate you looking after him for the week."

Gabriel walked over to her and pulled her into an embrace.

"You give excellent cuddles."

"I kiss great too," he whispered against her ear.

"Bighead," she muttered, hiding her grin against his neck.

He put her away from him. "Back in a few."

The door banged as he thumped outside, and Christina wandered to the lounge. This part of his house was more open. A large television hung on one wall. Two big doors led out onto a terrace, and she suspected the views over the native bush, and the land beyond would extend to the Hauraki Gulf.

A million-dollar view.

Now, all she saw was an expanse of darkness with not a single light twinkling.

A large bookcase took up most of another wall—mystery and thriller paperbacks and three framed photos filled the upper shelves while work-related non-fiction crammed the two lower racks. Titles such as cheese-making, land management methods, and animal husbandry told her Gabriel took his work seriously.

The stereo confounded her with its multitude of buttons, so she turned her attention to the photos.

One of a grinning Gabriel with a certificate in hand. Another from the same time with Gabriel flanked by his grandparents. Even as a teenager, he'd been close to his grandparents and spent the school holidays with them rather than at home.

Tucked behind these photos was one of an older Gabriel. He was with another man, and they were standing close, gazing at each other. Something about the image made her uneasy as if she were intruding on a personal moment.

The thump of the door and footsteps had her hastily returning the photo to its shelf and taking two giant steps toward the doors and the darkness beyond.

"I can't hear music," he called.

A pot clanged in the kitchen.

"Your stereo scared me. I don't have the correct class of license to drive it."

Gabriel appeared with a bottle of red wine, two glasses, and a plate of cheese and crackers.

"Is that your cheese?"

"Blasphemy. I'd never offer a competitor's cheese." He set everything on a coffee table and gestured her to take a seat on the couch. "Dinner will be another hour. I figured if we're drinking, we should have something to eat."

"Good plan."

"Want to watch a movie? I have Netflix. We can watch a box-set of something. Do you still enjoy mysteries and thrillers, or have you turned girlie and defected to the rom-com side?"

"I am an equal-opportunity viewer," she said. "How about a mystery? Have you watched the *Brokenwood Mysteries*?"

"The series filmed in North Auckland?"

"Yeah."

"I fall asleep if I watch television, so normally go to bed with a book. That way, if I nod off, I'm already in bed."

"Great strategy. I think you'd like the series. It's set in a small town with a police station at the center. I love the eccentric characters. There are several recurring ones, and the New Zealand flavor doesn't hurt. I rate the show as good as the English ones."

"Sold." Gabriel picked up a remote and pointed it at the TV. In a short time, he'd found the latest season, and they immersed themselves in the doings at the Brokenwood agricultural show and the resulting murder investigation. They sat shoulder-to-shoulder, thighs touching, casual and at ease as they'd been as teenagers.

Christina reached for a cracker and let Gabriel slice cheese for her. "You make excellent cheese."

"Yes," he said deadpan.

Her gaze jerked to his serious expression. The faint quiver of his lips gave him away, and she poked him in the ribs. "Bighead."

"How would you know? You haven't seen it."

"Gabriel!"

His deep chuckle had her bursting into laughter too. He refilled her wineglass and handed her more cheese. When the oven timer dinged, he paused the show and rose to sort out dinner.

Christina followed, not surprised to find herself unsteady on her pins. Gabriel had been right to serve a snack with their wine.

Gabriel opened a drawer and pulled out cutlery. From another drawer, he extracted placemats. "Set the table for me," he ordered, waving a hand at the dining table to their right.

By the time she'd done that, Gabriel had served portions of the beef stew, added a heaped spoon of fluffy mashed potatoes along with a mix of broccoli and carrots.

"Sit. I'm starving," he added. "I missed lunch."

Christina took a place at the table. "Maybe you should make sandwiches to take out each day. A thermos of soup or something like that."

"I never have time."

"You'll lose that sexy backside," she warned with a waggle of her finger.

He grinned. "Eat your dinner. Food will soak up the wine. Catch me up on what you were doing in Auckland. You're a trained accountant, right?"

"I used to work at Barker and Johnson. I loved it since I made close friends. We used to hang out together after work and during the weekends, and I shared an apartment with one of the women."

"What happened?"

"That transparent, huh?"

Gabriel shrugged and ate a mouthful of mashed potatoes.

"My friends married and left the firm where we all used to work. Everything changed."

"What about guys? Someone special."

Christina prodded at her carrots. "I've decided I'm too picky."

"No," he contradicted. "It's wrong to settle because you're lonely."

He got it. "I think I've been trying to find someone to share my life. I go on dates with high expectations and go home alone, disappointed. It's depressing."

Gabriel shot her a sharp look. "You don't need a man to be happy."

"True, but it's nice to have companionship and shared

interests. It's easy to get isolated, and life loses its sparkle." She shrugged. "Maybe that's why Bernice is making me mingle in the community."

"She wants you to grow roots." Gabriel leaned forward and placed his hand over hers.

Heat suffused her and zapped up her arm, sparking and firing against every nerve ending on the way. She barely suppressed her gasp. To her intense relief, Gabriel parted their hands and returned to eating his meal.

"Tell me about your friends."

A safer topic. "There's Maggie, Susan, Julia, and Connor. We're the ones who used to work together. Maggie and Connor married and have one daughter. Julia is with Ryan, and through them, I met Caleb, who has been Ryan's best friend since they were kids. They have two children. Susan wed Tyler after the reality show. They have a daughter and a son. My friends have children and are doing kid-related things, which makes me the odd-woman out."

"Yeah." He understood.

"They welcome me whenever we meet or visit, but their experiences are different from mine."

"I'm your friend, Christina. Don't forget that. Do you want to keep Bernice's cottage? What happens if you don't meet the criteria?"

"I receive ten thousand dollars. The balance goes to Bernice's niece and nephew. I want to keep the cottage."

"Can you do your personal shopper business from here?"

"Not here. I need to be in the city."

"Well, you have a job with me."

"Bernice suggested I sell my handicrafts at the market. I brought a few items with me. Susan stored the rest at her place."

"I've booked a stall for the upcoming weekend. Select some of your stuff and sell it along with my cheese. Put up a stand in the cheese shop."

"You don't even know if I have any talent," Christina protested.

"You do. Bernice told me. I used to ask how you were whenever we met over the fence or when Bernice walked Toby. She used to take him for walks into the bush on my property."

"Oh."

"If you take me up on my offer, you'll get an opportunity to explore what excites your prospective customers. What pushes your buttons."

Christina gave a decisive nod. "I will. Thanks."

"That's one positive move. Now let's discuss community activities. The obvious place to start is the various handicraft groups. Take half an hour to check out the other market stalls. See what's available and work out if there is a gap in the market. It's what I did when I started my farm. I listed my interests, looked at the competition, and chose to make cheese."

"You make it sound easy."

"It's not, but you can have fun. Bernice told me you love sewing and knitting and whatnot. You love fashion and makeup stuff." He waved his fork in the air, his earnestness kind of cute. "Isn't that why you started your business? You expanded on something you loved."

She opened her mouth to argue and clamped her lips together, her mind diverting and following the path his comment had sewn. For a long time, she'd vacillated. She'd experimented and started her business as a part-time hobby, gaining contacts and experience before she'd gathered the courage to resign and go full-time. Jumping feetfirst into important decisions wasn't her. She dithered. She fretted. She hovered on the brink, almost to the point of losing an opportunity.

"This is silly. Maybe I can get a job at the local accountant's firm. There is one, right?"

"And leave me in the lurch?"

Christina glowered at him. He was right, dammit. "I wouldn't do that."

"You're contradicting yourself."

His gaze flickered over her before returning to his almost-empty plate.

Suspicion rose in her. "Are you laughing at me?"

His lips quivered. "You haven't changed much. You still over-analyze everything."

"Only important things. I'm impulsive sometimes."

"When? Give me an example."

Huh! She had one for him without even straining her brain. "Not so long ago, I applied to go on the *Farmer Seeks a Wife* reality show."

"You're kidding." He stared at her with a narrowed gaze, then filled their glasses.

"Susan and I were both picked to go to the initial meeting. My farmer thought I was too bohemian with my bracelets and loose hair. He thought I'd scare his cows."

Gabriel spluttered then gave a belly laugh.

"I kid you not. Instead of asking questions to learn if we might be compatible, he raved about his cows for most of our speed date. Susan had better luck, although she didn't escape embarrassment. The cameraman filmed her with her dress hitched up and her panties showing. She ended up meeting Tyler, though, so there was a happy ending."

"Christina, believe me. A man with such...highly strung cows was not the one for you." He chortled again, the hilarity taking years off his face.

"Go on." Christina sipped her wine. "Laugh at my expense. Don't you get lonely?"

"Sometimes," he acknowledged.

"Keeping busy helps. I think that's my problem now. With the downturn in my business, I've had too much time to think. I get disheartened and that makes me indecisive." She swallowed hard since this issue wasn't a favorite discussion topic. She'd always thought she was a well-balanced human being. But Gabriel was a long-time friend, and she needed honesty between them. "If I'm not careful, I can slide deep into the blues."

Gabriel set down his knife and fork and reached for her hand. "Tell me."

"I get restless and tired, yet I can't sleep because my mind won't shut up. I stress about how I've messed up my life, and my friends have moved on, found someone to love. Then I'm ashamed because my friends are lovely and deserve every bit of happiness. I'm resentful toward them when they can't meet, even though I understand they have good reasons and aren't trying to hurt me. When I get like this, I withdraw into myself, and that makes my attitude worse."

"When was your depression diagnosed?"

"It wasn't—not until this year. You know I had moods when I was a teenager. My parents didn't think it was serious since I'd work on my craft or read a book. They called it my sulks. The feelings would pass, but it's been worse the last few years. You know the famous rugby player? The one who fronts the ads for depression on television?"

"Yes."

"I checked out the website he mentioned. Many of the mentioned symptoms—I had them. I did nothing about it because, well..." She shrugged. "I thought I'd be fine.

Then, about a month later, it was real bad. I couldn't stop crying and didn't leave my apartment for days. After watching a TV ad, I rang their helpline and followed their suggestions. Made an appointment with my doctor. We decided I should try the self-help measures first. Following the doctor's advice and the online suggestions has helped, but I can slip if I get too stressed."

"Bernice's death and the contents of her will have knocked you." It was a statement rather than a question.

"Yes."

"Continue with the coping methods your doctor suggested. You can talk to me. Share the coping strategies with me, and I'll try to help." His hand tightened over hers, and she glanced at him, her chest tight because of his understanding.

His brown eyes held sincerity and confidence, and she nodded. "Thanks."

"We should start now. What is one thing you do to regain a bit of balance?"

She wrinkled her nose. "You really want to know?"

"Yes," he whispered, leaning close enough for her to feel his breath against her cheek. The intimacy of it brought a shudder, a faint whimper of pleasure.

She breathed deep and focused on his question. It was challenging, and pricklings of warning blasted her. "I keep a journal, and each day I note at least one thing I'm grateful for."

"What are you grateful for, Christina?"

His gaze never left her, and a sharp spike of awareness struck her chest before shimmering downward to feather into her belly. "For having you as my friend and sharing this fantastic meal."

"My pleasure, sweetheart." He pressed his lips to her cheek. "You know you can visit my cows and goats any time, don't you? Your gypsy bracelets won't scare my livestock. I'm thankful for having your help in my farm store. To date, two female customers have propositioned me. One elderly lady pinched my arse. The women travel in packs, which makes them brave."

"Wow."

He nodded. "Really, truly grateful to you."

"Can I have more stew?"

"Yup. You have curves, but you're too skinny."

"Lack of interest in food and weight loss is another symptom. The doctor suggested I eat balanced meals and do regular exercise. He told me this would help."

"We can fix the regular meal thing by eating together." Gabriel took her plate and dished up another portion of stew plus a dollop of mashed potatoes. "What sort of exercise do you do?"

"I like to walk, which is easy now that I have to care for Toby. My friend Julia owns a club on K' Road. My other girlfriends and I used to take part in dance training with Julia and her dancers."

"You become more interesting by the minute, Christina Kingston. What other secrets are you hiding?"

A grin stretched her lips without warning, the meal and wine having relaxed her. "I dream about having a threesome with two men who focus on me. Oh!" She slapped her hand over her mouth, winced at the fiery heat that filled her face. "An alien kidnapped my mouth. Please, forget I mentioned it."

4

FANTASY ISLAND

CHRISTINA'S WORDS SHOCKED THE hell out of him since they'd emerged with not a whisper of warning. Pink seeped into her cheeks until they carried seven shades of red, and she refused to meet his gaze. The image of Christina naked and writhing on a bed with two men played through his mind. *Damn*.

"Please, please forget I said that," she ordered and reached for her wineglass. She gulped the contents.

"But the topic is such an interesting one." He worked on hiding his grin.

She bared her teeth at him. "Fantasy. I'm hardly likely to have two men when one is elusive. Now, please, change the subject."

He might cease his teasing, but he doubted he'd ever forget, not with the image now planted in his brain. *Hot damn.* "Okay, how about this? Along with meeting the conditions of Bernice's will, I challenge you to explore employment options other than selling your handicrafts. Step out of your normal routine. Use this chance to improve your future. I dare you, Christina."

"Why?"

Her eyes were wide behind her glasses and full of suspicion. Gabriel remembered this expression from the early days of their acquaintance when she looked askance at him because he was a boy. She'd considered boys noisy and smelly, especially when they farted. Her words, not his. Not a boy any longer, and now the stern school-teacher expression she aimed his way diverted his mind to more adult activities.

"Great having my friend next door again. Admit it, Christina. You need this opportunity. If you turn your back on it, what will you do? Slink back to Auckland and find a boring accountancy job instead of seeking a challenge? Sink into your sorrow and risk a bad case of depression?"

"Hey!" She leaned close and clicked fingers under his nose. "You should've stopped at the part where you enjoy my company. Are you sure I can do this?"

"Yes." He lifted his glass, saw hers was empty and poured her the last of the wine.

"Are you trying to get me drunk?"

"No, we should toast to the future."

Christina lifted her chin. "I'm game. Let's drink to your cheese and increasing your market share and to me for going ahead with this crazy scheme." She stood and wobbled a fraction before she straightened to her full height. "To our future."

Gabriel rose and clinked his glass to hers. "The future."

She slapped her free hand onto the back of her chair. "Whoa, that wine sneaked up on me. We shouldn't have opened the second bottle."

"Relax in the lounge while I clean up here."

"I should grab Toby and head back to the cottage."

"I'll walk you home in a few minutes. Go." He turned her and steered Christina into the lounge. "Sit. I won't be long."

Soft music started playing—a soulful saxophone taking the lead.

Despite her earlier complaint, Christina must've managed to work out his sound system. Gabriel found himself humming as he cleared dishes and stacked the dishwasher. Once he finished and wandered to the lounge, he spotted Christina slouched on the couch, her eyes closed.

"Hey," he said.

Her eyes popped open. "I'm awake."

"Dance with me," he said, extending his hand.

"Why?"

"Because we haven't danced before. Remember, we

were going to, and your dad had to go back to Auckland for work, so you missed the social. Had to show off my moves to other girls." He grasped her hand and tugged until she stood pressed against his chest. She swayed, and he wrapped his arms around her. When he moved a few steps, Christina stumbled.

"Your fault," she murmured.

"Maybe you should stay here tonight."

"In your ginormous bed?"

"I can find a T-shirt for you to sleep in."

"I've never seen such a large bed."

He grinned again, smiling more tonight than he had in months—no, years. "Told you. I like to stretch out. Enjoy my space." He still remembered their first kiss and holding her this way returned his thoughts to sex again. Sex with her. Something to consider.

Christina pulled back and yawned.

Gabriel's chest shook as he reclaimed her hand. "Let's get you settled. You have a big day tomorrow. Decisions to make. Cheese to sell."

"I should return to the cottage."

"Stay. I need to tell you something. A secret."

Her eyes grew wide. "What?"

"The dark scares me."

A snort escaped her. "Does that line work for you?"

"Don't know. Never used it before. Come on. Time for bed."

Christina yawned again, and he ached to care for her. He led her down the passage to his bedroom. Once there, he pulled a T-shirt from a drawer and handed it to her. "You'll find a new toothbrush in the top right drawer in the en suite. I'll grab you a towel."

"Do you have a face cloth?"

"I'll get you one of those too."

The woman listed from side-to-side, her eyes wide behind her lenses, and doing an excellent impression of one of the local owls that inhabited the nearby block of bush. Her bracelets jangled. She glanced at the door and took half a step in that direction as if she might flee. Not happening. He lengthened his stride and flung open the cupboard where he kept his towels while keeping one eye on his bedroom doorway. His breath eased out on his return. Christina sat on the end of the bed and was struggling to remove her socks.

"I'm more coordinated than this."

"Speech is fine."

"Y-yes. Stop looking at me that way."

"Like what?" He ducked into the en suite and set out the towels. While he was there, he grabbed the toothbrush for her. When he entered the bedroom again, her brow was furrowed. "Problem?"

"You're making me nervous."

Gabriel blinked and backed up a step, incredulous and vexed at the same time. How? How the hell had he made her nervous? Did he scare her? "Explain."

Her gaze held wariness as she lifted her head. "I like you. More than I should, and it'd be so easy to convince myself there's more there. Something real between us. I know myself well enough to worry about this. The last thing I want is to wreck our friendship because of something stupid."

"Two things. The bed is big enough for us to sleep without touching. If that's the problem, I can leave the bed for you and sleep on the couch. Second, you're insulting me if you think I'd walk away from our friendship because sex gets in the way. I can control myself."

"Not sure if I can," she mumbled.

Her disgruntlement had him laughing. "Get ready for bed. You're half-asleep now. Do you need help?"

She waved in dismissal and wobbled her way into his en suite. The door shut with a click.

Gabriel stripped while Christina was busy. Usually, he slept naked, but tonight, he retained his boxer-briefs. He switched on the two bedside lamps and turned off the main one, dimming his bedroom into more intimate.

Christina exited the bathroom, her steps slow and hesitant.

"Finished?"

"Ah, yes."

Gabriel tugged back the covers for her. "Should I sleep on the couch?"

She glanced at the bed, gave her head a hard shake.

Pleased, but clever enough not to make a smartarse comment, Gabriel strode away to clean his teeth. When he returned, Christina had slid into bed and turned off the lamp on her side.

Gabriel padded around the bed and plunged the room into darkness. From his side of the bed, he could hear Christina's soft breathing. He didn't think she was asleep yet. Instead, she lay on her side, holding so still it was unnatural. Every instinct urged him to close the space between them to wrap his arms around her. To spoon her and share body warmth.

He did none of those things, equally tense.

5

THE RUDE AWAKENING

CHRISTINA WOKE CONFUSED, HAVING no idea of her location. Warmth seared her back, and an arm curved around her waist. The room was dark, and a clock marked the seconds with an annoying *tick-tick-tick*.

What the heck?

For long moments, she sorted through different scenarios, her mind uncooperative and sluggish.

"It's early. Why are you awake?" A growly masculine voice. A familiar one.

Her confusion slipped into proper order. Waiheke. Gabriel. Dinner. Too much wine.

"You're touching me." A stupid thing to say. She caught her bottom lip between her teeth—a warning to think before she next spoke.

"That's bad?"

"Not what we agreed," she mumbled, her brain functioning better now.

"Want me to move?" His bigger body tensed behind her while she pondered his question.

She'd slept. Really slept for most of the night instead of lying awake with a hamster-wheel brain. For the first time in several months, she savored comfort and her rested state.

"Christina?"

She turned in his arms until they faced each other. "Thank you."

"Why are you thanking me?" His sexy rumble was deeper than normal.

Every feminine part of her jerked to attention, paused as if on the cusp of something magical. She stared into his brown eyes and gave him the truth. "I'll admit. This year has been a struggle. Spending time with you and feeling useful again, as though I matter and you listening to me without telling me to harden up and deal with my lot, has helped."

Gabriel stared at her, shook his head once, and eased even closer. He pushed his weight against her until her back hit the mattress, and he loomed over her. "You're my friend. Listening and acting as a sounding board is a friend's job."

Her traitorous body softened and yearned. Yeah, the stupid thing sent her warning signals then betrayed her. Her breasts prickled, her nipples hard and jabbing against his bare chest. Lower... She forced that thought away because Gabriel was her friend, not her lover. The silence between them lengthened, something dangerous hovering between them. Christina rifled through her mind, searching for a safe topic.

"I don't want to be your friend," he announced.

Hurt punched her in the chest, had her recoiling, struggling to escape.

"Don't," he warned in a hard voice. "Listen to me. Sorry. Too blunt. That sounded bad. Hell, I'm messing this up."

He wasn't wrong. He'd wounded her, and panic caused her to thrash against him.

"Stop!" he barked out. "Hell." He cupped her face with his callused hands and glared at her. "Want to be your lover. Means the friendship changes. Morphs into something bigger. Better. If that's what you want too."

She stilled. "You want me?"

He shifted his hips and settled against her. His erection was hard and firm. "Proof enough?"

"Morning wood," she said.

"Nope, it's all you. Wanted you since I saw you here. If I wanted feminine company to scratch an itch, it's easy to find. I don't. Not lately."

"You're not playing me?"

"Hell, no." His brows drew together, and his stormy features suggested she'd insulted him.

Too bad. Join the club. "You don't consider lovers can be

friends?"

He groaned. "Didn't phrase that well. Hard to think with this spike in my pants."

Christina licked her dry lips. "I never want you to hate me."

"No guarantees in life, babe. All I know is the minute I saw you again, everything seemed balanced. Like it did when we were kids. What if us together works? Strengthens us? Makes us better. Think about that." He brushed his knuckles over her cheek. "Worth the risk."

Christina studied his expression. He meant it. Yeah, she could see that even though the edges of his profile were fuzzy without her glasses. "Yes," she whispered.

"Be certain. Hate you to cry foul later."

"You mean a friend with benefits thing?"

"Sex."

"Gabriel. I need details, boundaries. Specifics. I also need caffeine."

"You're pretty when you're agitated." He stroked her cheek again, displayed tenderness before his face returned to hard-edged determination. "Can't predict the future, babe."

Christina sucked in a deep breath, expanding her chest and creating a delicious friction that rippled down to her sex. Holy Hannah. She wanted this, wanted him so much. He was right. Life was a risk and sometimes a person had to take a leap of faith.

"Yes." She wrapped her arms around his neck and kissed him.

He muttered against her lips, his meaning garbled as their mouths collided. Gabriel took control, his skill leaving her in no doubt he'd done this a time or two since their first kiss. He pulled away and grasped the hem of the T-shirt she was wearing. In seconds flat, he whipped it over her head. He dragged down her panties and his boxer-briefs. Then he was touching her again, his hands shaping her face, her breasts, her hips. His mouth sucked one of her nipples, and Christina clung to him, caught in the whirlwind that was Gabriel.

"You on birth control?"

"No."

"Have to fix that."

The hand on her hip shifted, and he drew away.

A croak of protest escaped Christina.

"Condom," he muttered in explanation.

He was back in seconds, his blunt fingers gliding between her legs. Stroking. Teasing. Playing her flesh like an instrument. Then he sucked on her clit, and she saw stars, her orgasm racing through her, tossing her into uncharted waters.

"Beautiful," he murmured, and he took her mouth, hard and uncompromising, driving her up again, taking her by storm.

A brief pause to don the condom, then he pushed inside

her. One smooth, determined stroke stole her breath. He pulled back and thrust again. Hard and deep.

Christina clutched his shoulders, gasping in shock and pleasure.

He stilled, his gaze golden. "Too much?"

"No. More," she said. Although she'd known Gabriel for a long time, she hadn't sensed these steely depths to him. He filled her, commanded her body, and gave, satiating every empty part of her. "Give me more. Please."

He took her at her word, increasing the strokes and propelling her toward pleasure again. She climaxed around him, crying out as the spasms rippled through her pussy. He gave a soft, satisfied laugh, then focused on his own pleasure. His drive dominated her, slaked her hunger. Destroyed her and rebuilt her with his strength. He took her mouth. Mastered that too, as his big body shuddered and relaxed.

He kissed her collarbone, nipped her neck, then settled in to kiss her again. This time it was softer, gentler, and Christina realized that even if this was a mistake, even if they stuck to a platonic friendship, he'd given her a gift. He'd given her honesty and the best sex she'd ever had. Yep, he'd ruined her for other men—the ones in her past came up lacking. Still, it was a gift of acceptance.

"Why are you smiling?"

"That was great sex."

His expression softened. "Yeah, it was." He parted their

bodies and disposed of the condom. "We'll do it again."

Her gaze darted down to his cock. He was still erect. She raised her eyes and found him smiling.

"You think I can't." He reached past her for a condom, his eyes predatory.

This time, he moved slower, touching and kissing her everywhere, teasing out responses she'd never known she had in her. She tried to explore his body, too, but he seemed more interested in getting his fill of her. Finally, he rolled on the condom and pushed into her. He kissed her sweet and deep, building the passion between them. He was rough and commanding, yet he never hurt her. She came again with a wail, and he chuckled, containing the cry with his mouth. His next thrusts were rougher, harder as he prolonged her pleasure. Gabriel climaxed with a growl, his big body stilling. She held him, exhausted but so happy.

Gabriel separated their bodies and ditched the condom. When he returned to her side, he hauled her against his chest.

"Have to get up soon. Got to milk the cows."

"It's still dark."

He nuzzled her neck. "Not for long."

Christina relaxed, let her mind drift. It took her a while to realize Gabriel had stiffened beside her. He pushed up on his elbow, and she, too, heard the noise. Footsteps on the wooden floor.

"What the fuck?" he muttered.

Before Gabriel could act, the bedroom light came on, dazzling her eyes and making her blink.

"Hi, honey. I'm home!" the man standing in the doorway shouted.

6

RECONNECTING WITH OLD FRIENDS

CHRISTINA HAD LEFT BY the time Aidan returned from Oneroa. He strolled into the kitchen and checked on the pot roast he'd left cooking in the crockpot. Satisfied the meat was almost ready, he started on his vegetables—baby carrots, green beans, and Brussel sprouts.

Christina was an interesting woman. Not his type or so he'd thought until he'd caught her checking out his butt. That had intrigued him as had her competent and relaxed manner with the customers. The bit about the cave...

He chortled. He had to tell Gabriel that gem. The customers who'd arrived on the bus had listened spellbound to the tall tales she'd woven about cheese. Yes, Christina was a woman with hidden talents, and he could see why Gabriel had befriended her.

His smile faded a fraction as he recalled finding them in bed. It was obvious what they'd been doing. Even though hours had passed, and he'd had time to process, he knew it wasn't fair to resent Gabriel sleeping with someone else. But the hurt lingered.

He'd wanted to hate Christina until Gabriel had told him he could bunk in his room. While he'd let go a little of his anger—because aye, he'd been the one to leave Gabriel—a sliver of jealousy bloomed to nag him. What if Gabriel wanted Christina more than him? What if this time, Aidan had created irreparable damage by placing his selfish needs first?

The door opening and closing wrenched Aidan from his angst. Aye, angst. A new condition for him since he was the one who had walked and never glanced over his shoulder. Truth—until he'd seen Gabriel and Christina in bed together, it hadn't hit him. How much he loved Gabriel. How much he counted on his lover being there for him when Aidan needed him. How much he'd hurt if Gabriel chose Christina rather than him.

The glimpse of his lover with another had struck like a punch in the face. Aidan took a measured breath, fixed a grin to his face, and turned to face Gabriel. His heart did a funny, irregular thump as he witnessed Gabriel's fatigue.

"Are you finished for the night?"

"Done everything that needs doing. Something smells

good. Do I have time to have a shower?"

"Take your shower and I'll serve dinner when you're ready."

"Thanks." Gabriel turned away without another word.

Aidan blinked, his hands clenching as he watched his man stride away. No hello kisses. No cuddle. Hell, he'd screwed up bad this time. His mother had tried to warn him. She'd told him if he loved Gabriel, he had to compromise. She'd accused him of using Gabriel when it suited him.

And now, when he was ready to act the responsible adult, it was too late.

Aidan removed the pot roast from the crockpot and placed it on a serving plate before he made gravy. Fear had his right hand trembling while he heated oil and added a spoonful of flour. The flour fluttered from his spoon and hit the counter with splotches of white before he regained control.

Damn, he couldn't tear himself apart like this. He needed to man-up to Gabriel and ask his lover where he stood. If Gabriel didn't want him any longer, Aidan needed to ken. Aidan added meat juices to his pan and stirred to avoid lumps forming.

"That smells good. I'm starving," Gabriel said.

Gabriel's sudden appearance had Aidan starting. He waited until his pulse rate settled before he turned to face Gabriel. As always, the man made his breath catch.

Although no one would call Gabriel handsome, the man possessed a presence that compelled people to take a second glance. His strength and confidence drew people in, and once they got to know him, his solid core of integrity made him someone to rely on. Amazing, given his parents had kicked him out of the family home when he'd been seventeen.

Aidan still didn't ken why, but he hoped Gabriel would confide in him one day. All he'd said was there'd been a blow-up, and his grandparents had invited him to live with them for as long as he needed. Aidan loved Gabriel's grandparents and always would because they'd stood by the man he loved.

Aye, loved. Aidan cursed, wishing his stupid head and heart had worked in concert a year ago.

"Hey," Gabriel said. "Everything okay?"

"Just a lot of thoughts rattling my brainbox tonight."

Gabriel nodded and didn't push. Aidan liked that about him too. The man never pried into private matters, but he always lent an ear if required.

"Want a beer?" Aidan asked.

"I'll get it," Gabriel said. "You want one?"

"No, I'm drinking water tonight. The last six months, I've been drinking too much. Doing stupid shit because of it. I'm cutting back since my head works better when I'm not hungover."

"I'll drink water too."

"No, I won't slip because you're drinking a beer. If that's what you want, have a drink. I'll serve dinner."

"Did you see Christina?"

"Aye."

Gabriel frowned, and Aidan caught the grimace before Gabriel smoothed out his expression.

"Sold a lot of cheese today."

Gabriel nodded and retrieved a beer from the fridge. He twisted off the top and drank.

The easy company that had existed between them had faded, and Aidan wondered if he'd lost Gabriel's trust. The idea bothered him, yet his behavior, the way he'd left Gabriel not once but three times...

Aye, Gabriel had a right. Somehow, he had to fix this.

"How was Christina?"

"She seemed fine," Aidan said, surprised by the question. "Didn't you visit her earlier?"

"I did."

Aidan set two plates on the table and retreated to fetch a jug of his gravy.

Gabriel took his seat and glanced at the meal Aidan had made. "Looks great. What did you and Christina talk about?"

Aidan frowned. "What aren't you asking me? You don't normally hedge around a topic."

"Things I know aren't mine to share," Gabriel said. "Don't want anything to happen to Christina. I care for her. She's my friend."

"Okay." Aidan thought back and pictured Christina. She'd been quiet. Understandable, given the situation. "She arrived as I was filling the cheese cabinet. Things were awkward, but we dealt and acted like adults. I came to the kitchen and made more scones. When they were done, I took Christina a mug of tea and a scone. I lingered and eavesdropped on her conversation with two customers. They were elderly ladies, and one of the ladies had her family coming to visit this weekend. I got that the son-in-law was a dick, and the lady wanted to prove Waiheke is an awesome place to live. Christina understood what the lady meant, and she told her to serve three of your cheeses with local olives, bread, and lavosh. She described each cheese and told her you had a special cave on your farm where you age the blue cheese. Christina said it was experimental cheese, so to-date you haven't made a lot. She told the woman this cheese was excellent and in demand. She gave the lady lots of info to slip into the conversation—the stuff that impresses a food snob. Your friend is great with people. She also hosted a bus tour and sold all the scones I made plus a hell of a lot of cheese. I had to restock the cabinet for her."

"You took her tea and a scone?"

"Aye. I told you that. I asked her to dinner too, but she turned me down. Said she had things to do."

Gabriel acknowledged this with a nod, then his mouth

curled into a smile, amusement traveling to his eyes. "A cheese cave, huh?"

"Yeah. The people on the bus tour enjoyed that touch too. The day's takings are over there." Aidan jerked his head in the direction of a canvas bank bag, which sat on the far end of the counter. "Christina said there was a lot of money, and she didn't like to leave it in the shop."

"Thanks," Gabriel said and started eating.

Aidan stared down at his plate. Whatever he'd said about Christina had reassured Gabriel. Aidan cut his slice of meat. "I met the real estate agent this afternoon. One property wouldn't work, but the other one is perfect. It's right in the middle of town. Prime position right next to the bank."

"The old ice cream parlor?"

"Aye. It's smaller than I wanted, but it has a deck outside. During the summer, I can have tables on the deck. It's better to start smaller and build rather than to start too big and ambitious. This way, I can play with my hours. Maybe close Monday and Tuesday. Those days, I can help you, experiment with recipes, and do my travel thing." Aidan stopped chattering and started eating before his dinner turned cold.

"You're really doing this?"

"Aye." Aidan tried to keep the snap from his voice, but some bled through. "I've signed a lease for a year and paid the deposit."

"Give me a break, Aidan. You're not known for commitment."

Aidan froze, forced himself to bite his tongue. He deserved this from Gabriel. His unthinking behavior and restlessness had caused this rift between them. It was up to him to prove his reliability. At least Gabriel was talking to him, allowing him to stay in his house. Share his bed. Getting physical might help.

Gabriel ate his dinner, pleased at Aidan's presence. Surprised his lover had signed a lease on a property. That was a new one. What had his grandmother said last week? Adulting. He'd heard the phrase before, but not from his grandmother, and it fit what Aidan was doing.

The product of wealthy parents, Aidan had always owned anything he desired, done what he wanted while Gabriel hadn't possessed the same financial cushion. Yes, his grandparents had stood for him, but he hated the idea of them spending their retirement egg on him. So he'd worked part-time while at school, and once he'd left school, he'd put in more hours.

One thing about Aidan, though. The man wasn't a dick. Never threw his family's wealth in Gabriel's face.

Aidan was Aidan. Footloose and fancy-free, drifting around the world whenever the urge took him. Another thing Gabriel liked about Aidan. He never bludged off his parents, expecting them to pay for his expenses. He'd started a blog about food and travel, attracted an audience, found sponsors. Aidan had always come back to Gabriel. Each time Gabriel told himself this would be the last time, but when Aidan was with him, his life gained in richness. He settled and became more at peace with himself, and the sex always rocked.

But as he got older, this wasn't enough. He wanted someone he could turn to on a rainy day and bitch about the mud, the cold, the stubborn cow who kicked him when he was trying to help her. He sensed Christina could be that person, yet if he was honest, giving up Aidan was impossible since the man was so much a part of his life.

Aidan's hand settled over his, and Gabriel flinched at the unexpected touch. "Heavy thoughts?"

"Thinkin' of the past. You and me."

Aidan stiffened and withdrew his touch. "Aye?"

"I love you. Always have."

Aidan sighed. "Aye, I ken."

Gabriel shot him a quick glance. This man always had Scotland in his speech, but it was sparse. This was practically a full sentence. Demonstrated the upheaval in his mind.

"Gabriel, what are you trying to tell me?"

Gabriel shoved away his empty plate and reached for Aidan's hand. "Love having you here with me, but I can't do this anymore. Not if you intend to leave again."

Aidan straightened on his chair. "Christina."

"She's part of it. What I'm saying is I don't want casual anymore. I want a relationship. Maybe kids. I want my hard work to mean more than it does."

"I can't have your children."

Gabriel barked out a laugh, the sly humor from Aidan lightening the mood. "Know that, smartarse. I'm talking a future. A solid one with no doubts on either side. Lazy Sunday afternoons. Trips together. Meals. Happy times. Sad. I want it all."

"I've come home."

"You leave," Gabriel said bluntly.

"I've signed a lease."

"Could still leave."

"Is this a threat?" Aidan demanded. "Do you want me to go?"

"No, dammit. This is me laying out my feelings. You wanna trample them, go right ahead." Gabriel rose and collected their empty plates. "Thanks for dinner. Best meal I've had in ages."

"Where does Christina fit in?" Aidan asked, standing too.

"She's a friend."

"But you have a history."

"You and I have history," Gabriel countered.

"You slept with her. I found you in bed together."

Gabriel's brows rose at the faint accusation in Aidan's words. "You haven't been here for over twelve months.

Was I meant to put my life on hold when you'd given me no promises?"

"I called."

"Twice," Gabriel said. "The connection was so bad I couldn't hear, and the other time, you left a message."

"But you slept with her."

Gabriel glared at Aidan. This was a variation of several discussions they'd had over the years, and this rehash pissed him off. "You had sex with anyone since you've been away?"

"No," Aidan snapped. "I inferred that earlier."

And it still surprised the hell out of Gabriel.

"You're it for me. Always have been," Aidan muttered.

"Funny way of showing it," Gabriel said, eyes on Aidan. "Can't handle this way any longer."

"Aye, I get that," Aidan said. "For the last time, that's why I'm here. I don't want to lose what we have."

Gabriel studied Aidan, saw the desperate truth glittering in his bloodshot eyes. He nodded. "Wanna watch TV, or do you need to hit the sack?"

"Bed. I'm having trouble keeping my eyes open."

"I'll clean up in the kitchen and watch the rugby. Sleep, mate."

Aidan studied him for a long time before his shoulders slumped. "See you later. Who's playing?"

"It's the provincial games. Super rugby is over for the year."

After Aidan headed to the bedroom, Gabriel cleared the kitchen, wiped the counters, and grabbed a beer. He turned on the television, but the game failed to hold his attention. Christina filled his mind, along with Aidan. Christina's blurted fantasy curled around him, into him. Crazy, but these two gave him different things. So what if it was non-traditional? His grandparents never judged him, and they were the only ones who mattered. Apart from Aidan and Christina.

Gabriel twisted the idea to and fro. Some negatives. Yeah. But the positives pushed ahead, winning to his mind. Instead of blundering in, as usual, he needed a plan. A solid one to give him what he wanted. Christina and Aidan. First, Aidan needed to get to know Christina. Get a friendship going. Knowing them both, he couldn't see them hating each other. They had him in common. Both were smart people. Should be easy. Wouldn't be, though. He sensed it in his gut. But he'd fight for this. Now he'd tasted Christina, he hated to let her go. Wanted Aidan too, which made him a selfish bastard. He grinned. Christina's fault. She'd put the idea in his head.

Yeah. Couldn't force this. Had to take his time. Had to watch Christina too, without hovering. Vulnerable now. Last thing he wanted was to make her drop farther into her depression. She'd told him she could deal if she did things right. A death. Him. Aidan. Added together, this might push her over the edge. He scrubbed his hand over his face, worrying for her. He'd wanted to check on her again, but questioning Aidan had reassured him.

That reminded him. The shop takings. He had time to sort out the banking. He grabbed the canvas bag and his deposit book. Not much cash. No problem. He added up the EFTPOS receipts and smiled. Not bad. Bloody good, in fact. If he could keep this up, he could repay the last of his debt, repay his grandparents, and give Christina a pay rise.

CHRISTINA DRAGGED HERSELF FROM bed. She hadn't slept much—not with her mind driving in circles. Gabriel. The sexy Aidan. Her failure yet again. The necessity of staying on Waiheke. Her friends. Everything whirled through her mind, flitting like butterflies yet leaving their mark. When she slept, she woke with tears sliding down her face.

While her preference was for more sleep, Toby's bark told her it was time to move. Toby needed his dinner and a walk. Fresh air wouldn't hurt her either. Christina chose clothes at random from the closet. A faded yellow T-shirt. Jeans with holes in the knees. A pair of red gumboots. A denim jacket.

When she fed Toby, he didn't seem interested in his dinner, but he drank water.

"Hey, boy. Are you missing Bernice?" She smoothed her hand over his head, and he sidled closer for a cuddle. "Want to go for a walk?"

Toby brightened at the W-word, and she snapped on his lead and headed for the river walk instead of the bush on Gabriel's land.

"I don't know what to do about Gabriel," she told Toby. "I like him so much, but now Aidan is here. How can I compete with him? He's pretty, and they have a history. I have to stay here for six months. What should I do?"

Toby didn't have answers. Instead, he nosed in the undergrowth—the blackberries and long grass that bordered the river walk.

With each breath of fresh air, Christina shoved away her fatigue. She paused at a vantage point and watched a mama duck herd her ducklings into the water. Christina stretched and ran through her special breathing exercises. Although her mind remained sluggish and her thoughts raced in turmoil, forcing herself from the house had been a positive move. Her thoughts skipped ahead, told her there were a lot of empty hours in her future, and her shoulders slumped. The black beast pushed at her mind, smothered her positive thoughts, whispered of loneliness, informed her no one wanted her.

Gah! Not again.

She didn't want to be like this. Dependent on others for her happiness. Bernice had loved her. Her parents loved her. Her friends, even though she hadn't seen them for ages, loved her.

She could ring Susan. Ask her if she'd kicked the flu's butt.

Before she could second guess herself, she plucked her phone from her pocket and sent a text to Tyler. *Is Susan okay now? Well enough for me to ring her?*

Her phone rang a few seconds later.

"It's me," Susan said. "I'm right beside Tyler."

"Are you busy?"

"Never too busy for you. I'm so bummed I was sick, and it was worse when the others told me they put off the meet-up too. Are you at the apartment? Should I swing by to pick you up for coffee?"

Christina laughed, giddy with relief and pleasure at Susan's response. Then she realized Susan didn't know about Bernice. Her friends hadn't met her godmother, although she'd mentioned Bernice over the years.

"I have so much to tell you. First, the apartment owner gave everyone notice because he's tearing down the building. He offered compensation for moving, so I signed his papers."

"So, where are you staying?" Susan asked. "Why didn't you say something? Do you have a place?"

"Give me a chance to speak. My godmother wasn't well, and my parents are overseas on their trip, so I'm staying at Bernice's cottage on Waiheke Island."

"That's not far."

"Still my turn," Christina said.

"Sorry." Laughter sounded in Susan's voice, and it was easy to picture her friend with her long black hair, her eyes crinkling with humor.

"Bernice died. It was sudden."

"Oh, Christina. I'm so sorry. Can I help in any way? I know how close you were."

"Yeah." Christina swallowed hard. The lump in her throat didn't shift, so she gulped again. "Bernice left me her cottage, but there are conditions. I have to live here for six months."

"Oh," Susan said. "Is that a good thing?"

"The timing is perfect since I have somewhere to live, but I miss Bernice so much."

"You were close. It's understandable. What are you doing for a job?"

"I have a part-time job selling cheese. The shop is shut on Monday and Tuesday. I'm thinking I'll make soap and scarves and sell those at the local market. Give myself breathing space."

"Hmm," Susan said. "I guess there's not much market for a personal shopper in Waiheke."

"No. Business had dried up in Auckland too. The economic downturn hasn't helped."

"If I were my mother, I'd lecture you about returning to accountancy. Do they have those on the island?"

Christina snorted, amused at her friend. "It's a forty-minute ferry ride from Downtown, Auckland. We're civilized over here."

"Good to know," Susan retorted, but Christina could tell she was laughing. "How did you get the job in the cheese shop?"

"The guy who owns the farm next to my grandmother's cottage makes the cheese. I knew him when I was a teenager."

"Is he cute?"

Christina hesitated, and heat gathered in her cheeks. "Y-yes."

"Y-yes?"

"He was my first kiss, and he's aged well."

"Have you kissed since?"

Christina hesitated.

"Christina? Are you still there?"

She closed her eyes. "We slept together."

"Right. That does it," Susan said. "I'll round up Maggie and Julia. We're coming over to Waiheke for the day. You're off Monday and Tuesday, right?"

"Yes."

"Give me a week because it's like herding cats with everyone going in opposite directions."

"Gabriel won't mind me taking a day off. As long as it isn't a Sunday because I want to test the vibe at the market. But we could go wine tasting and have lunch at one of the vineyards."

"That sounds lovely," Susan said. "I'll let you know once I've organized everyone."

"I can meet the ferry. The four of us will squeeze into Bernice's car."

"Great, I can't wait. Don't be a stranger, huh? If you ring and I'm busy, I'll tell you, then I'll call you back as soon as I have a chance. Don't hesitate because you think I'm too occupied with family. Same goes for Julia and Maggie. They'd tell you themselves if they were in on this conversation. I know what you're like, Christina. That's why I'm so pleased you rang today. I get that you feel left out since all of us married and have kid stuff to do. We care for you."

The warmth that suffused Christina this time was the right kind. A cozy embrace of the emotional type. She'd done the right thing in calling Susan. "Thanks," she muttered, her mood swinging from wanting to cry with relief to laugh with delight.

"Can I tell Maggie and Julia everything you've told me?" Susan asked.

"Yes," Christina said.

"What about the first-kiss guy?"

"It'd be easier for me if they were up-to-speed."

Susan chortled. "Don't you worry. Now that I have your permission, I'll grab them for coffee today. We'll have a gossip session."

"I wish I could be there," Christina said.

"Don't you have cheese to sell?"

"True and soap to make."

"The lavender soap you used to bring home?"

"Yes."

"Save some for me," Susan ordered.

"I'll give you some."

"No, not this time. I'll pay for it," Susan said. "Oops, gotta go. Tyler is late for work, and I want the car today. Talk to you soon."

Christina ended the call, the weight pressing on her shoulders now lighter. She'd pushed away from her friends because they'd gone in different directions. She'd allowed herself to linger and resent their fortune in finding the perfect one. A mistake. One she had to own and put right. Hadn't the five workmates been known as the Tight Five, taking the name of a rugby term where players bind together in a scrum? Susan had made her see they were still friends, but friendship, like all things, didn't flourish when untended.

She hadn't put in the work with her friends.

Not an error she'd make again.

She was a person who needed a plan. It kept her focused with eyes on the prize, and it helped her to control her depression.

Christina whistled for Toby. He came, but he wasn't his normal happy self. She crouched beside the tan-and-white dog and made a fuss of him, scratching behind his ears. He missed Bernice. She made a mental note to check dog health on the internet and keep a close eye on him.

7

Kisses In The Cheese Shop

Gabriel had meant to visit Christina after milking to check on her. Shit had piled in the way. His grandmother called, distraught.

"James is sick," she said. "I need to take him to the doctor, but I can't do it on my own."

"Do you have an appointment, Gran?"

"Not yet."

"Make one as soon as you hang up. I'll clean up and come to collect you."

His grandmother hesitated. "What about your other chores? I know you're busy."

"That's silly talk. You need me, I'm there. Besides, Aidan is here. Turned up yesterday morning. I'll ask if he can do a few things for me."

"What about your cheese?"

"I have a friend selling it for me. You remember Christina?"

"Christina?" His grandmother sounded more alert. Curious. "Christina and Aidan. I hadn't heard. Maybe I should've gone to the bake sale at the church yesterday. James told me to go, but I wanted to keep an eye on him."

Some of Gabriel's worry faded at her words. "I'll be there in fifteen minutes. You make that appointment."

"Fifteen minutes. Hmm, that will give me time to think up nosy questions."

Gabriel barked out a laugh, pleased her panic had dispersed. "You do that, Gran. 'Course, I don't have to answer them."

Ten minutes later, after a quick shower, he was on the way to pick up his grandparents.

His grandmother met him at the door. Concern creased her forehead. "James is adamant he doesn't need a doctor."

"What time is your appointment?"

"There was a cancelation. We need to be there in ten minutes."

Gabriel followed his grandmother to the kitchen. "Grandpa, you're worrying Gran. You need to go to the doctor. Otherwise, I'll never hear the end of it. This will be my fault."

His grandfather's face was pale, and today, his age had settled into his body and features. Gabriel helped his grandfather dress, concerned when the older man's balance was off. He slung an arm around his grandfather and supported most of his weight on the way to his vehicle. His grandmother grabbed her purse, locked up after them, and climbed into the rear.

"Tell me about Christina. She the one you kissed?" his grandfather asked.

More of the anxiety he'd held close to his chest dispersed. A nosy grandparent was one who wouldn't die today. His gaze met his grandmother's in the rear-vision mirror. "Didn't take you long to tattle."

"We worry about you, boy," his grandfather rumbled, a little of the color returning to his cheeks.

"Christina is beautiful," Gabriel said in an understatement. "She's helping me in the cheese shop, and after two days, she's drawing in customers. Told a tour group I have a special cave just for my blue cheese." He shook his head, a tiny grin playing with his lips. He knew this because he fought it from growing bigger. No sense giving away too much before he was ready.

"Have you kissed her? How does it compare?" his grandmother asked.

"Nosy question," Gabriel countered.

"What about Aidan? You kissing him?" his grandfather inquired.

Gabriel shot him a side-eye. "Nothing wrong with you, old man."

"I told Beth it is the flu."

"Best to check," Gabriel told him.

"I agree," his grandmother said. "Now, back to the kissing conversation."

"When I have something worth mentioning, you'll be the first to know."

"Keep an ear to the gossip, Beth," his grandfather said. "Locals on this island pick up things fast. Two possible lovers. That will get the bigmouth juices running. Probably get an irate call from your parents."

"Jesus," Gabriel said, pleased they'd reached the doctor's surgery.

"Gabriel Fletcher!" his grandmother said. "What have I told you about cursing?"

"Sorry, Gran," Gabriel muttered. The last thing he wanted was to worry about his parents' and his sister's actions. He'd walked away from that when they'd kicked him out of the house. They might try to use his relationship with Christina and Aidan to hurt his grandparents or his lovers. They'd already attempted to force him to leave the island. Thanks to his grandparents, he'd won that battle. Once he maneuvered Christina and Aidan together and laid out what he wanted from the future—their future—he'd have to tell them about what had gone down with his parents, his sister. Telling them his side of the story, which was the bloody truth—even though his Mum and Dad didn't see it that way.

"Done woolgathering, boy?" his grandfather

demanded. "Much as I hate to admit it, I need help here."

"No problem." Gabriel climbed from his SUV and jogged around the hood to the passenger side. His grandmother had already hopped from the rear and was doing her hovering thing.

"You get the door for us, Gran," Gabriel suggested.

She did, leaving him alone with his grandfather. "You serious about this girl, boy?"

"As serious as I am about my farm."

"You giving the boy the flick?"

"No," Gabriel replied.

His grandfather frowned, and Gabriel helped him out. "I'm keeping both of them, Grandpa. If they agree."

He had the satisfaction of watching his grandfather doing a goldfish impression and couldn't help his smirk.

"Boys, do hurry up," his grandmother called. "The doctor is waiting."

As Gabriel helped him along the footpath leading to the front door of the surgery, his grandfather said, "You're a maverick. You never take the easy way, boy."

Gabriel sighed. "I enjoy the challenge. I hope I don't muck up this one. Too much at stake."

His grandfather shot him a sharp look. "Your heart involved?"

"Think so, Grandpa."

His grandfather nodded several times. "It was like that for me when I first saw Beth. Fell for her straight away, although I fought it. Knew I was off to war. I didn't want to risk leaving her without a husband, but I couldn't leave her alone. She got pregnant with your uncle, and I married her. Worried the whole time I was away, she might find someone else."

"Gran would've never done that," Gabriel said with certainty.

"I know that now, but things happened fast at the beginning. With the war and everything, we never spent much time together. Not until after. What I'm saying, Gabriel. You find someone who makes you happy, you hold on to them. Don't let others dictate how your life should go. You want both of them, you make it so. Never forget, Beth and I are on your side. Consider you our boy. Anyone you love, we'll love too simply 'cause they mean so much to you. Proud of you."

"James," his grandmother called, her tone impatient now. "We're not leaving until the doctor sees you and tells me I can stop worrying."

"Beth, stop fretting. I needed to tell our boy something. Was important."

Her scowl softened and filled with love, even if it bore a tinge of exasperation.

Gabriel hid his grin even as he prayed he'd settle into this kind of love with Aidan and Christina. He helped his grandfather into the doctor's room and left him with the doctor and his grandmother.

"Hey, Gabriel," a feminine voice said.

Gabriel turned, froze for an instant, and strode outside without giving her the time of day. *Bitch*. If she thought she could speak soft and friendly and he'd forgive her, she could fuckin' think again.

He leaned against the hood of his vehicle, pulled out his cell phone, and rang Aidan.

"Hey," Aidan said, and the tinge of Scottish in Aidan's voice soothed his angst. "How is your grandfather?"

"He wasn't so good when I arrived to pick him up, but some of his feistiness returned during the ride to the doctor's surgery. They're in with the doctor now."

"That's great. Tell them I said hello."

"How is Christina?"

"She seems cheerful. Talked about going over to Auckland to purchase some supplies for her soap-making and scarves. The Tourism Board called me, and they want me to do a piece on Matakana and Goat Island. Also, one on Puhoi, Piha, and the wine-growing region north of Auckland. Matakana will be on a Sunday because that's when they have their market. I wondered if it would be okay if I asked Christina to go with me. Give me a woman's point of view."

"When were you thinking?"

"I need to go to Puhoi and Piha plus the vineyards next week."

"Have you asked her?"

"Not yet. I thought I'd run it past you first. Don't want to step on any toes."

Gabriel watched the doorway to the doctor's surgery for his grandparents. He wished he and Aidan were having this conversation in the same room. Because right now, he wanted nothing more than to kiss the man stupid. No sex. He wanted them on the same page before sex came into the equation, but kissing would work fine. "You're not steppin' on toes. I want you and Christina to become friends. Ask her. Depending on things here, I might try to take time off, and we could go to Matakana together. Heard the snorkeling at Goat Island is fantastic. Have a friend who owes me a favor. He and his wife might do the milking for me for one weekend."

"You mean it?"

"I'll try to make it happen."

"Aye! Gabriel, I..." He drifted off. "Thank you. This means a lot to me."

"My grandparents have finished. Later."

"The doctor gave us a prescription to fill," his grandmother announced.

"We'll drive home via the chemist," Gabriel said. "Do you need groceries?"

"We'll get them another day," his grandmother said in a firm voice. "James needs to rest."

Gabriel helped his grandfather into the passenger side of the vehicle and closed the rear door for his grandmother.

"What did the doctor say?" Gabriel asked as he backed out of his parking space.

"It's not the flu. James has high blood pressure. He's one of the lucky ones who have symptoms. The doctor has prescribed medication, and once James takes the tablets, he'll be fine."

"Excellent news, then," Gabriel said.

Five minutes later, he parked near the pharmacy and strode inside to get the prescription filled. Coming out, he spotted his bitch sister and Darcy. Seeing that woman once today had been bad enough. Twice just pissed him off. He scowled and ignored them when his sister drove past.

"Was that Stacey?" his grandmother asked.

Sharp as a tack. She didn't miss much. "And Darcy," Gabriel gritted out.

"I heard she was back. Sarah Baker told me at the last book club meeting. She wondered if you knew she was back."

"I do now." Gabriel strove for calm. "The woman tried to speak to me today while I was waiting for you."

"None of that family has much class, despite their money," his grandfather said.

Gabriel headed home. "You got that right."

After dropping off his grandparents and making sure there was nothing they needed doing, he drove home. For once, he had someone waiting for him. Two, actually, and that lightened his mood.

When he arrived, two cars and a mini-bus were parked in front of the cheese shop. Curious, he strode around the back. Both Christina and Aidan were talking with customers, and the place smelled like delicious food. Gabriel lingered out of sight and listened to Christina spin tales about his cheese. He smiled, his satisfaction growing big and wide until he realized his jaw hurt from grinning so hard. The bus passengers left, each of them with a purchase while the driver lingered to speak with Christina. He shook her hand, delighted by whatever she'd told him, and left.

Gabriel entered the shop, his gaze tracing her face. She shoved her glasses up her nose, and her golden bracelets made a jingling sound.

"You're back," she said.

"I am." He seized her by the shoulders and hauled her into his arms, acting on impulse. Once he touched her, the notion cemented into certainty. He needed his mouth on hers. *Yesterday*. He drew her closer, smiling at her widening eyes before his lips touched hers, and he settled into seduction mode. Not too decadent. There was one remaining customer. Unwillingly, Gabriel drew away and ran the back of his knuckles over her silky cheek.

"Oh, my," the woman said, patting her chest. "I wish I received a greeting like that."

"You should leave before I shock you," Gabriel said. "I aim to kiss him in the same way."

If Gabriel thought the woman would scuttle off in distress, he was wrong. Shrugging, Gabriel pressed another kiss to Christina's soft lips and turned to Aidan.

Aidan looked hurt, but he didn't move straight away. When he tried to escape, Gabriel blocked Aidan and stepped into his personal space. He gripped Aidan by the shoulders and stole a kiss from him too. This kiss tasted just as good. Different, but still hot, it diverted Gabriel's blood to his dick.

"Oh, my." The woman patted her rust-colored sweater at chest level again, her blue gaze full of nosy interest.

"Um, I thought you were in a hurry," Christina said to her in a soft voice.

The woman straightened, her blue eyes skimming each of them before she shook her head. Her lips, shaded with bronze lipstick, ticked upward. "Finding one person to love is hard. Believe me, I've gone through several users and arseholes. Finding two is stealing everyone else's chances, Gabriel. Do your grandparents know?"

Gabriel's shoulders stiffened, and he narrowed his gaze on the single mother. While he knew her, it was only to say good morning or offer other pleasantries. "Not discussing this with you."

Her smile widened to gleeful. "I'll say goodbye then. I'm looking forward to eating the goat's cheese." Then, she hotfooted it out of the cheese shop, leaving them alone.

8

THE PROPOSAL

AIDAN GAPED AT THE rapidly departing woman before turning his disbelief on Gabriel. His bloody knees threatened to buckle, and he gripped the edge of the refrigerator unit to bolster his strength. While he fought his physical balance, he attempted to shore up his mental equilibrium too. He could still taste Gabriel on his lips, and the spear of jealousy at watching Gabriel plant a kiss on Christina dug into his heart.

"What the fuck was that?" Aidan's quick glance at Christina told him Gabriel had flummoxed her too. She didn't know what to make of Gabriel's kisses. Aidan licked his lips and sidled closer to Christina.

In the short time he'd known her, he'd discovered he enjoyed her shy humor and the more confident persona she projected for the customers. She made him laugh, and the woman had a gift for selling cheese. He'd invited her to go with him on his trip. She'd accepted on the condition she could visit a wool shop to stock up on supplies. Now, he slipped his arm around her shoulders. She trembled but didn't reject his touch. He fit her closer to his side, and together, they stared at Gabriel.

Gabriel didn't answer. Instead, his gaze turned distant, as if he were chewing over what to say.

Aidan waited, his mind sorting through different scenarios and coming up empty. Christina's expression had blanked, and he didn't know her well enough to guess her thoughts.

Finally, Gabriel straightened. "I refuse to choose between you and Christina. I want both of you. Finally decided this while I was scared as shit about my grandfather's health and trying to keep it together for Gran. Life is too short to fuck around and make myself unhappy. I could love either of you. All I needed to do was choose. But I don't want to pick one over the other and lose one or both of you. Which means, I choose you both."

"But..." Aidan broke off when his brain refused to string together words.

"Blame Christina," Gabriel said with a wink. "She gave me the idea."

"Christina?" Aidan turned Christina in his arms, so she faced him. Her gaze ducked his and focused on his shirt buttons. He stroked her hair and smoothed a lock away from her face. A delicate pink filled her cheeks, and Aidan placed his fingers under her chin, directing her eyes upward to meet his. "Is that true?"

"Um, yes?" Her gaze darted away and back.

"She told me she fantasized about loving two males," Gabriel said in his deep rumble. "I've been thinking about it ever since because it'd solve my problem of caring for both of you."

Shock rippled through Aidan, and he gave his attention to Christina. "You told Gabriel you wanted two men in your bed?"

"Y-yes."

Aidan breathed deep and caught a hint of her flowery perfume. It was old-fashioned, yet nothing about the scent on Christina screamed out of touch or outmoded. In two days, he'd come to enjoy the whiff of flowers and freshness. "That's what you want, honey?"

"The customer you just scandalized mentioned it's difficult finding one person to love. Experience had taught me this already, so her opinion wasn't a surprise. I've dated a lot. My girlfriends, too, before they each found their one. I've always fantasized about having two men caring for me, loving me, but I figured since finding one was hard, a pair would be impossible." Christina checked her purple watch and tugged from Aidan's grip. "It's time to close the shop. I'll swap out the open sign at the gate."

Her bracelets jingled as she let her arms relax at her sides.

Aidan's gaze slipped to her butt and the sway of her hips when she strode outside.

Silence fell in the shop.

"Do you have anything to say?" Gabriel asked.

"Aye," Aidan said. "I'll have a lot to say once I figure out where my head is at. I didn't—I've never considered anything like this."

"Won't be easy. I get that. Worthwhile though. Something special."

"Waiheke is an island. It's a small town that's landlocked. Have you considered the gossip?" When Gabriel opened his mouth, Aidan raised his hand. "If we go ahead with this fool idea, all of us will be in the firing line. What happens if the locals blackball your cheese? Refuse to buy from you? Have you thought about that?"

"Considered lots of things since the idea entered my head. I hesitated, but as I told you, my grandfather's illness jolted my thoughts. Both you and Christina mean something to me. Refuse to choose, knowing the other will get hurt. It's much better this way."

Aidan threw up his hands. "How? How is it better?"

"Think of a pot with three legs compared to one with only two legs. The one with three legs is solid. Robust. The three of us together fit, and we'd be stronger since we'd have each other for support. That's if you intend to stay."

Aye, and there it was. Aidan's proof he'd damaged his relationship with Gabriel. His inability to settle had broken trust. His selfishness in following his desires. Despite his assurances he intended to—wanted to stay, Gabriel didn't believe him.

"How do you envisage this working?" Aidan asked.

"Haven't thought that far," Gabriel informed him, his brown eyes flashing with impatience. That determined chin of his—today covered in stubble—lifted.

Gabriel was serious. He meant every word.

Christina returned, her jaw as set with determination as Gabriel's. Aidan wasn't sure what she intended to do, but she had her strop on. Her eyes flashed with magnificence, and her bracelets tinkled. She stomped toward him and Gabriel. Figuring Gabriel was her target, Aidan sidestepped to give her room to pass him. She dodged with him, gripped his biceps, and stared up at him. Searching. Aidan had no idea what she was hunting for, but her face softened from its determined mask. She removed her hands, took half a step back while still watching him.

"Angel's stardust," she muttered, and she closed the distance between them again, gripped his shoulders, and kissed him.

Aidan froze at her velvet-soft lips against his. He'd told the truth about remaining celibate, and for him, that meant kissing on the mouth. Gabriel was the last person he'd kissed, last person he'd fucked. Christina drew closer and pressed her breasts against his chest. She opened her mouth and traced his lips with her tongue. Her scent filled him. Flowers and sweetness. Her softness seduced him. Heat surrounded him, permeated him.

Wait, what?

He flinched, and Christina pulled back, but she didn't remove herself from his space.

"It's me, Aidan," Gabriel said from behind him. His mouth was warm against Aidan's ear, and Gabriel nibbled his neck, sending darts of pleasure through him. He stopped, lifted his head, leaving Aidan quivering with arousal. For a long second, neither Gabriel nor Christina did anything. Aidan opened his eyes. Hell, he hadn't even realized he'd closed them. He caught the tail end of a silent Christina and Gabriel exchange. Intriguing. Undecipherable to him, at least.

Christina gave an imperceptible nod and claimed Aidan's mouth again. This time, Aidan was more prepared for her soft lips and her floral scent. He wasn't prepared for the twin assault. Gabriel pressed close to his back until Aidan felt the prod of Gabriel's erection. Gabriel's mouth claimed a spot on Aidan's neck to suck and kiss and tease.

Desire roared through Aidan, blanketed as he was between Christina's softness and Gabriel's unrelenting muscles.

Then Gabriel's heat disappeared, and Aidan groaned, wanting it back. Christina stepped away, and he mourned the loss of her touch as keenly. Aidan's body hummed and pulsed, every nerve ending reverberating with pleasure.

"Are you closed?" a man asked.

"Yes, I'm sorry," Christina said.

"Oh, I was hoping to organize a cheeseboard for an office party next week." The man cast curious gazes at him and Gabriel.

Christina turned to us. "You two go. I've got this. I'll head home after this since I'm worried about Toby. He's not doing well at the moment." She turned back to her late customer and smiled, dismissing him and Gabriel.

Gabriel hesitated, and Aidan decided it was his turn to talk, and they'd do it in private.

"Gabriel, Christina said she's got this." Aidan prodded Gabriel toward the rear exit of the shop and outside.

"I want Christina to stay," Gabriel stated, planting his feet.

"Have you considered she wants space to think? I do after your declaration."

The hard determination in Gabriel's expression faded. "You didn't mind both of us kissing you."

"It was an ambush." Aidan prodded Gabriel again, shoving him to get the man to move. "Please. Christina is busy tonight, and she wants to check on Toby."

Gabriel took his gaze off the rear door of the cheese shop and focused on him. As always, heat punched Aidan in the gut. "What's wrong with Toby?"

Aidan shunted Gabriel toward the house. "Toby is off

his food. Christina is worried he's pining for Bernice. She told me if he doesn't start eating again, she'll take him to the vet."

"That dog loved Bernice. She'd had him since a puppy," Gabriel said.

"Christina told me."

"Where is Christina going tonight?"

"She informed me she wanted to become involved in the community. There is a book club meeting at the local library tonight, and she figured she'd go." Aidan laughed. "Apparently, she enjoys reading, but if they're reading something literary, she won't last long and will need to try something else."

Gabriel barked out a laugh. "She reads romances with burly dudes on the covers."

This time, Gabriel let Aidan grab his hand and tug him into the house. "How do you know?"

"It's what she used to read as a teenager. She'd get them from Bernice. Sometimes, she'd read a paragraph to me, sigh, and tell me that was the way to treat a lady. A few times, I consulted with my grandmother, and she agreed, so I placed the information into my seduction repertoire. She also reads mysteries, but doesn't enjoy too much blood and gore."

"Cozy mysteries?" Aidan asked.

"Yeah. That's the term. How do you know?"

"My mother reads cozy mysteries. She says they relax

her after dealing with stubborn, chauvinistic males in the boardroom." Curiosity filled Aidan. "What ways to treat a lady?"

Gabriel shrugged and stalked to the fridge. He pulled out two bottles of beer, opened them, and handed Aidan one. "Things like opening doors, carrying bags, and helping in small ways that cost nothing but make a person happy and treasured. Bringing coffee. Giving them the last cookie." He shrugged. "Small things."

Aidan thought back, frowned. "You do those things for me." He gestured at the bottle of his favorite beer.

"I care for you." Gabriel met and held Aidan's gaze.

"Aye," Aidan breathed. "I'm beginning to realize I've taken you for granted. Finding you in bed with Christina gave me a big clue. You've been giving, and I've been taking but not doing the reciprocal thing. A relationship shouldn't be like that."

"No."

Enlightenment swept over Aidan, filling him with understanding and remorse. Hell's bells. Due to his stupidity, he'd almost lost Gabriel. He set his bottle on the kitchen counter and strode toward Gabriel, intent on kissing him.

Gabriel's mouth was firm rather than soft, the sensation of stubble against his face different but no less arousing than Christina's smoothness. Gabriel allowed the kiss, but when Aidan tried to take it deeper, he stepped away.

"What?"

"I'm not kissing you or Christina alone. Told you what I want. The next step is up to the two of you. Refuse to touch either of you when there is no agreement between us. Refuse to choose. Refuse to play games. It's all or nothing." He downed the remaining beer in his bottle. "Gonna shower."

Gabriel sauntered away, and Aidan stared after the man. He'd always acted confident, a little arrogant. Aye, and bossy. Yet Gabriel was a gentleman and never played games. All along, he'd told Aidan women and men attracted him. For him, it was the personality beneath the skin that caught his attention. He'd also told Aidan he didn't cheat. When he was with someone, he believed in loyalty. His honesty had grabbed Aidan from the start. His maturity when the rest of their friends were placing notches on their headboards and having competitions to see who could drink the most and get wasted.

Aye. He'd been stupid in treating Gabriel as a convenient body to fuck. Could've had Gabriel all to himself if he'd dragged his head out of his arse in time. Now, Gabriel had feelings for Christina, and while Aidan wanted to hate the woman, he couldn't. He liked her, which was why he'd invited her to go on his first travel gig.

Crap. Aidan plonked his butt on one of the chrome barstools that stood at the breakfast bar. Even in this modern age, he didn't ken if a three-way relationship could grow strong enough to withstand local gossip and smartarse comments. People would talk. He remembered what it was like when he'd visited during school holidays. His mother's amusement at the small-town nosiness. On the plus side, Gabriel was right about strength in numbers. Aidan's parents might look askance at his choices, but they kenned Gabriel. Gabriel had earned their approval when he'd stepped in and stopped a local bully from stealing a young girl's ice cream money. His mother always asked after Gabriel. While his parents were cool with his sexual choices because he, like Gabriel, was bisexual, he wasn't sure if they'd approve of him taking one of each sex.

Hell's bells.

Was he considering this?

Aidan climbed to his feet and grabbed a glass of water. He needed to speak with Christina.

The idea that he'd lose Gabriel...

Anger flashed through him. Anger at himself. Anger at Christina for impeding what should've been a simple reconciliation and a happy-ever-after. Then, there was Gabriel. Trust him to make this complicated. But that was the guy Gabriel was—full of layers of light and shade. Aidan reminded himself that complicated had attracted him, kept him coming back. Made him realize his behavior toward Gabriel was crap, and he needed to fix it with decisions, or he'd lose something valuable.

Aidan yanked open the fridge and pulled out two steaks

he'd defrosted plus fresh vegetables. By the time Gabriel appeared in the kitchen, he had dinner almost ready. He turned to face Gabriel, wishing he had the right to walk to him and claim a hug. He'd have to earn that again, understood it even as he castigated himself for his stupidity.

"I need to talk to Christina. Get to know her better since I only met her two days ago. Is there a timetable on this suggestion of yours?"

"No timetable," Gabriel replied. "We have six months to work this out. Know what I want since I've been thinking about it for a few days now. I can wait for you and Christina to catch up."

"What if one or both of us say no?" Aidan asked.

"Then, I'll still have two good friends," Gabriel said. "Told you before. It's all or nothing."

And that, Aidan thought, was that.

9

POOR TOBY

CHRISTINA SCOWLED AT HER book club selection while she spooned up breakfast cereal. As she'd figured, it was a book she'd never give a second glance if she saw it in a bookshop or library. But, bonus points for her—she'd dipped her toes into community events and made tentative plans to go for coffee after the market on Sunday. The women had acted standoffish though, some of them whispering when they didn't think she'd notice.

Small towns. Ugh!

Toby whined, drawing her attention. His food bowl sat nearby with his morning meal uneaten. "Hey, Toby." She clicked her fingers, and he glanced in her direction but didn't move. "Maybe it's time to take you to the vet for a check-up."

Christina checked Bernice's address book and found the

vet's contact details as she suspected she would. An hour later, she was on her way to the vet's surgery with Toby in the back seat. He still hadn't eaten.

She clipped Toby's lead in place and led him toward the surgery. He started shaking, and Christina crouched to comfort him. "I get it, boy. I don't enjoy a doctor's visit either, but sometimes they can see things we can't." When he continued trembling, she picked him up and carried him inside. After checking in with the receptionist, she took a seat. She and Toby were the only ones waiting, although the vet was with another patient.

"You look familiar." The receptionist's badge informed Christina her name was Stacey. Stacey had jaw-length brown hair with blonde highlights and was a little heavy. Her smile was on the mean side. Mean in that it barely shifted the line of her mouth to a curve.

"I'm Bernice's goddaughter. I used to spend my school holidays on the island with Bernice. If you live here, you might've noticed me around," Christina said.

"You live opposite Gabriel Fletcher's farm." Stacey's words sounded like an accusation.

"Yes, my godmother left me her cottage."

The vet, an elderly man with a relaxed manner, appeared on the heels of a woman carrying a tabby kitten in a cage. "You should be all set," he said with a nod before smiling at Christina. "Ah, Toby. Come on in."

Christina set Toby on the floor, then picked him up

again when he trembled. She followed the vet and placed Toby on top of a stainless-steel table.

"Now, what's the problem?" the vet asked.

"Toby isn't eating, and he's not enjoying his walks like he used to."

The vet slid his hand over Toby's head. "I was so sorry to hear about Bernice. I'll miss her at the theater club."

"Thank you," Christina said. "I miss her a lot. She was a special lady."

"She was," the vet agreed, compassion shining in his features. "As for Toby, we'll give him a once-over, but I gave him his annual vaccinations a month ago. He was in perfect health then. My best guess is he's missing Bernice. Dogs get depressed, just like people."

"They do?" Christina had never considered dogs might suffer from depression. "I know a little about depression. But dogs can't talk and tell you their symptoms. How do you help them fight their sadness?"

While he carried out his examination, he talked to Christina. "Well, you could introduce another dog, so Toby has a companion. If that's not an option, you could try finding him a part-time doggie companion. Doggie daycare would be ideal. Take him for lots of walks and take him with you as much as you can. But you don't want to coddle him either. You need to sail a line between giving him attention and not spoiling him. You need to distract him and give him other things to think about instead of missing Bernice."

The vet took Toby's temperature, checked his teeth and paws, and finally, stroked him.

"I'm confident there's nothing physically wrong with Toby. I want you to spend time with him, play with him, give him extra walks, and doggie company if possible. From memory, Bernice told me he enjoys the beach. Try him with some of his favorite meals, but don't overfeed him. Also, make sure his water bowl is full at all times. Give it a week, and if he's still not eating, there is medication we can try, but each dog is different. The medication might work, and it might not. It should be a last resort."

"All right," Christina said. "Thank you."

"You're very welcome," the vet said. "I have some treats out at reception. Let's see if he'll eat one."

To Christina's relief, Toby accepted a cracker from the vet and swallowed it.

"Excellent," the vet said. "Call me if you have further concerns."

"Thank you."

The vet turned away to greet a mother and child. The mother carried a cage with a blue budgie inside.

Christina paused at the reception desk and presented her credit card.

The woman processed her payment, her manner tense. As she handed Christina a receipt, she said, "You should stay away from your neighbor. He's not a decent man."

"Pardon?"

"Gabriel Fletcher is a two-faced liar," she stated.

The bell on the door rang, announcing a new arrival.

Stacey smiled at the elderly woman. "Clara came through the operation well. She's awake and ate dinner this morning."

Dismissed, Christina led Toby from the vet's surgery, her mind whirling at Stacey's bitterness and open dislike of Gabriel. The woman wasn't familiar to Christina, but as a kid, she'd only hung out with Gabriel. Of course, she'd met Bernice's friends too, and if they'd had children or grandchildren staying, she'd spent time with them. Not this Stacey woman, though.

What had Gabriel done to incite such dislike?

It was apparent Stacey actively hated Gabriel, and given what Christina knew of him, she couldn't fathom why.

10

MARKET DAY AND A PISSY YOUNGER SISTER

CHRISTINA DIDN'T GET A chance to ask Gabriel about Stacey since he didn't appear at the cheese shop. With Toby still moping, she'd spent her time worrying about her dog rather than stressing about Gabriel and his preposterous suggestion. Because it was ludicrous, wasn't it?

Sure, she'd fantasized about a threesome ever since she'd first read a romance featuring one. She'd even told her girlfriends she wanted two male lovers at the same time.

But that was a fantasy, and this was real life where people suffered hurt feelings.

She might get burned.

One positive though—with Toby, Gabriel, and Aidan

filling her mind, there hadn't been room for negativity. Her depression had eased because work crammed her hours, along with sorting through Bernice's possessions, planning her scarves, and looking forward to seeing her girls when they visited Waiheke. Plus, the three males in her life. She'd spent time with Toby, obsessed about Gabriel, and now, she was currently sneaking peeks at Aidan whenever he wasn't watching.

He was cute, his appearance edgier than Gabriel's with his long black hair. Today, he wore it in a man-bun, and the look worked for him. The trace of an accent that deepened when he became passionate about a topic held charm.

"Are you going to keep peeking at me all day, or are we going to face the invisible Gabriel in the room?" Aidan said.

Christina jerked, her gaze flying to him. "You know, Bernice saved a heap of cane baskets—the type that comes with gift baskets. What do you think about making up a few baskets with cheese, crackers, and maybe a chutney to sell at the market tomorrow?"

"That is an excellent idea. I can make an onion marmalade tonight. It won't take long." He grinned at her. "Changing the subject won't work. You need to tell me where you are with Gabriel's suggestion. You kissed me." Accusation shaded his tone, yet his face didn't echo the sentiment.

Christina inhaled and did her four-second breathing

exercise before she decided how to answer.

"What are you doing?"

"I suffer from depression, and this is one of the coping methods I use. I do it when I'm stressed."

His dark brows arched. "I'm stressing you by asking questions?"

"I didn't say I was anxious now."

He glared at her. "You implied it."

"My mind is full of uplifting stuff and questions. There is no room for depression today."

"What sort of questions?"

"Cheeseboards," she said, valiantly trying to maintain an impassive expression. "Is it a good idea to sell cheeseboards at the market? Will customers want them? Should I chuck away the cane baskets I've pulled out of storage? And if we decide to sell them, should I line them with colored tissue paper or as an alternative one of my silk scarves?" She risked a direct glance at Aidan and pursed her lips. "So what do you think? Cheeseboards or not?"

Aidan stared at her, and she couldn't guess at his thoughts. A master of enigmatic, which might prove difficult in the future.

When he didn't answer, she continued. "I'm leaning toward the tissue paper, three types of cheese, a packet of crackers or lavosh. Lavosh would be my preference and some of your onion marmalade if you have time."

"Stop." Aidan held up his right hand in a halt signal.

When her inner devil prompted her to open her mouth again, he stepped close and gripped her shoulders.

"Do I have to kiss you to shut you up?"

"Do you want to kiss me?"

Aidan growled, and seconds later, his mouth slanted over hers. Christina froze, yet didn't offer any other form of protest. Deep down, she admitted his kiss was what she wanted to help her in this decision. Sure, they'd kissed before, but she required another one where she wasn't rigid with shock. If it was like kissing a brother...

His mouth coaxed hers to widen, and a spike of heat struck her. Instinctively, she crowded close enough for her breasts to flirt with his chest. He was taller than her, but not as tall as Gabriel. He was, however, solid with broad shoulders, and she gripped them to anchor her in place. When she tried to lead the kiss and take it deeper, Aidan pulled away.

"Stop trying to drive the boat."

"I'm participating," she countered.

"No, you're trying to force me to go in the direction you want."

Christina sniffed. "You don't have to kiss me." She tried to step away, but he held her in position.

"I didn't say I was averse to your kiss."

For a long moment, Christina stared at him, and he stared back. Heat entered his gaze, and she found herself curious. "Have you slept with a woman before?"

"Aye. I thought you understood Gabriel and I are similar in that regard. We're attracted to people rather than a particular sex. And so you're as clear as Gabriel. Although I haven't been here for over a year, Gabriel is the last person I slept with."

"You love him."

"I do."

Christina licked her lips, discomfort washing over her. "It must be difficult—a shock—learning he is interested in me."

"Seeing you together in bed hurt." Aidan gave her honesty. "I've tried to internalize my pain because I haven't been fair to Gabriel. I didn't give him assurances when I left, and he thought my leaving meant I was leaving him too."

"Messy," Christina blurted.

"Aye. My fault, you ken."

"Have you decided what you want to do?"

"I want to ken you better," Aidan said. "Cheeseboards. Tissue paper. Three kinds of cheese. A jar of my onion marmalade. When I go to Oneroa to purchase plastic pottles for the marmalade, I'll get the ingredients for lavosh. I suggest we do ten baskets as an experiment. Do you have that many?"

"Easily," Christina said. "How do you intend to get to know me? Will it involve more kissing?"

"I haven't decided yet," Aidan said.

"Will you give me a warning? I wouldn't want to eat garlic and put you off."

"Not a problem for me," Aidan said with a wink.

Christina's phone rang, and she glanced at the screen. "Susan."

"The stars have aligned, and we can come next Tuesday," Susan said. "Does that work for you?"

"Awesome. Oh, Susan. That's brilliant. Which ferry will you catch?"

"Maggie checked the ferry schedule. She said there's one that arrives at Waiheke around ten."

"Excellent, I'll be at the ferry terminal to pick you up. I'm looking forward to seeing you so much."

"We're excited too," Susan said. "Julia's nanny is looking after the babies, and Ryan and Caleb volunteered to do the school run. Do you need us to bring anything?"

"Not that I can think of."

"Great. See you on Tuesday."

Christina disconnected, happiness making her want to sing and dance.

"Good news?"

"Three of my friends are coming over from Auckland for the day next Tuesday. I promised to give them a tour and lunch at a vineyard."

"A wine tour?"

"Well, my friends enjoy a glass of wine. I don't think any of them are pregnant at the moment, although we haven't caught up for a while."

Aidan smiled at her, and it lit up his eyes.

"You have dimples," she whispered. "They're so cute. It makes me want to kiss them."

"Do you always say what you think?"

"Normally, I bottle up things, which is part of the reason my head gets so busy, and I get depressed if I'm not careful."

"I suggest we ask Gabriel if we can borrow his vehicle. I'll drive and use the time to do a piece on Waiheke Island for my travel blog. That way, you and your friends can have a few glasses of wine and enjoy yourselves. It would also be nice to have photos of pretty ladies on my blog."

"You'd do that for me?" Christina whispered.

He nodded, another smile wreathing his mouth. This time, she stepped nearer and fingered one of his dimples. His smile deepened, and she found herself grinning too.

"I would," he said. "It will give me a chance to spend time with you and meet your friends."

"You can't kiss my friends," she said. "They're all married women."

"That's fine then because you're the only one I'm considering kissing."

"On your program."

"Aye, that's right." He glanced at his watch. "I'll walk to the gate to turn the sign around, then head off to shop for supplies."

"I have tissue paper we can use inside the baskets, plus clear cellophane to cover the baskets once they're filled. What will you use for the lavosh crackers?"

"I'll give it some thought." Aidan strode past her, pausing at the last moment to brush a kiss across her lips. Then he was gone, marching up the gravel driveway to the signage.

"Be still my heart," Christina muttered, staring after him for long seconds before she turned her attention to readying the shop for business. Sleep this coming evening would be full of these two men. She didn't understand what she was doing, but at least her mind was full of positive things rather than negative.

MARKET DAY MEANT AN early morning wake-up. When the alarm jerked him awake, Gabriel untangled himself from Aidan and climbed out of bed. Despite the king-size bed and starting each night on opposite sides with a decent amount of space between them, Aidan always rolled closer to him during the night. Each morning Gabriel woke with a warm body tangled with his and a hard-on. Each morning, he ignored his erection and took a cold shower before he started his day.

He was determined to wait until Aidan and Christina sorted themselves out before he dived into intimacy again.

Some mornings were harder than others. He grimaced. No pun intended.

After his quick shower, he prodded Aidan awake and headed for the kitchen to make coffee. Aidan always moved faster once he caffeinated. The week had been busy in the shop, and Gabriel had high hopes for the market. Aidan and Christina had worked wonders with their baskets, which sat on the kitchen table, prepared to be sealed after cheese and relish were added.

A knock sounded at the door, and when Gabriel answered, he found Christina and Toby. Christina was carrying a box.

"Hey, come on inside." Gabriel stood back to let Christina pass.

"Can I bring Toby inside with me? He's clean since I washed him yesterday."

"No problem."

She set down the box. "These are my scarves—the ones I want to sell if possible. Is your vehicle locked? I don't want to leave them behind, so I'll put them in the trunk now."

"It's not locked." Gabriel gave her a quick kiss even though her hands were full. Heat and desire—lust—roared through his veins. Sleeping next to Aidan and seeing Christina most days was not tamping down his libido. Something needed to give and soon. He stepped back from Christina. "I'll pour you a coffee."

Christina arrived back and claimed a seat at the breakfast

bar. Aidan wandered out from the bedroom dressed in a pair of boxer-briefs and nothing else. He still looked half asleep and hadn't noticed Christina's presence. Aidan preferred to sleep in the nude, but Gabriel—for his own sanity—had vetoed that inclination.

Gabriel watched Christina's reaction with interest. Her gaze darted to Aidan and fixed, scanning his length twice before settling on his chest. Aidan kept fit by trekking and water sports during his days jaunting around the world. Since he'd arrived on Waiheke, he'd helped Gabriel with farm chores. No doubt about it—the man looked good.

"Coffee?" Gabriel asked.

"Please." Aidan blinked on seeing Christina gawking at him. "Like what you see?"

"Turn around," Christina ordered.

Gabriel hid his grin as he poured another mug of coffee.

"What?" Aidan sounded confused.

"Turn around. I wanna see the entire package."

"There's nothing wrong with my package," Aidan growled.

"Turn around so I can judge for myself."

Aidan let out a huff and rotated his body in a full circle. His brows rose when he faced Christina again. "Well?"

"Very nice," Christina said. "Can I touch?"

"No," Aidan growled.

"Spoilsport," Christina whispered.

"How would you like me to ogle you?" Aidan

demanded.

"I suspect you will." Christina took a sip of her coffee. "But just so you know. I have average-size breasts, and I'm pear-shaped. I—"

"There is nothing wrong with her body," Gabriel interrupted. "She's curvy where she should have curves and soft. FYI, I dislike skinny women, and you need to regain the weight you've lost."

"Same," Aidan said without hesitation. "Give me soft, lush curves anytime."

"Changing the subject," Christina said in a stern voice. "Can I take Toby with us? He won't mind if he's tied up at the stall, but I thought if he could see people, he might perk up a bit."

"Is he still depressed?" Aidan asked.

"He's eating a little, but he's not his usual happy self. I'm following the vet's instructions, and I guess it's early days yet, but I'm worried."

"We'll find a spot for him," Gabriel said. "Aidan, we have half an hour before we have to leave. If we're late, they'll give our booking to someone else."

Aidan grabbed his coffee mug and headed for the bedroom. "Won't be long."

"Are you two sharing a bed?" Christina asked, her tone curious.

"We are, but we're not having sex."

"Because?"

"Because now you've given me the idea, it won't leave my mind. I'd like some action, but I'm willing to wait on you and Aidan. I refuse to push either of you into a situation if you're not comfortable."

Christina downed the last of her coffee and stood. "You're a good man, Gabriel Fletcher. Can you grab the box of cheese marked gift baskets for me? The rest of the stuff is already in the kitchen. I'll start assembling the baskets. It won't take long." She produced another bag and pulled out two pale blue T-shirts that bore navy-blue lettering to match the labels he used on his cheese. "I made us matching T-shirts so we'll look professional. I'm already wearing mine." She lifted her jacket to show him.

A knot formed in Gabriel's throat as he accepted the two shirts. "That's such a great idea. Thank you! I'll take this one to Aidan."

They arrived five minutes early, but Gabriel decided half of the residents of Waiheke had beat them to the market. Their assigned table wasn't in the best position, but they'd make do. It had been a while since he'd attended a market here, and it'd be interesting to see if their products sold.

Gabriel started dumping wedges of cheese onto the table.

"Stop," Aidan instructed.

"Not that way," Christina said. "We have a plan."

"How about I take Toby for a wander and survey the rest of the market while you carry out your plan?"

"Go," Aidan said, waving him away.

Gabriel untied Toby's lead and grinned from Aidan to Christina. Neither of them noticed his amusement or his happiness, but spending time with them brought satisfaction. Contentment. The pair were working as a team. They acted comfortable together and frequently touched even though they'd met mere days ago. Quietly happy, he led Toby along the sidewalk.

His gaze skimmed the various stalls. No cheese. Excellent. Less competition.

One face caught his attention.

Crap.

The last person he wanted to see.

Then another woman turned. His sister.

Fantastic. A double bonanza.

He hoped they stayed the hell away from him, and he'd return the favor.

No harm. No foul.

He loitered at a stall selling clothing and ducked behind a dressmaker's dummy when the two women wandered past.

"Love affair gone wrong?" a wry voice asked from behind him.

Gabriel jumped before whirling to face the wizened woman with long white hair who was unpacking clothing from a crate. He'd been so engrossed with his hiding he hadn't noticed her presence. "Something like that."

"Two against one. It's best to hide when the odds are against you."

Gabriel gave a jerky nod, tossed back into the past. His sister and her best friend had ganged up on him. They'd lied so convincingly his parents had taken their side. The pain at the betrayal still cut deep. "Thank you for letting me hide. I think it's safe to leave now."

"Anytime, laddie." She beamed at him, displaying a gap in her smile.

With a wave, Gabriel headed back to his stall. Their stall. In the short time he'd been away, Aidan and Christina had transformed their allotted area into a magical splash of color. They'd set the attractive and tempting gift baskets on the left. They'd placed the portable refrigerator unit in the middle, and the three types of cheese he'd wanted to sell—the cheddar, the goat's cheese, and the blue—were front and center. On the righthand side, Christina displayed her scarves, grouping like colors together, so they looked like a silken rainbow.

Aidan noticed his arrival first and held out a plate full of crackers and thin slivers of his cheese. "Sir, can I tempt you with a morsel of our blue cheese?"

"Or if you prefer a tasty cheddar, sir, try one of my crackers." Christina offered him her plate, a noticeable twinkle behind the lenses of her glasses.

Gabriel swallowed hard and sent them both a stern look. "Don't call me *sir* unless you mean it."

Aidan exchanged a glance with Christina and winked. Gabriel watched a tinge of pink slide over her cheeks. They turned back to him.

"Yes, sir," they chorused.

Gabriel stiffened all over. *All over.* "Toby and I are checking out the market stalls in this direction." Gabriel stomped off with Toby, and Christina's sweet giggle and Aidan's deeper chuckle followed him. A grin tugged at his lips, and he let it grow, confident in his mind that this teasing was an excellent thing.

Most of the stallholders were set up and ready for business. Gabriel checked his watch. The first wave of day visitors from Auckland should arrive soon. He and Toby wandered the aisles, studying the handicrafts and food items available. Olive oils. Olives. Several of the wineries had stalls. Soap. Clothes stalls. Ice cream. A sausage sizzle. A stall selling homemade dog biscuits. He stopped to purchase three for Toby and grabbed coffees and pastries before heading back to their stall.

Aidan was already giving out samples of cheese and flirting with passing women to get them to stop. Christina was serving a customer, and it looked as if they'd sold at least one gift basket.

Gabriel settled Toby with a biscuit and set down the coffee and pastries. He ripped off his jacket and tossed it in a pile with Aidan's and Christina's discarded clothes. He grinned because he liked the way they looked jumbled together, then he set on his business head and jumped in to help.

About two hours later, there was a lull in business.

"I'm going to grab more coffee and have a quick peruse of the other stalls," Christina said.

"Coffee truck is that way." Gabriel gestured. "There's a stall selling soap in the same direction. A couple of the stalls in the opposite direction are selling scarves. Take your time."

Aidan nodded, leaning into Gabriel. "We've got everything covered."

"What happens if someone needs help with a scarf?"

"Go," Gabriel urged. "If a lady or a gentleman wishes to purchase a scarf, Aidan and I can offer masculine advice."

Christina laughed. "Should I bring coffee or something to eat?"

"I'm good," Aidan said. "I have a yearning for fish and chips and a walk on the beach later, though. Anyone up for that?"

"Me," Christina said.

Gabriel nodded. "Sounds good."

"Should I take Toby?" Christina asked.

Gabriel glanced at Toby, who was still chewing on his biscuit. "He's happy here."

Christina arrived back about half an hour later, carrying three coffees and a bulging cloth bag of mystery purchases.

Aidan was busy flirting with a mother and daughter and

matching scarves to their eyes. It seemed to be working, and he sold three before Christina handed him his coffee.

"People like the way you've displayed the scarves in a palette of colors," Aidan commented. "Most of the women who stopped to browse have a color in mind to go with an outfit. You take the guesswork out of their selection, and they don't have to paw through piles of scarves to find what they're searching for."

Christina nodded, pleasure scoring into her expression. "I'll add the scarves I held back."

"Aidan has already done that," Gabriel said.

"What?" Christina's brows bounced upward, and she turned away to check the box she'd packed her scarves in. "It's empty."

"That's what I meant." Gabriel slipped his arm around her waist and hugged her against him.

"Some of those scarves were secondhand. They were Bernice's. I didn't think they'd sell."

"Bet they were expensive and high-quality," Aidan said. "Some women acted as if they'd won a huge prize."

"A lot of them were from Paris and were designer scarves. Bernice had so many. I kept a few for myself, and thought if there were any left, I could use them as bows on the cheese baskets next week."

"Only one basket left," Aidan said with satisfaction.

"I believe that basket has our name written all over it," a masculine voice declared.

"Henry," Gabriel said, offering his hand to Bernice's lawyer. "Justine." He smiled at Henry's wife. "You know Christina, but have you met our friend Aidan Wayland?"

Gabriel made the introductions before Henry turned to Christina. "Justine told me she met you at the book club. I'm pleased you're entering the spirit of the community."

"How are you going with our assigned book?" Justine asked.

Christina wrinkled her nose. "I've had trouble," she confessed. "I prefer genre fiction, and romance with the odd mystery to spice things up. Our read might have received public acclaim, but it's full of sadness. It dragged down my mood in the first chapter. I much prefer an uplifting romance." She leaned closer. "The sexier, the better."

"Can you tell our organizer that during our next meeting? Please," Justine said. "She won't listen to reason. There are about six of us who prefer romance. Seven with you."

"What's stopping your club having a selection of two books each time? I have no problem listening to others talking about a book. Reading it firsthand—no. It's depressing. When I read, I want entertainment and fun. Romance."

"Exactly! Can I ring you later in the week to discuss tactics?" Justine asked.

The two women exchanged numbers while Henry paid

for the last cheese basket.

"Aidan, it's your turn to research the other stallholders," Christina said.

"Thanks. I'll go, but I've decided to focus on local produce for my dishes. That makes more sense than going with a particular regional cuisine. Nice to meet you," he said to Henry and Justine.

Not long after, Christina nudged Gabriel. "Do you know that woman? I met her at the vet's surgery, and she's been glowering at us for the last five minutes."

Gabriel glanced up to meet the glare of his sister Stacey. Her mouth curled in distaste before she stomped around a family group and disappeared into the crowd.

"That'd be me she's aiming at. That's Stacey, my younger sister."

Christina clapped her hand to her forehead. "That's why she looked familiar the other day. I couldn't place her even though she wore a nametag. She knew about me, though, and told me you were trouble."

Gabriel snorted. "She holds a mean grudge. I'd prefer not to discuss her or my family. One day I'll tell you and Aidan the reasons my parents kicked me out of their house and why they and my sister treat me like a bad smell."

"If they hate you so much, why do they stay on Waiheke?" Christina asked, seconds before she smiled at a newly arrived customer.

Gabriel didn't want to discuss his family and what

he suspected their reasons were for staying. He had his suspicions, although he didn't want to spoil his day by debating them. He turned his attention to a new arrival while Christina talked scarves with two teenage girls.

Around one, vendors started packing up their remaining stock, and Gabriel, Christina, and Aidan did the same.

"A suggestion," Aidan said. "Why don't I grab the fish and chips now, and by the time I'm back, you should be finished. We can find a more private beach and have a chat." He gave a chin-jerk in Christina's direction.

Gabriel's pulse started racing as he shifted his gaze from Aidan to Christina. "Excellent plan, but can you get sausages instead of fish for me? For location, I know the perfect beach."

11

TOGETHER WE'RE STRONGER

"ARE WE ALLOWED TO drive through here?" Christina asked.

"Gave Gavin a call while you were talking to the two ladies who arrived as we were trying to pack up. Promised him a cheese basket in return, and he jumped at the chance to score points with his missus," Gabriel said.

Christina smiled when she spotted the expanse of white sand, currently empty except for a flock of seabirds. She itched to kick off her shoes and enjoy the sunny spring day and the warm sand beneath her feet.

"This is the beach only accessible by boat," Aidan said.

"That's right." Gabriel parked his vehicle. "And select friends. We walk from here."

They didn't have a picnic blanket, but Christina didn't mind sitting on the ground. Rocks guarded the outer edge of the private cove. Two gnarled pohutukawa trees offered shade while the sand glistened in the sun, pristine and free of flotsam. Beyond the beach, the water was a striking turquoise. A yacht sped past, the colorful red-and-white sail billowing in the wind before it disappeared from sight.

Toby settled on the sand, in the shade cast by one of the pohutukawa trees, with a doggy sigh. She, Aidan, and Gabriel sat nearby.

Aidan had also purchased three cans of L & P—a classic New Zealand soda with a citrus flavor. He handed a newspaper-wrapped package and a can of soda to her.

"Where's the tomato sauce?" Christina asked.

Grinning, Aidan plucked several tiny packets from his pocket along with a whole lemon and a pocket knife.

"Aidan was a boy scout when he was younger," Christina commented to Gabriel.

"I was a scout. I loved the outdoor activities and excelled at them," he added with cheer. "My Swiss army knife comes in handy whenever I'm traveling. An impulse told me to bring it today."

"Almost warm enough for a swim," Gabriel said, digging into his parcel and picking up a battered sausage.

Christina shivered. "*Brr!* Not for me. I refuse to swim in the sea until at least December."

"That I remember," Gabriel said. "I also remember your bright red bikini."

Cursed heat invaded her cheeks. She'd thought she'd

conquered this bugbear tell, but these two men slid beneath her control. "Aidan, when are you taking over the premises in town?" she asked. "You never said. Do you need to do much work on the interior before you can open? And if you've thought about the menu, does that mean you intend to open soon?"

"The kitchen isn't perfect, but it will do for now," Aidan said. "The main dining area needs painting. I thought I'd go for rustic. For the menu, I'll do platters and have one dish of the day, which will change according to produce availability. I intend to open for lunch from Wednesday to Saturday and for dinner on Saturday night only. Not sure about Sunday yet. I'm experimenting and getting a sense of what might work. It's different running a business rather than working in a restaurant. Maybe I won't enjoy this, which is why I'm dipping my toes in the water rather than going all-in as I'd originally intended." He stopped talking, and the left side of his mouth hitched upward. "Tell me more about this bikini. Was it tiny?"

Gabriel heaved out a gusty sigh. "Oh, yeah. She looked hot. Started to think about more than a kiss. The wait was worth it."

Christina realized her mouth had opened and snapped her teeth together. He'd wanted to sleep with her back then? She'd been a goody-two-shoes. Their kiss had been fantastic, but her mother had put the fear of god into her about teenage pregnancy. With the way she'd blushed back then, it had been difficult enough hiding the fact she'd kissed a boy, and she'd liked it.

"Makes sense," Christina shared with Aidan, ignoring the red bikini topic. "You still have your travel gig."

"Which is why I'm giving myself at least two days to travel to different destinations. I can fly anywhere in New Zealand and not waste too much time," Aidan replied. "Do you still have the red bikini?"

"Not the same one."

"Pity," Gabriel said, his fingers running from her knee and up her thigh.

His touch lit every nerve on the way, each jumping to attention. Even through her jeans, the slow slide of his fingers prodded her libido, made her recall her night with Gabriel, and the best sex she'd had in forever.

"What about you?" Aidan asked, his eyes on her. He took in the caress of Gabriel's hand, and his mouth quirked into that amused hitch again. "Did wandering around the market help with your decision about whether to make soap or not?"

"Can we talk about us?" Gabriel asked before Christina replied.

Her pulse had grown choppy, arousal dampening her panties, yet she didn't move her leg. Instead, she counted the seconds between each mesmerizing, each sensual, each maddening glide of Gabriel's work-rough fingers. Her body grew warmer, and although she wore her favorite pair of jeans, she was tempted to grab Aidan's pocket knife and hack off the denim to allow Gabriel direct contact with her legs.

Aidan turned to Gabriel. "We mightn't have made up our minds yet. This is a weighty decision."

Gabriel growled, and Christina barely suppressed a smile even as a tic started in her jaw. Gabriel was a man who thrived on action. He worked out what needed doing and bulldozed ahead to achieve his goals. Now, he'd decided he wanted her. He wanted Aidan. Done deal. And he was pushing forward. While she was oh-so-tempted, now that reality inserted into her fantasy, all she could see were the roadblocks and the possible consequences.

She worried and decided apprehension was smart.

Aidan's usual humor dropped away, and he grew serious. "My main problem is I don't want to lose our friendship. Although Christina and I haven't known each other for long, I like her a lot."

"Thanks," Christina said, warmth suffusing her chest because she could see he meant every word.

"Going quietly crazy," Gabriel stated. "After spending the night with Christina, I want her again, and waking up with you wrapped around me every morning, Aidan—I'm sick of having cold showers."

Christina glanced at Aidan, and he held her gaze before a slow smile crept across his visage. Her pulse rate leaped yet again and, in that moment, she decided she'd jump with both feet. If these two sexy men wanted her, she was inclined to agree to Gabriel's proposal.

But caution led her to ask a question. "What if this is a mistake? I like you both. You make great friends. I agree with Aidan on this part. The last thing I want is to lose your friendship."

Gabriel opened his mouth, no doubt, to pour out a serving of his rough charm and persuasion, but before he could speak, Aidan cut in.

"I ken there is a possibility of us getting together and things going bad, but what if us together is spectacular? Aye, we each have our faults, but together we balance out. We're like the three-legged pot Gabriel mentioned. United, we're stronger."

"What faults?" Christina asked, part curious and partly disturbed by the way he saw her. The fact he'd spent time diving deep and thinking about her. *Them*.

"Gabriel is a workaholic because he wants to prove to his family he doesn't need them. I drift and allow circumstances and my itchy feet to keep me moving. It was fun at first—traveling and getting paid for it because of my blogging, but it's lonely. The friendships I make are transient, and I want more, which is why I'm here on Waiheke. I want to prove to Gabriel, and now to you, that I have what it takes to have a long-term relationship. To commit."

"And me?" Christina asked.

"You haven't made your depression a secret. A successful relationship won't necessarily help you since I ken depression and associated anxiety can reoccur at any time. You've been low because of your godmother's death. Gabriel helped you when he dragged you to his place and forced you to sell his cheese. The truth is you have a better chance of a normal life if you surround yourself with people who love and care for you. People willing to listen when you need it and who have your best interests at heart," Aidan said, sounding more Scottish than usual.

"I'm not a workaholic," Gabriel protested.

"You are," Christina stated, seeing it now that Aidan had pointed this out. "You work long hours, and before Aidan and I arrived, you rarely saw other people for days. Aidan is right. On paper, we'd be stronger together. More balanced."

"And the physical?" Gabriel asked, a challenge in his voice.

Christina sucked in a deep breath, puffed it out, and jumped. "I don't know about Aidan, but I'm in. I'm willing to give this a shot."

She and Gabriel focused on Aidan.

"Aye," he said with a slow nod, his brown eyes serious. "I'm in too."

Gabriel kissed Aidan—quick and hard—before turning to her and repeating the kiss. "Been going crazy worrying about how you'd both decide. This is gonna be great."

"How will this work?" Aidan asked.

"Been thinking about that. My suggestion is to take our time and not rush." Gabriel glanced at both of them before he continued speaking. "If the three of us are together and in the mood, we should fool around, but there's no reason the two of you can't sleep together or any other combination of us. But I thought we should have one rule. Say, for example, if you and Christina have sex, give me details later. That way, I won't get left out. Less likelihood of jealousy. If I sleep with Aidan, one or both of us will give you a rundown and answer questions. Same if it's you and me, Christina."

Christina nodded in agreement. An excellent idea, and a way that was less likely to cause bad feelings or arouse the green-eyed monster.

Aidan stood and walked around Gabriel's extended knees to sit beside Christina. "Can I kiss you?"

Christina swallowed a mouthful of L & P. A shudder sped through her, and it wasn't nerves. Instead, anticipation frisked her breasts then raced downward to pulse at the juncture of her thighs. She stared at him, her heart beating faster than average. Since they'd arrived at the beach, she'd been in a state of heightened expectation, as if she were balancing on a tightrope stretched over a mighty canyon.

Gabriel's warm hand landed on her thigh again. He restarted his finger strokes while Aidan cocked his head, a quizzical smile flirting with his lips.

"Christina," he prompted in his Scottish-tinged voice.

It brought to mind braw Scottish warriors in their plaids, marching through a misty glen in the Highlands. Another shiver worked down her body.

"Kiss her," Gabriel whispered, his tone a smidge away from daring.

"Christina?" Aidan repeated. "Can I kiss you?"

"Yes, please." Her voice emerged in a whisper filled with uncertainty and anxiety. This was big. Huge. She hadn't fretted like this since she'd agreed to perform onstage at Maxwell's, her friend Julia's burlesque club.

Aidan's gaze dropped to her lips. "So polite. Polite girls get rewarded."

The first touch of his lips was a faint caress. Christina sighed, and Aidan smiled against her mouth, an instant before he deepened their kiss, taking it from flirtatious to serious. He traced his tongue along her bottom lip, the slide achingly slow and tortuous. He nipped the same spot with his teeth, the sharp jolt of pain morphing into something darker. Edgier. Christina lifted her hands and settled them on Aidan's shoulders. Aidan nibbled on her top lip and soothed the ache with another of those slow, gliding licks.

Then, heat covered her back, and she jumped in surprise.

"Steady, Christina. It's me," Gabriel whispered against

her ear. "I can't have Aidan having all the fun." His warm mouth nuzzled her neck, just as Aidan deepened their kiss.

Christina gasped against his mouth, her insides growing tight, the sudden burst of disquiet fading as flutters beat at her chest. Her nipples hardened when Gabriel trailed kisses down her neck. When he reached the base, he brushed aside her T-shirt and sucked.

She moaned against Aidan's mouth, and he took advantage, sliding his tongue inside to dance with hers. An unexpected flush of warmth slid down her torso, the glide and suck of Gabriel's mouth along with Aidan's kiss almost too much. Better than anything her imagination had conjured when she'd tried to envisage two lovers.

One of Gabriel's hands slipped under the hem of her T-shirt. His fingers ran up and down her ribs, firm enough not to fall into the ticklish category yet distracting. Arousing.

Aidan lifted his mouth. "Open your eyes, Christina."

"I didn't realize I'd shut them."

Beside her, Gabriel laughed. "Did I distract you?"

"My mind is bouncing all over the place. Too many sensations. Aidan's mouth. Your hand on my bare skin. I'm excellent at multi-tasking but the pair of you..." She trailed off and shook her head, a tentative smile for each man.

"Blew your fuses?" Aidan asked with a wink at Gabriel.

"No explosions," Christina replied. "But I thought my

heart might beat out of my chest."

Gabriel chuckled, his amusement evident.

"You think it's funny, but wait until you have two people focusing on your pleasure and see how you cope. Everything is magnified. More. Better." She gave an irritable shrug and reached for her can of soda. "It's hard to explain. I just hope I don't expire from a heart attack when the three of us are naked in bed. That might be embarrassing."

Gabriel chuckled, and he and Aidan did a high-five. A guy thing. Christina rolled her eyes.

"Sounds like fun," Aidan said. "Have you finished your meals?"

"Yes," Gabriel said.

Christina scrunched up her newspaper. "I've eaten enough. Why?"

"Because I'd enjoy privacy with both of you. Some of the ideas running through my mind aren't suitable even for this private beach," he muttered.

"Plan." Gabriel stood and held out his hand for Christina. When she took it, he tugged her to her feet. "Any second thoughts, say so now."

Christina glanced from Gabriel to Aidan and back. Both men wore intense expressions, and the lust and desire emanating from them set an echoing beat throbbing in her pussy. She hesitated, double-checked her inner thoughts, and gave a decisive nod. "Let's do this. Can Toby stay with your dogs? He seems to prefer their company to mine, anyway."

The drive back to Gabriel's house happened too slowly and also too fast. Anxious heat clung to her skin while her heart raced, and she wondered if the organ might drill out of her chest. Her mind kept darting back to when Aidan had been kissing her, and Gabriel had caressed her neck with his mouth and his tongue. The cascade of pleasure she'd experienced at the dual touch. She'd read about threesomes, dreamed of how a loving with two men might proceed, yet none of that had prepared her for the drugging bliss of being the center of their attention.

She licked her lips while her left hand ran over Toby's head. Instead of staying with her frenzied thoughts, she forced herself to inhale, do her four-second breathing exercise, and focus on Bernice's dog. Toby had seemed better today, happier and more alert after hanging out with them.

She petted along his back and leaned closer to the dog that now belonged to her. "Hopefully, this lasts for both of us," she whispered to Toby.

"Did you say something?" Aidan asked.

The two men had been murmuring back and forth in the front, but she hadn't been paying any attention to their actual words.

"I was talking to Toby."

Gabriel's phone rang. "Get that for me, Aidan," he said

as he rounded a bend on the gravel road.

"Gabriel's phone," Aidan said. He paused and listened before reporting to Gabriel. "It's your grandmother. She wants to know if you'd like to go to her place for dinner. She says she has cooked roast pork with all the trimmings."

"Put it on speaker for me," Gabriel ordered. He waited for Aidan to do that, then spoke. "Gran, I've got Aidan and Christina with me."

"Oh good," his grandmother announced, and Christina was positive she heard an excited clap of hands. "There is plenty of food. Bring them to dinner too. I haven't seen either of them for years. Six o'clock," she announced and hung up before Gabriel commented either way.

Aidan laughed. "She reminded me of my mother in the way she couched her request as an order."

"Do you mind?" Gabriel asked. "I'm sorry it means we won't have alone time, but I'd intended to stop by to check on my grandfather, anyway."

"We get a free dinner, and there's still time to fool around," Aidan said.

"Gotta squeeze in the milking."

"If we both help, the milking will be quicker," Christina offered. "I don't mind. Think about the shower together before we head out to dinner. In that nice, big shower of yours. That decadent wet-room of a shower with no doors and only walls. The one with the convenient seat and the extra taps and showerheads. Your excellent shower paired with my favorite lavender shower gel. Pure indulgence."

Aidan and Gabriel were quiet for a moment, exchanging a glance. Aidan grinned back at her and winked.

"Christina," Gabriel said. "I love the way your mind works, and I'm so glad you enjoy my shower. It's my favorite renovation so far."

"I favor the kitchen," Aidan commented. "The flow is awesome."

"Listened to some of your plans and comments," Gabriel acknowledged.

In the end, they'd stopped at Christina's cottage so she could pick up a set of older clothes suitable for farm work plus tidier clothes to wear to dinner.

Toby had crawled out of the car, trotted around the garden, then climbed into his kennel and gone to sleep. Christina had put out food, refilled his water bowl, and left him there since he seemed happy and settled. It meant she'd stay at the cottage rather than with Gabriel but she decided she'd continue with a slow approach, so she didn't become overwhelmed.

Now, with the milking finished, they were wandering back to the house with an hour to spare before they had to leave to drive to Gabriel's grandparents'.

"I still need to feed the dogs and check on the batch of cheese I'm making," Gabriel said. "Go ahead. Shower." He took two steps and came to an abrupt halt. Gabriel turned and nailed them with a stare. "Details."

Seconds later, he had gone.

"Well," Aidan said. "We're not bots. We don't have to follow his orders. If you want to shower alone, tell me."

"Getting naked for the first time is awkward," Christina said, and while she started with her gaze firmly on Aidan's handsome face, it ended up aimed at her feet.

A pair of hands landed on her shoulders. She flinched. An insistent finger beneath her chin had her gaze lifting. "If you've changed your mind, it's all right. You can take the first shower. I'm not forcing you to do anything."

"I'm nervous. What if this is a mistake?"

"What if it's not?" he countered. Aidan studied her for a moment longer and kissed her. The second his lips touched hers, every bit of tension seeped through her shoes and into the floor. She inched closer until her breasts flirted with his chest, and she wound her arms around his neck.

Despite their work in the cowshed, he smelled of sunshine and something woodsy and fresh. Without warning, he pulled back and slapped her arse.

"Shower. I'll get us a drink. Do you want a beer or a glass of wine?"

"Wine, please."

"Sure thing, honey."

Aidan strode from Gabriel's bedroom, and she stared after him. If she changed her mind, Aidan would take a step back. Gabriel would do the same. She never doubted that for an instant, which told her she trusted both men.

Did she want that? Heck, why was she hesitating? Aidan was gorgeous, and she'd already slept with Gabriel. She liked both men, was physically attracted to them, and when she spent time with Gabriel and Aidan, she didn't experience her usual loneliness.

This was what she wanted.

Besides, it was she who'd shoved the idea at Gabriel.

She plopped on the edge of Gabriel's bed and slid off her socks. She stood and lifted her T-shirt over her head. Soon, she was naked. She padded through to the en suite bathroom and placed her glasses on the counter.

Aidan arrived as she stepped under the warm water in the wet-room area. She hadn't exaggerated when she'd told them she'd enjoyed using Gabriel's shower the first time she'd stayed overnight. The tile-lined area, with its lack of walls, meant it was comfortable and roomy enough for three people. The seat, she realized with a start, would work perfectly for blow-jobs instead of needing to kneel on the hard tiles. With the entire area waterproofed with decorative blue-and-white tiles, splashes didn't matter. Crowding would never present an issue in this shower. Not for three adults.

Christina beckoned Aidan closer and watched him set down the drinks he'd brought from the kitchen.

"Do you want me to leave?"

"Stay. Shower with me," Christina said. "I had a

moment of panic. I'm good now."

"Sure?"

"Positive," Christina said.

Without taking his eyes off her, Aidan stripped. Naked, he joined her under the stream of water.

"How well can you see without your glasses?"

"Enough to see you're delighted I agreed to let you shower with me."

"You're beautiful. A bit skinny, but I figure I can make sure you eat proper meals."

Christina snorted. "You can talk. From where I'm standing, you're not much past skinny yourself."

"I lost weight when I succumbed to malaria. But we're talking about you."

She snorted. "You're as bad as Gabriel. It's true I've lost weight. When I'm down, I don't always eat. Everything that has happened—I'm eating better now. Lots of fruit and vegetables. I promise."

"Clock is ticking," Aidan said and reached for the bar of soap Gabriel had left sitting on a mesh tray.

A bottle of supermarket shampoo sat on a shelf. No frills for Gabriel.

"I should've brought the soap Bernice has stacked in her bathroom cupboard. She has homemade bath salts too. I've been dying to try out Gabriel's roll-top bathtub ever since I spotted it."

"Tomorrow," Aidan said as he slid the bar of white soap

over her back and shoulders.

Weirdly, shyness no longer harried her. Perhaps because they were both naked and busy scoping each other out.

"Do you mind if you get your hair wet? I doubt Gabriel has a blow-drier."

"It's fine," Christina said and started doing some touching of her own. He had dark hair on his chest. Not too much but enough to show he was a mature adult. While his muscles weren't quite as defined as Gabriel's, the man was in shape with broad shoulders, narrow hips, and muscular thighs. She ran her hands over his shoulders and worried a flat masculine nipple. Her fingers traced lower over his abs until she cupped his hips.

When she glanced up, Aidan's intense gaze burned her.

"Don't stop," he urged her, his black hair plastered to his scalp. "You have full rein to touch me anywhere you choose."

Such a powerful, handsome man. Her focus drifted to his erection, and she licked her lips. One thing she loved was to have a man in her power, to draw him under her spell. Sucking a man's cock worked magic, although she'd only done it with a few of the men in her past. Most hadn't deserved this gift.

"Let me sit," she murmured, tugging him with her as she sat on the tiled seat. Obligingly, Aidan followed her, planting his feet as she ran her fingers along the length of his cock. The ruddy head had her licking her lips, and she lifted his shaft to her mouth while seeking his eyes. They burned with heat and lust and passion, yet he didn't hurry her. Merely stood in front of her with the water pounding his back.

Her tongue snaked out, ran over the head of his cock, and Aidan moaned. The sound vibrated through his body, and he growled when she enclosed his tip in her mouth. Aidan shoved his fingers into her wet hair and clasped her head. Yet he didn't overwhelm her with his strength, his need to thrust. He let her taste and explore and go at her own pace. She cupped his balls and took him deeper, enjoyed both his ragged breaths and mutters along with the steamy mist and water surrounding them.

Aware of the passing time, she upped her pace until Aidan's legs trembled, and his appreciation became louder. Curses and moans. Grunts.

"Beautiful, I'm going to come. If you don't want me to do that in your mouth, you need to pull back."

Christina ignored his warning and, instead, slurped and sucked and licked. His hands tightened on her head, and his hips moved, pushing him deeper into her mouth. He came an instant later, his big body shuddering, a curse ringing out and echoing in the bathroom. Christina eased back, kissed the tip of his cock, and stood. His arms came around her in a tight embrace.

"Thank you, honey. That was amazing." As always, his accent was stronger when his emotions were aroused.

"We've used up our time allowance. It's quarter to six."

Christina had known that and didn't care. "We should turn off the water before the hot runs out. Gabriel shouldn't need to have a cold shower."

"Tomorrow," he said. "A date. You and I. I want a turn to explore that pretty body of yours. Aye, the first thing I intend to do is kiss and suck on your breasts. All right?"

She nodded.

"Here's the soap. Wash up and finish." His hand slipped over her butt, and she jumped when he slapped it. He reached for Gabriel's shampoo and lathered his hair.

Christina hustled and was soon drying herself with a navy-blue bath towel. In Gabriel's bedroom, she slathered on rose-and-lavender scented body lotion before pulling on underwear. A miracle of miracles, she'd found a matching bra and panties in black lace. She wriggled into a short denim skirt and a low-necked lacy steel-gray top.

Aidan strode into the bedroom as she started dealing with her hair. She hadn't washed it, but it was damp. She ended up braiding the longest lengths and pinning them up. Tonight, she kept her makeup light with a tinted moisturizer and a natural lipstick.

"You look gorgeous," Aidan said as he dressed in boxer-briefs, a pair of newish jeans and a cream button-down shirt. He sat on the end of the bed to don socks and boots. "Are you staying here tonight?"

"No, not since Toby decided he wanted to stay at the

cottage. I'd prefer not to leave him alone."

"What will you do tomorrow?" Aidan asked. "Your friends are visiting this coming Tuesday, right?"

"They are. I thought I'd make soap tomorrow and sort out more scarves to sell. As long as it's all right with Gabriel, I might put up a display in the cheese shop. The guy who conducts the mini-bus tours of Waiheke told me he'd be back. I figure tourists might like to buy soap or a scarf along with their cheese."

Gabriel arrived and started stripping as soon as he entered the bedroom. In seconds flat, he was naked and striding for the en suite.

Christina stared until Aidan nudged her with his elbow.

"I thought you'd seen Gabriel naked?"

"I didn't get to see or explore as much as I wanted. Gabriel was an action-man." Christina's words held a faint complaint because she'd wanted to run her hands over Gabriel and learn the touches he enjoyed most. She'd love to chip away at his control and drive him crazy.

"Aye, Gabriel prefers to do things his way. He focuses on a subject or in our case, lovers."

"We should break him of that habit. As much as I enjoy sex and pleasure, I think giving myself to a lover and teasing them until they lose their minds is fun too."

Aidan's brows lifted. "Like what you did with me?"

Christina beamed. "While I'm still aroused and twitchy, I figure when we do get together, the sex will be beyond excellent."

"If you intend to sleep on your own tonight, will you get yourself off?"

Heat climbed into her cheeks, but she forced herself to meet Aidan's gaze. "Possibly."

"These are the rules. If you touch yourself, you have to either describe the process to me tomorrow, or you need to do a repeat and show me," he said, his eyes twinkling with mischief. "That sounds like the perfect way for me to get payback."

Christina narrowed her eyes, although she wanted to smile. She fought the impulse, struggled to maintain her glower. "I thought you enjoyed me sucking you off."

"Aye, I did, but like you, I find giving pleasure increases my own. Let's make each other extra happy."

"Does that charm work on all the ladies?"

He offered a solemn nod. "Men too."

"You're a flirt," she accused.

Gabriel stalked out of the en suite, naked. He'd overheard part of their conversation. "Yes, he is a flirt. Cute sometimes." He prowled to a drawer, opened it, and pulled out underwear while giving Christina and Aidan a glimpse of tight buttocks. "Other times, it's a pain in the butt."

Christina studied his body, and he caught her staring.

"Like what you see?"

"Yes," Aidan spoke for her.

Gabriel huffed, and suddenly, they were all laughing.

This set the tone for the evening. On the way to Gabriel's grandparents' house, they stopped to buy two bottles of wine and a six-pack of beer and piled back into Gabriel's vehicle.

"It's a five-minute drive to my grandparents' house." Gabriel glanced at Christina, who sat in the passenger seat. "Tell me what you and Aidan did while I was doing chores."

"Me?" she asked.

"Yes."

In the rear seat, Aidan sniggered, and Christina shot him a glare. "Sometimes, you're annoying."

"Me?" Gabriel asked.

"Both of you," she confirmed.

Gabriel reached over and placed a hand on her knee. "Talk fast, babe. Four minutes now."

His touch sizzled up her leg. There was no other word to describe his caress. This time, his hand had direct contact with her skin. Just as effective. Just as distracting.

"Babe," he warned, centered her mind again. "We're not getting out of this vehicle until you do as I ask."

"Bossy, much?" she muttered and cursed at the whoosh of heat pooling in her cheeks.

"He says nothing he doesn't mean," Aidan said.

"Why can't Aidan tell you?" Now, she appeared sulky.

"Want to hear it from your sexy lips," Gabriel informed her. "Almost there. Do you want me to tell Grandma we sat in our vehicle for ten minutes while you poured hot tales of sex out of your pretty mouth?"

"Gabriel!" she burst out, horrified at the idea.

"My grandparents know about sex," Gabriel stated. "First, I'm here and proof of them having sex. We'll skip the parents' part in the equation. Second, when I wanted to kiss you for the first time, who do you think I asked for advice?"

Christina swallowed hard and was fiercely glad of the dim light in the SUV interior. Aidan didn't help matters by hooting behind them, his hilarity silenced as if he'd slapped his hand over his mouth.

Christina dragged in a quick breath. "We got naked, and I sucked off Aidan in the shower," she blurted.

"Details," Gabriel demanded as he indicated a right turn into a driveway.

Gabriel wasn't joking. Fine. She'd stumble through this and find a way to embarrass Gabriel at a later date. She shot a glare over her shoulder at Aidan, who was still sniggering. Two sets of payback.

Christina closed her eyes and began. "I stripped off all my clothes and started showering first. Aidan came into the wet-room, which I adore by the way. He was naked, and we kissed and cuddled and wandered hands up and down limbs and backs and chests. Butt cheeks. I copped lots of touches. I grew curious about Aidan's cock, and I stood back a bit. You have the seat in the wet-room, so I suggested Aidan stand there while I appeased my curiosity. I used my hands on his length," she whispered. "I licked the swollen head with my tongue and tasted him. He tastes fine, which made me decide to take him into my mouth and suck him like a lollipop. His cock grew bigger, and his pre-come dripped from his tip. I explored his balls with my hands, and once he started moaning, I let him use my mouth, let him thrust. His moans made me so hot. It made him hot too because he warned me he was about to explode inside my mouth. I let him because I wanted him to enjoy himself."

"What about you, princess?" Gabriel asked in a gritty voice.

Christina's eyes popped open, surprised to find the vehicle was stationary. "What about me?"

"Did you climax?"

"No. Aidan wanted to, although he warned me we were running out of time. I told him later would be fine."

"But Aidan mentioned you wanted to stay at the cottage tonight," Gabriel said.

"Right, which means you and Aidan will have lots of description for me tomorrow," she said. "Are we done?"

Gabriel leaned over and grasped her shoulders, holding her in place before she made good on her intention to open the vehicle door. He kissed her slowly and thoroughly, using his tongue and mouth to excellent effect. When he lifted his head, she was breathing hoarsely, and that edgy, unfulfilled sensation had zapped her center.

"Well done, babe. I enjoyed your description." He cupped her jaw and gave her another slow kiss before pulling back and exiting the vehicle.

"That was hot," Aidan murmured. "The more I see and experience with you both, the more I think this is a great idea. Sex between the three of us will rock."

Before she could answer, her door opened, and Gabriel stood there waiting. He also opened the door for Aidan.

"I've got the wine and beer," Aidan said.

An outside light switched on, burning away the darkness and highlighting pots of cyclamens, freesias, and daffodils.

"You're here," a female voice said. "Right on time."

Christina remembered the times she and Gabriel had arrived at his grandparents' house for lunch or afternoon tea. She'd always liked his grandparents, and apart from more wrinkles, his grandmother appeared the same.

"It's so good to see you both," Gran said. "I recall you both spending time in my kitchen during school holidays and you and Aidan eating as many cookies as Gabriel. Never at the same time, though. Had the two of you met before?"

"They've only just met," Gabriel said.

"You too?" Christina whispered to Aidan.

He nodded. "Happy memories."

They found Gabriel's grandfather carving the pork roast

in a huge kitchen. "Perfect timing," he boomed.

Christina's gaze wandered the kitchen. It was as she remembered with white curtains decorated with red poppies at the windows. Pots of herbs sat on a sunny windowsill. In décor, it was a twin of Bernice's kitchen and always put her at ease. The kitchen table where she and Gabriel had sat years earlier with cookies and milk bore a pretty lace tablecloth and five place-settings. A bunch of yellow freesias sat in the middle of the table, releasing their delicate fragrance. The tiles on the floor gleamed while a roast meat scent permeated the air. It was like walking into a welcoming embrace.

"They were happy times," Gran said. "You brought wine. Excellent. Aidan, will you have a glass of wine, or would you prefer beer? Gabriel, I take it you'd prefer your normal beer?"

"Yes, please, Gran," Gabriel said.

"I'll have a beer too, please," Aidan said.

Soon, they sat around the large kitchen table, and chatter and laughter flowed between them despite the gap in years.

"I'm so glad Gabriel has someone to help him on the farm," his grandmother said. "He works too hard."

"We had fish and chips on the beach today," Christina said, earning a grateful glance from Gabriel. "So, he's not all work."

"We're hoping to wean him from his workaholic ways,"

Aidan added.

"Excellent," Gran said. "You have our blessing."

Christina talked about handicrafts, and Gabriel's grandmother invited her to attend the Women's Institute meeting with her.

"It's not all oldies, dear," Gabriel's grandmother said. "We have quite a few young mothers and single women too. We do handicrafts, arrange trips, go walking, and raise money to fund our scholarship program. Next month, we're holding a zombie run. I can't wait to dress up as a zombie."

Christina stared at Gabriel's grandmother. "Zombies?" She glanced at Aidan and saw it intrigued him. Gabriel bore a grin.

"Are you dressing as a zombie too?" she asked Gabriel's grandfather.

"Not me," he stated. "But I am helping with zombie makeup. Can't be much different from painting a fence."

Before any of them could comment on that nugget, Gran said, "I have entry forms here and will sign you up after dinner."

"What day is it?" Gabriel asked.

"It's a Saturday. We're holding it on the Everetts' farm and using part of the obstacle course they built for the rugby team to train."

By the time they left for home, Gran had extracted entry fees from each of them. She was the same force of nature

Christina recalled from her teenage years.

Gabriel pulled up outside her cottage. "Sure you don't want to grab Toby and come home with us?"

"Not tonight. This Women's Institute group meeting—will it send me balmy like the book club?"

"My mother and sister used to go," Gabriel said. "So I know there are different age groups. I think Henry Wainscoat's wife goes too. Perfect group to join to fulfill the terms of the will. As far as I know, Bernice was a member too. Gran will know."

"All right," she said. "I'll do it."

"Dinner tomorrow night," Gabriel said. "At my place. You're staying the night."

"You need to curb that bossy gene of yours," she murmured.

"I like it," Aidan stated.

"Excellent. You can tell me all about his bossiness tomorrow," Christina said and climbed out of the SUV. "Don't misbehave too much."

12

GABRIEL AND AIDAN

GABRIEL DROVE THE SHORT trip to his house, his mind on Christina. While she'd acted happy enough, he sensed she'd turn tail if this situation became too intense or if they reached a point where they stumbled.

No relationship was easy. A typical connection between a couple took work. Juggling the opinions and needs of three people would require exceptional skill. They'd need to learn together. There'd be compromise and hurt feelings.

He'd considered this before he'd made his proposal, decided the outcome was worth the effort. Yeah, he was all in, and he intended to prove this to Aidan and Christina. Of the two, he figured Christina might take the most persuasion or think short-term rather than the permanent that was his aim.

She'd lost Bernice and had her world turned upside down. Stressful enough for most people, but with her depression, he wanted to make sure she thrived. With him and Aidan. Her sultry voice as she'd told him what she'd done to Aidan—hell. Still had an uncomfortable erection.

"Do you think she's okay?" Aidan asked.

"After she told me she suffers from depression, I read up on the subject. Basically, we have to be there for her when she needs us."

"Are we pushing her?" Aidan asked.

Gabriel parked and switched off the headlights. "She'd prefer to drift with our relationship. Last thing I want is to press her harder than she can cope with."

"I agree."

"Hate to force you into something you're not keen on either. Both of you have to want this. No going through the motions." Gabriel climbed out of his vehicle, and once Aidan stood beside him, he locked his SUV.

"Does it make me a prick if I say I'm glad that it gives me an opportunity to have a sexy night alone with you?"

Gabriel's gut bucked, and he shot a sharp glance in Aidan's direction, trying to read the man. "Do you not want Christina?"

"You're putting words in my mouth." Aidan strode closer to the front door, and when the security light flicked on, he turned and placed his hands on his hips. "Christina barely took the edge off earlier. I haven't had sex for ages—apart from my hand. I want you to focus on me tonight. Tomorrow, I'll sing like a canary to Christina."

Gabriel nodded. "Forgot about your trip. You and Christina still going tomorrow?"

"Next Sunday. Sorry to miss the market here, but my Tourism contact wants me to check out the Matakana market."

"Perhaps I could swing two days off and still go with you."

"Aye?" Aidan cocked his head, and his eyes shone with excitement at the prospect.

"I want to support your job in the same way you're helping mine. Part of the compromise thing. Plus, figure I'm due a break."

"You and Christina can drink wine and pose for my photos." Aidan beamed enthusiasm and offered Gabriel a quick hug. "I can't wait. Need to rejig my plan of attack. This'll be epic."

Aidan had asked Gabriel to go with him before—a long time ago, when he'd been doing a piece on Auckland. Gabriel had declined, but now he saw how much this meant to Aidan, saw he'd acted selfishly.

"A mini-holiday spent with my two favorite people. Should be good."

Gabriel promised himself he'd try harder to socialize and to participate in the hobbies Christina and Aidan enjoyed instead of burying himself in work. In the past, he hadn't mingled because he didn't want to run into his parents or his sister. The island was like a small town where a person couldn't help meeting the same people repeatedly.

He doubted his parents would ever move elsewhere, and he'd grown roots here, the climate and his slice of land perfect for his needs. Sure, he could shift to the mainland, but his grandparents were here. They'd supported him when he needed their help, and he loved them. Hated that because of him, his grandparents and parents seldom spoke.

Yeah. Instead of avoiding his parents, he'd do his thing—socialize with Aidan and Christina, and act with politeness should he encounter his mother, father or sister.

"Gabriel, are you listening to me?" Aidan's impatient tone jerked him from his reverie.

"No," he confessed. "I'll try to do better."

Aidan blinked. "I asked how serious this zombie run thing might be. Do we need to train?"

"We can go and do a run-through of their obstacle course. I was at school with John Everett, and we've kept in touch."

"How close a friend is he?"

Gabriel unlocked the door and tugged Aidan inside. "Not that kind of friend. You are the only guy I've ever slept with who lives on this island. Christina, the only woman in recent history. Long story, but if I wanted sex in the past, I picked up someone whenever I left the island on a buying trip."

"You've never mentioned that before."

Gabriel flipped the internal lock, turned, and prowled toward Aidan. "Didn't seem important. We were together, so I didn't look elsewhere. Since you left the last time, I've been busy. Christina is the only one since you." By the time he'd finished speaking, he'd backed Aidan against the wall. He placed one hand either side of Aidan's head, caging him in place with his bulk. "Anything else you want to know?"

Aidan's throat worked in a swallow, and Gabriel savored the heat coming off his chest. Gabriel bent his head and licked along the spot where Aidan's neck met his shoulder. He repeated the move, and Aidan shuddered.

"Nothing else," Aidan whispered.

Gabriel nipped a spot then soothed it with his tongue. "You sure?"

"Shut up and kiss me." Aidan gripped Gabriel's shoulders and lifted his head, his impatience clear.

Gabriel chuckled. "Couldn't have said it better myself." He settled against Aidan, letting his lover experience his weight. His readiness. His impatience.

He fitted their mouths together and dived straight into a heated kiss. Tongue. Teeth. Mouth. Aidan cupped his face and gave himself to Gabriel's kiss. He moaned his appreciation and wriggled their lower bodies together. Aidan rocked his hips, his brown eyes darkening with the same lust that filled Gabriel.

Part of Gabriel wanted to hurry. He didn't. He dallied and teased himself and Aidan until ragged gasps filled the entranceway of his home.

"Are we going to do it here in the hall?"

The atmosphere thickened even further with the silent acknowledgment that this time would be more than quick cuddles or untangling bodies that slid together during sleep.

Gabriel lifted his head to grin at Aidan. "We have a comfortable bed at the end of this passage."

"My point," Aidan murmured.

Gabriel's body hummed with residual pleasure as he pulled away from Aidan. He held out his hand, and when Aidan curled his fingers around his, he tugged him toward his bedroom. His pulse skittered, excitement, and desire plus a genuine need to lie close to the man he'd chosen to be his. A part of him wished Christina was here too, but commonsense told him slow was better in this case. They had plenty of time to ease into this relationship and grow trust and respect and love along with the lust.

Crap, he had it bad, and he hoped like hell they didn't crash and burn. He switched on the light, stared at the bed for a few seconds, and shuddered, his cock hard and wanting.

Once he ushered Aidan inside, Gabriel undressed the man. He batted Aidan's hands away when he tried to help, refusing to go fast. *Words*. Aidan needed Gabriel's words, so he understood Gabriel's intentions and the way his mind was working. He sucked in a deep breath and sought the right words. Honest ones. Heartfelt ones.

"Let me. Please," Gabriel whispered before pressing a soft kiss to the middle of Aidan's chest. "I want to undress you and remember everything about this moment. One, so I can tell Christina and two because this time is important to me. It feels as if I'm making a promise, and I want to appreciate this moment and recall every second."

Aidan froze, his brown eyes wide and surprised. "You mean it. In the past, it was always a race to get each other off."

"Neither you nor Christina understands how serious I am about making our threesome work. This is one way to prove it to you. Make this moment special. Make this moment stand out as *the one* amongst the others."

"Christina isn't here," Aidan pointed out.

"She will be soon. Still needs time."

"This was her idea."

"Yes," Gabriel agreed. "But taking a fantasy and turning it into reality takes an adjustment in thinking. That's why I didn't push Christina when she preferred to stay at her cottage. Small steps."

A pucker formed on Aidan's brow before it cleared, and wonderment replaced his confusion. "You're wooing us both."

Gabriel started, surprised at the old-fashioned term, yet

it fit what he wanted to do. He barked out a laugh when Aidan's expression turned smug. "You got it."

His hand trailed down Aidan's face before he unfastened the remaining buttons of Aidan's shirt to reveal hard flesh and muscles. Different from Christina yet spellbinding. He pushed the shirt off Aidan's shoulders, let it drift to the floor.

The decorative leather belt with its fancy silver buckle dropped next, his patience fraying at the edges. Gabriel made quick work of Aidan's boots, jeans, and underwear. His socks. Once he had Aidan naked, he backed him to the bed.

"I wonder how much it would take to break your restraint and get you to go crazy?" Aidan whispered.

"Not much," Gabriel confessed. He retreated a few steps and ripped off his own footwear and clothes. That done, he turned on one bedside lamp and switched off the main light. He grabbed condoms and lube from his nightstand, slapped them on the top within reach. "Much as I want to, don't think I can go slow," he admitted.

"Aye," Aidan breathed.

He joined Aidan on the bed and wrapped his arms around the man who'd become his friend, his lover, and now if things went the way Gabriel wanted, his future.

He fused their mouths together and slipped into the easy way they'd always had between them, despite the urgency thrumming through his veins. Aidan slid his thigh between his, and the first brush of his cock against Aidan's had him hissing.

Gabriel reached down to grip Aidan's shaft even as he kissed the man, dancing their tongues together and relearning Aidan's taste.

"Want you inside me," Aidan whispered. "Want to feel this tomorrow."

Gabriel tightened his grip on Aidan's cock, so grateful for this man and his return. "Missed you. Glad you're back."

Aidan stilled for an instant before firming his grip on Gabriel's shoulders. "I worried when I saw you in bed with Christina. I thought I'd screwed up and lost you."

"Took me a while to work out the truth."

"Will your grandparents approve?"

Gabriel chuckled. "They already know what I want. What about your parents?"

"My mother wants grandchildren," Aidan said. "Can we talk later?"

In answer, Gabriel reached for the bottle of lube and squeezed a dollop onto his palm. "Hands and knees," he barked.

He teased and stroked and prepared Aidan while kissing and caressing his butt and sliding one hand around his thigh to stroke his cock too. He'd missed this, Aidan's departure having left a massive hole in his life. No, he doubted he'd shock his grandparents.

"You okay?" he asked Aidan.

"Aye. So ready."

Gabriel stroked deep, twisting his fingers until Aidan jolted at the burst of electricity through his body. Right spot. Perfect. He glided a digit over the same place and smiled at Aidan's gasp.

"Gabriel!"

"Soon," Gabriel promised, grabbing the lube. He pushed more inside Aidan until heat seared his fingers instead of the chill of the lube. Then, he picked up a condom, rolled it on his aching dick, and smoothed lube on that too.

Seconds later, he lined up his cock and entered Aidan. Despite the urgency drumming through him, he loved at a snail's pace, intent on pleasuring Aidan and teasing himself until he knew he wouldn't last much longer.

"Aidan?"

"Not breakable," Aidan whispered. "Please, Gabriel. Move."

After aiming a kiss at the back of Aidan's neck, he upped the pace, stroking into his body while gripping Aidan's cock and giving his lover more stimulation.

"Not too much, aye? Too close. Want to savor."

Gabriel never let up on his thrusts or his stroking. His own climax beat at him, and he gave up trying to hold back. He reached for it, loving the heat of Aidan, the way he gasped and strained, and the pre-come that aided him in jacking off his lover. His balls tightened, his orgasm sizzling to full life. For an instant, he experienced light-headedness as if all the blood had left his brain and drained to his cock. Automatically, he stroked, tried to keep his rocking and hand stimulation even rather than jarring.

Aidan groaned, and wetness splashed against his palm. Aidan's channel flexed and rippled around him, and Gabriel soared. He thrust deep and held still, his cock pulsing, and pleasure filling him with satisfaction and contentment. He pressed a kiss to Aidan's shoulder and carefully pulled out.

Aidan flopped forward until he lay face-down on the mattress, and Gabriel ran his fingers down Aidan's back.

"Aidan?"

"Give me a minute," Aidan murmured.

Gabriel rose and strode into the en suite. He ditched the condom, washed up, and took a warm cloth back for Aidan.

Ten minutes later, they lay under the covers, wrapped in each other's arms. For the first time in years, Gabriel relaxed in both mind and body. Since age seventeen, when his family life had imploded, he'd fought and struggled for balance. This was fuckin' balance with Aidan, with Christina.

"I want to have children," he murmured to Aidan.

Aidan, who had been trailing a finger over his biceps stopped. "I love you, man, but I don't ken how I can do that."

"Idiot," Gabriel said. "You, me, and Christina."

Aidan moved from his arms and switched on the lamp on his side of the bed. "I need to see your face. You want to father a child with Christina?"

"One of us would be the father if Christina agrees. Don't care who the father is."

Aidan's frown cleared, and he grinned. "You truly want this—a future with both of us."

"Yeah."

"What if Christina doesn't want to have children?"

"We could adopt or foster kids."

"What if Christina doesn't want to have children?" Aidan repeated.

"Something to discuss," Gabriel said. "Confident she will. You?"

"I could handle children," Aidan said after a pause. "Not something I've thought about before because I've always traveled."

"Family is important."

"You don't talk about your parents. By the time we met, they weren't in the picture."

"They live on the island," Gabriel said, his gut hardening as it always did when he mentioned his parents. "They accused me of doing something and refused to believe me when I denied wrongdoing. Instead, they kicked me out of the house and dumped my belongings on the lawn. If it weren't for my grandparents, I'd have been fucked."

Aidan's eyes grew wide. "I kenned it was something big." He hesitated, as if he wanted more details, but he didn't ask. "My parents wanted me to go into law like my father, but they'd never cut me off."

"Lucky," Gabriel said. "My parents were strict. Controlling. Don't believe in second chances."

"It's lucky you have your grandparents," Aidan said.

"Yeah, I owe them a lot. One day, I'll tell you and Christina what happened, but rehashing it makes me angry. Just know if you ever meet my parents, and they act like arseholes, it's me they're cutting. Not you. Not Christina."

"Do you want me to tell Christina?"

"No, I'll do it."

Aidan reached for the light and turned it off again. He cuddled back against Gabriel and soon fell asleep. Gabriel didn't sleep straight away. First, he thought of Christina and hoped she was doing okay alone. His parents came to mind, and not for the first time, he wondered why they hadn't believed him, why they hadn't allowed him to explain. They'd taken his sister's accusations and those of her best friend as gospel.

He dreamed of babies. His babies. Other people's babies. A judge with a pounding gavel. Gabriel in isolation.

He awoke with a hoarse shout, bolting upright in bed,

his heart beating like crazy.

"Gabriel?"

"I'm fine," Gabriel barked. Aware he'd snapped, he sighed. "Bad dream." He climbed out of bed.

"Do you want to talk about it?"

Gabriel shook his head. "No. Gonna watch telly for a while."

"I'll come with you."

"Go back to sleep. I'm fine. I'll come back to bed in a bit." Gabriel left the bedroom before Aidan replied. Hell, he hadn't had that dream for years. His parents had fucked with his head. His sister. Her friend. He had deserved none of the crap they'd dished him, and now he had something substantial in his life, he refused to let his parents wreck it for him.

He'd do anything for Christina and Aidan because they were his future.

13

GETTING INVOLVED IN THE COMMUNITY

TOBY WASN'T EATING AGAIN, and he was doing his moping thing. He was also shivering as if he was cold. Christina rang the vet, but he was booked for the entire day. Before she could ask for an appointment the following day, the receptionist told her she had an urgent case and hung up.

Unsure of what to do, Christina picked up Toby and cuddled him. He ceased his shivering, and she carried him into the kitchen. She placed him in his basket and continued to talk with him while she boiled the jug to make tea.

Her phone rang. Gabriel.

"Sweetheart," he said, his husky voice doing a number

on her knees. She leaned against the counter as she pictured his face. "Did you dream of us?"

"Yes."

"Did you masturbate?"

"Gabriel!" Her lips twitched on hearing Aidan's laughter on the other end of the phone.

"Answer," came Gabriel's implacable demand.

"No, I did not. I thought about it and decided to wait."

"Aidan and I had great sex," Gabriel said. "Your turn next time."

A spike of anticipation ran the length of her body, and she smiled. "Promises. Promises."

"Done deal, sweetheart. Mark my words."

"Gabriel, Toby looks sick again. I rang the vet, but the receptionist told me they're busy all day. I don't know what to do."

"Suggestion," Gabriel said after a long pause. "Find a jacket or a sweater or something that still carries Bernice's scent. Put it in his basket with him and see if that helps."

"Perfect," Christina said. "I haven't summoned enough bravery to clear Bernice's bedroom yet. I've done the other rooms, but I need more time before I attack hers."

"No need to make excuses. I get it. You do it when you're ready. Aidan and I will help. Okay?"

"Thanks."

"Unnecessary. Aidan is helping me this morning with the milking and a couple of other things that need two people."

"Go ahead. I found enough ingredients in the store cupboard to make soap, so I thought I'd do that today."

"Come for dinner and plan to stay the night."

Christina gulped.

"Christina?"

"I heard you."

"You'll come for dinner?" Aidan had taken possession of the phone. "I'll make a lasagna."

"I'll be there. Oh, no. Wait. I promised your grandmother I'd pick her up and take her to the Women's Institute meeting. She wanted to introduce me to her friends."

"Come for dinner anyway. We'll make sure we eat early," Aidan said.

"We'll miss you," Gabriel said in the background. "Think of us today."

"I will," she whispered. "What time?"

"Come around five. See you later," Aidan said. "I'm looking forward to it. Oh, one thing. Think about if you want children. Gabriel asked me last night."

He disconnected the call before she gathered her scattered thoughts. Children? She set her phone on the counter and smiled. She loved children but had almost given up on having one or two of her own.

CHRISTINA DROVE FROM HER cottage to the farm at quarter past five. She'd wasted time while dithering over what to do with Toby. After giving him the comforter off Bernice's bed, he'd settled and seemed happier. He'd gone for a short walk before dragging the quilt halfway to his kennel. She'd intended to take Toby with her, but he'd refused, sitting his butt in the middle of the comforter and remaining in place, outfoxing her with his stubbornness.

In the end, she'd let him have his way and left him sleeping in his kennel with Bernice's comforter.

Gabriel met her as soon as she pulled up outside his house. He opened the car door. "You're late."

"I wasn't sure what to do about Toby." She smiled up at Gabriel. "He wanted to stay at the cottage."

Gabriel pulled her into his embrace the instant she exited her vehicle. "I missed you." Without giving her a chance to reply, he urged her inside his house.

A rich aroma of herbs and tomatoes and cheese greeted them, and she gave an appreciative sniff.

"That smells amazing."

"Aidan is a fantastic chef," Gabriel said. "He uses heaps of garlic."

"Which will be great for me, meeting lots of new faces this evening," Christina said. "Hi, Aidan. The delicious scents in here are making me hungry."

"Do you not eat garlic?" Aidan asked.

"I do, but I don't like to breathe it over people. I'm

meant to join in with the community, not scare them away."

"They're not vampires," Gabriel said.

"Aye, but some of the single men might fit into that category," Aidan said. "Recall that I've met your friends when you dragged me along to a social rugby game."

"Good point," Gabriel deadpanned. "Add more garlic."

Before Christina could add an indignant retort, Gabriel turned her into his arms and kissed her. It wasn't a casual kiss between friends. It wasn't much like the first kiss they'd shared all those years ago. This kiss made promises, forced her mind to passion, and stole her breath. When Gabriel lifted his head, his brown eyes glowed with satisfaction.

Aidan slapped an oven mitt on the counter and strode over to her. Adeptly, he inserted himself between her and Gabriel. "My turn."

Aidan's kiss was different. Less dominating and more persuasive. Still sexy and sensual and decadent. Christina clung to his shoulders while trembling at the heat coming off Gabriel, who remained standing behind her.

"Are you sure you want to go to this meeting tonight?" Gabriel whispered. "I owe you details. I could show rather than tell."

"I promised," Christina said. "Your grandmother is amazing, and the last thing I want to do is disappoint her."

"Can you come back after the meeting?" Aidan asked.

"How about a raincheck for tomorrow night? I'd like to check on Toby since this is the first time I'm leaving him alone."

"Tomorrow," Gabriel said. "But call us once you get home." He exchanged a gaze with Aidan, who winked in return.

"Are you two plotting?"

"Perhaps," Aidan replied. "You won't know until we act."

"I have to concentrate at the meeting, not daydream."

The oven timer buzzed, and Aidan turned away to remove the lasagna from the oven. He'd already set the table.

"Do you want a glass of wine?" Aidan asked.

"Not tonight. I prefer not to drink at all if I know I'm driving. Water is fine."

Aidan served the lasagna, and Christina helped herself to salad.

After the first mouthful, Christina moaned in delight. "This is amazing. You should have this as one of your dishes of the day. Not many people will turn up their noses at lasagna."

"I second that." Gabriel sent her a sly glance. "It's almost worth the garlic breath."

Aidan chuckled and grinned at Christina. "What is your answer about children? Enquiring minds want to know."

Christina spluttered. "Isn't it too early to discuss

children?"

"I'm all in," Gabriel said. "I want children."

"Well, I do, too, but early days."

"Would it bother you which one of us fathered our child?" Aidan asked.

Christina stared at Aidan then at Gabriel. "You want me to answer that?"

"Yes," Gabriel said.

"Aye," Aidan said at the same time.

Christina sucked in a deep breath, doing a four-second hold while she did it. Immediately, the tightness around her chest eased as her coping habit kicked in. She scanned Gabriel's and Aidan's faces again and realized they were serious. They wanted an answer. So she considered their question then tossed out her thoughts. "If I were in a committed threesome, it wouldn't matter to me who fathered a child because the child would belong to us all. It would be no different if we adopted a child. The genetic material doesn't make a man a father or a woman a mother. It's the love and nurturing that makes a good parent. The advice and lessons they impart. The opportunities they give their child. The way they talk to them or spend time with them. All of those things contribute to being a parent."

"Couldn't have said it better myself," Gabriel murmured.

Aidan nodded. "We'd both like children."

"And if I can't have children? I'm not getting any younger."

"We can adopt or foster," Gabriel said.

"Might be difficult if the authorities learn we're three," Christina countered.

"Excellent point," Aidan said. "But I say we work on the relationship and learn each other before we worry about things like families and marriage. The three of us together will cause gossip. I'd take a bet that Christina will get the worst of it. Are we ready for that?"

"I'll smack anyone who gives Christina a hard time," Gabriel snapped.

"It will be other women," Christina said. "Women can be bitchy. Believe me, I know. I might have stepped out of bounds myself once. Susan and I were bitches to our friend Maggie when Maggie started dating Connor. We were lucky Maggie forgave us, and our friendship returned to normal. Ever since, I've tried not to judge others because I hated the way I behaved."

"I'm looking forward to meeting your friends tomorrow," Aidan said. "I've mapped out a plan of attack for us. All you need to do is enjoy yourself."

"Thanks," Christina said.

"What time are they heading back to the mainland?" Gabriel asked.

"They're playing it by ear since they've sorted childcare, but probably about five."

"I'll finish work early so I can meet them before they leave," Gabriel said.

"That'd be great." Christina glanced at her watch. "I should head out now. Your grandmother said we shouldn't be late arriving at the church hall. Thanks for dinner, Aidan."

"No problem, sweetheart." He took her in his arms and kissed her soundly. "The garlic isn't too bad," he said once he pulled back.

Christina rolled her eyes. "Lucky for me, I have mints in the car."

Gabriel kissed her too—slow and passionate—until she clung to him. When he pulled back, his eyes danced with humor. "Thank you for taking Gran with you."

"She's lovely," Christina said with honesty. "I like your grandparents. It's no hardship picking her up. Besides, I might get some inner knowledge about the zombie contest."

"Gabriel and I checked out the course today. Gabriel's friend told us we can do a run-through if we want. There are obstacles and mud pools. It looks like fun."

"Mud?" Christina asked, appalled at the idea.

"Mud is excellent for the skin," Aidan informed her. "I did a research trip in Fiji where they had a mud spa. We have them in New Zealand."

"Interesting, I'm sure." Christina wrinkled her nose at him. "Gotta go. See you tomorrow morning. Are you sure you want to drive us around?"

"Aye, I'm positive."

"Okay, then. Bye!" Christina hurried outside and was soon pulling up in the driveway belonging to Gabriel's grandparents.

Gabriel's grandmother came outside to meet her, carrying a container of food along with her handbag. Christina jumped out of her car and ran around to the passenger side to help the elderly lady settle herself.

"Should I have brought a plate?"

Gran patted her hand. "No, dear. I bought enough cakes for two. There's always too much food for supper, anyway."

Soon, they were on their way to Oneroa and the church hall. Once they arrived, the number of vehicles in the parking lot surprised Christina. She took possession of their supper contribution and walked with Gran to the entrance.

"Mrs. Fletcher, I didn't think to ask how long the meeting will take," Christina said.

"Call me, Gran, dear. We should be on our way home by nine-thirty. We start our meeting promptly and save our chatter until after the formal part of our evening."

Christina followed Gran inside, and within minutes, they'd taken a seat with several of Gran's particular friends.

"This is Christina, Gabriel's friend," Gran announced. "Oops, we're ready to start. I'll make introductions later."

As they started proceedings, a prickling sensation told Christina someone was watching her. With a casual glance, she checked to her right. It was Stacey from the vet's surgery and another woman of the same age. They whispered to each other, heads close together, then both scowled at Christina.

Christina pretended not to notice and instead concentrated on the chairwoman. An older woman with a chic pixie cut, her hair was a smooth glossy black. She wore a charcoal-gray skirt and a cream blouse and appeared as if she'd stepped out of an office. Her bright red lipstick shouted confidence, and she smiled widely to display her white teeth while she ran through matters of business, including the upcoming zombie run fundraiser.

There were several craft classes on offer, and Christina listened with close attention. She wondered if perhaps there was a call for her makeover services and made a mental note to talk to Gran. Maybe she could offer a makeover as a prize to help raise funds. That would help her gauge the viability of her skill in this area.

The attention to detail for the zombie run and the members' enthusiasm impressed Christina. Several of the elderly ladies, including Gran, were excited about dressing as zombies, and they'd cunningly recruited their children and grandchildren to join their ranks.

Christina had a thought and raised her hand during question time. "Have you considered getting people to sponsor the zombies for the number of kills or ribbons they claim from the runners?"

There was a silence before a woman seated behind Christina said, "That's a great idea. Have a contest between ourselves. I like it."

The chairwoman beamed at Christina. "Wonderful suggestion. Would you be willing to organize that for us?"

"Sure, I can design a sponsorship form and email it to everyone. All they'd need to do is print it out and collect sponsors. For those who don't have a printer, I can print out extras. Perhaps they could drop by the cheese shop to pick one up? Or I could bring some to the next meeting."

Once the formal discussions had taken place, Gran introduced Christina to her friends and some of their daughters. Soon Christina was deep in discussions about knitting. Every woman she spoke to bemoaned the lack of a craft store on Waiheke and the need to travel to Auckland for supplies.

"Supper is ready," the chairwoman called.

Everyone drifted to another room off the main hall. Gran and her group of friends claimed a table, and Christina volunteered to collect cups of tea for them. After running through her order, she made her way to the tea counter and lined up behind earlier arrivals to await her turn.

"Hello," a voice said. "Christina, isn't it?"

Christina turned to find Stacey and her friend in the line

behind her. Something in their expressions had Christina's welcoming smile freezing.

"Hi," Christina said. She'd found Stacey standoffish at the veterinary clinic and later when she'd spoken to her on the phone. "How are you, Stacey?"

"This is my friend Darcy."

Christina offered a friendly smile at the pretty dark-haired woman. "Pleased to meet you."

"Darcy has a son," Stacey said.

The abrupt introduction of this topic confused Christina. "You do? How old is he?"

Darcy's eyes narrowed. "He's almost ten."

"Wow! You don't look old enough to have a son that old," Christina said, which was nothing less than the truth.

The line shuffled forward, and Christina found herself willing the woman in front of her to hurry. This conversation was making her uncomfortable.

"I understand you work for Gabriel Fletcher," Darcy said.

"That's right." Christina forced a smile. What was taking the woman so long? How hard was it to pour a cup of tea?

"He's a liar," Stacey said. "You can't trust him."

"Pardon?" Christina gaped at the pair. One thing she loved about Gabriel was his honesty and integrity. He was blunt and never promised something he couldn't deliver. He'd been that way ever since their first meeting when they were teenagers.

"He's a liar," Stacey repeated. "Don't fall for him because he'll trample all over you and walk away without looking back."

Finally, the woman making her tea finished, and it was Christina's turn. She turned away from the two women intent on blackening Gabriel's name, set out seven cups and poured tea, and added milk to six. She grabbed a tray and walked away without speaking to Stacey and Darcy again.

"Well!" Stacey's indignation followed Christina as she left.

Christina distributed the cups of tea as one daughter arrived with two plates bearing assorted cakes and sandwiches. Christina slipped into the seat next to Gran. During a quiet moment when the lady sitting on the other side of Gran was speaking to someone else, Christina tapped Gran's arm.

"I've just had the oddest conversation with Stacey."

"Humph," Gran said after a brief glance at the two young women. "We'll talk later."

"All right," Christina said.

Three-quarters of an hour later, they set off for home.

"Did you enjoy the meeting, dear?" Gran asked.

"I did. I arranged to meet two of the girls for coffee next week. Daphne and Claire."

"Ah, they're both lovely girls. Gabriel dated Claire for a

while. I had high hopes, but she met Steve during a trip to Wellington, and that was that."

"Has Gabriel dated a lot?"

"He did when he was in his early twenties, but then he purchased his land and became a workaholic. It's good he has you and young Aidan to drag him away now and then."

For an instant, Christina wondered what Gran thought about Gabriel having two lovers. No way did she intend to approach the topic. She was leaving that tumultuous sea for Gabriel to navigate.

Christina hesitated, then asked, "Stacey said some nasty things about Gabriel."

"Stacey is so different from her brother."

Gran's disapproval had Christina veering to the middle of the road before she corrected her steering. "I never met Stacey because she was always staying with friends when I visited during the school holidays." She thought back and shook her head. "Why is she so nasty about Gabriel? I don't get it. What about the woman she was with?"

"Darcy was or still is, I suppose, Stacey's best friend. I'd heard she and her son were back on the island, although I try to steer clear of Stacey, so I hadn't seen her until tonight," Beth said. "I can't tell you anymore, dear. If you have questions, you must ask Gabriel."

14

HER FRIENDS GIVE WARNING

EXCITEMENT FILLED CHRISTINA AS she and Aidan waited for the ferry to berth. She bounced up and down on her toes and clutched Aidan's arm while her gaze remained on the passengers waiting to disembark.

Beside her, Aidan chuckled. "Should I give you something to take your mind off your friends?"

"What?"

Aidan pulled free of her grip, grasped her shoulders, and kissed her.

Her startled *eep* remained trapped, and she tensed for an instant before she relaxed and settled to enjoy their kiss. Heat roared through her, but Aidan didn't deepen their kiss.

He loosened his hold and grinned at her. "Are you more relaxed now?"

"We're here," a familiar voice exclaimed.

Christina whirled, her golden bracelets jangling. Her three friends: Maggie, Susan, and Julia, stood in a group, each woman grinning at her. Each smile held curiosity.

"This is Aidan," she said. "Aidan, this is Maggie. Susan. Julia. Aidan volunteered to be our driver today, which means we can have a glass of wine or two."

She hugged Maggie, a full-figured brown-haired woman with an impish smile before turning to repeat the greeting with Julia, a slim blonde. She gave a third hug to Susan, who had her straight brown hair twisted up in a messy bun.

"This way, ladies," Aidan said. "Your adventure awaits."

"Aidan has a popular travel and food blog," Christina told her friends as they wandered from the terminal to where they'd parked Gabriel's SUV. "He has planned a tour for us and will do a blog post. I told him I thought it would be all right for him to take our photos to go with his post."

"I'm fine if you'd prefer not to be on my blog," Aidan said as he unlocked the vehicle and opened the rear door. "Who is sitting in the back?"

"Christina, you take the front. We can interrogate you from the back," Susan said with a broad grin.

"See what you've done," Christina said to Aidan.

"I kissed my girl," Aidan said and winked at her. "Ladies, do you have enough room back there? Is there anything you want to put in the trunk?"

Once her friends settled in the rear, Christina climbed into the front, fastened her seatbelt, and braced for questions.

"I'm so sorry about Bernice, honey," Maggie said. "She was a special lady."

"It's hard to believe she's gone," Christina said. "I miss her. Toby misses her too. The vet says he's depressed."

"Is Toby not eating again?" Aidan asked.

"He's eating, but he's listless, and he doesn't want to walk. Bernice had him from a puppy," Christina told her friends. "He seemed happy enough when I left this morning. Gabriel offered to look after him, but he refused to leave his kennel."

"Ah! Gabriel is the first guy you ever kissed," Susan said. She belatedly clapped her hand over her mouth, her eyes wide above her fingers.

"Not the thing you should blurt out when Christina is with her boyfriend," Julia chided.

"Sorry!" Susan said.

"Aye, 'tis no problem. I ken about Gabriel."

"Ooh, a man with an accent," Maggie said with a grin. "Scotland, right?"

"My mother is Scottish," Aidan said. "I went to school in both New Zealand and Scotland. That's how I met Gabriel—during a visit to Waiheke with my parents."

"He's an excellent cook too," Christina said. "Now, how

are all the kids? What time are we aiming to have you back at the terminal?"

"Connor told me to enjoy myself and have a great time," Maggie said. "It's such a treat not to have to worry about strollers and the other kid paraphernalia."

"Hear. Hear," Julia agreed. "Ryan told me he and the nanny had things under control. He's having a few weeks off and is enjoying chilling. I think Caleb was going to hang out with him for the day. My manager at Maxwell's is on top of everything. I don't have a curfew."

"What about Tyler?" Christina asked Susan.

"He's working on an art project today. Ryan and Caleb are doing the school run for him. We're here until you tire of driving us around," Susan said.

"Sounds great," Aidan said. "I don't ken about you ladies, but I could do with a coffee and a pastry. We'll head toward Oneroa and maybe go for a walk on the beach since it's such a nice morning before we hit the vineyards."

Christina relaxed and enjoyed catching up on the gossip about Maxwell's plus the things happening in her friends' lives. She told them about her godmother's will and how she needed to live on Waiheke for at least the next six months. She described the book club, the Women's Institute zombie run she was doing with Aidan and Gabriel.

"I'll get muddy," Christina wailed.

"Aye, you will," Aidan agreed in amusement.

"It's almost worth a return trip to see this zombie run," Julia mused.

"I'm trying to imagine a pack of elderly ladies dressed as zombies," Maggie inserted into the conversation.

"You won't once you meet Gabriel's grandmother," Aidan said. "She's brilliant."

"Gran is special," Christina agreed. "She's excited about dressing up as a zombie."

"I'm trying to imagine my mother donning zombie clothes and makeup." Susan shook her head. "Nope. Not happening."

Christina giggled, having met Susan's strict mother.

By the time they'd visited four vineyards, sampled different olive oils, had lunch and wandered around Stoney Batter, a World War Two site with gun emplacements, the women were relaxed and giggly.

"One last stop," Aidan said late afternoon. "We'll stop at Gabriel's place and sample some cheese."

"*The* Gabriel?" Julia asked.

Aidan chuckled. "The Gabriel." He sent Christina a wink, and she turned gooey inside. She was so lucky with him and Gabriel.

Aidan pulled into Gabriel's driveway at around twenty past four. As soon as Aidan parked, the door of the cheese shop opened, and Gabriel strolled out. While Aidan opened the door for her friends, Gabriel came to her. He pulled her into his arms and kissed her. A quick but thorough kiss that left her clutching Gabriel's shoulders. When she stepped back, her friends were all staring at her.

"Clearly, we didn't ask the right questions," Julia said.

"Come inside and taste Gabriel's cheese," Aidan said.

"You're involved with Aidan *and* Gabriel?" Susan whispered.

Christina straightened her shoulders. "Yes," she said with a false calmness. This was the part of their threesome that made her hesitate. The reactions of outsiders.

"Christina," Gabriel said, offering his hand.

She took it and clasped their fingers together, savoring his closeness, the contact, and the little tingle that sped through her because of his finger calluses. *Sex.* Every time that slide of his fingers across her skin reminded her of sex and intimacy. With Gabriel. With Aidan. Gabriel's hand tightened, the sharper contact bringing her back to the present.

She glanced at Susan, collected her thoughts. "I have a part-time job working for Gabriel in the cheese shop," she told her friends once they stood inside. "We have locals and tourists coming for tastings and to purchase cheese. Gabriel, these are my friends Susan, Maggie, and Julia."

"Pleased to meet you," Gabriel said. "Christina often mentions you. She's missed having you around as often, so I was glad you could visit today."

"Ladies, another glass of wine?" Aidan asked.

While Gabriel cut samples of cheese, Aidan poured

wine for everyone.

"Both of them?" Susan hissed.

"Take off your judgment hat," Christina countered.

Susan's expression softened, and she squeezed Christina's arm before accepting a glass of wine from Aidan. "Right. You're right. I-I just don't want you to act hastily. Your godmother passed away, and you're alone with these men without your sounding boards." She gestured at her other friends who were chatting with Gabriel and by the sounds of it, discussing cheese and the production process.

"I'm making friends here," Christina said and cursed herself when this came across as defensive. "And you're a phone call away." She didn't add that her three friends weren't as accessible these days because that wouldn't go well. The last thing she wanted was an argument. "I'm trying new things and working on a business. I have a part-time job. Susan, don't worry." She sipped her wine and caught Gabriel's gaze. He crooked his finger and pointed at the cheese. "Come and try Gabriel's cheese. It's amazing."

Gabriel pulled Susan into the cheese conversation while Christina joined Aidan. He slipped an arm around her waist. His silent comfort was what she needed, and she leaned into him.

"Is your friend giving you a hard time?" he murmured.

"Yes, she's worried about me. Before my friends married

and started having children, my moods were up and down a little. It was after I was on my own more, and the advertising campaign regarding depression started playing on television that I wondered if my low moods were depression and anxiety. I haven't told my friends how low I was for a time there, and how I'm getting better at managing my moods."

"You told Gabriel and me." Aidan nuzzled her hair and placed a soft kiss on the patch of skin right behind her ear.

Christina drew in a sharp breath, his affection tempting her to turn into his embrace and seek a more intimate kiss. "I did." Her voice emerged breathlessly. "I've known Gabriel for a long time, so it was easy with him. You—you're important to Gabriel, and I like you a lot."

Aidan kissed her jaw. "Only a lot?"

Christina grinned and poked him in the chest. "That's all you're getting right now."

Maggie approached them. "Did you get the photos you wanted?"

"I have some awesome photos," Aidan said, excitement lighting his face. "Let me grab a business card for you. It has my blog on it. I'll get the post up tomorrow. If there are any photos you'd like copies of, flip me an email."

"Thanks," Maggie said. "I'd love a photo of the four of us girls together."

"Let me get that business card," Aidan said.

Christina watched Maggie's friendly grin, and when

Julia and Susan joined her, she guessed she was in for more questions.

"A threesome can be fun," Julia said. "I've had one or two in the past, but they're never permanent. They can't be. There's too much pressure from outside sources. Gossip and contempt from some people. Insults and slurs. Whispers behind your back. Even if you can get past that, jealousy can be an issue."

"Stop," Christina said in a sharp voice. She scanned her friends' faces, holding their gazes in turn. "I get that you're doing this because you're worried about me, but I've known Gabriel since I was seventeen. I trust him. Gabriel has also known Aidan for a long time. I trust them both. I've supported each of you over the past years." She turned to Maggie. "Apart from you, Maggie. I was a bitch to you at first, but I love how you and Connor are together. I'm happy for all of you. You found good men, and you're moving on and making families."

"That's it," Susan said. "You don't have to push a relationship to keep up with us."

Without warning, Gabriel pushed in beside Christina. "Stop bullying Christina," he stated in a quiet voice. "She was so excited you'd squeezed in a visit. Don't spoil it for her."

Susan sucked in an audible breath and her smile was forced. "You're right, of course. We're not handling this the right way. I'm sorry. You're our friend, and we want you to be happy."

"We do," Maggie agreed. "You know you're welcome to call or come for a visit. If you need to talk, we're all only a phone call away."

"I'm sorry," Julia said as she squeezed Christina's hand. "I've had a lovely day, and we were wrong to gang up on you. If you want to talk, you know my number. I hadn't realized how beautiful it is here. I'll see if Ryan and the kids would like to spend a weekend over here. Maybe I can persuade Caleb to come too."

"That'd be nice. You could stay at my cottage if you'd like," Christina said. "Same goes for you two. If you'd like a weekend break, there's room at my cottage."

"Thanks," Maggie said. "And on that note, we should make a move for the ferry. Gabriel, can I buy some of your cheese to take home with me? I've already got the wine. I should take cheese too."

Five minutes later, her friends piled into the SUV. During the journey to the ferry terminal, Christina kept a smile pinned to her lips, and she teased her friends. Susan recounted the story of Mr. Blue, her bright blue vibrator that'd caused a storm of gossip during her appearance on the *Farmer Seeks a Wife* reality show. By the time they arrived, her smile had turned more natural, yet inside, her thoughts scuttled around like a colony of ants.

She and Aidan walked her friends into the terminal, and they chatted while the newly arrived ferry tied up to the wharf, and the passengers started to pour off.

As she waved off her friends and giggled at their clinking bags, the weight of a stare distracted her. When she spotted Stacey Fletcher, she stiffened.

"Something wrong?" Aidan asked, moving closer to her and placing an arm around her shoulders. His comfortable and protective presence stifled some of her building anxiety. Her friends and now Stacey Fletcher.

"Have you met Gabriel's sister?" Christina asked without taking her gaze off Stacey.

"No. He never discusses his family. I mean, he told me they kicked him out of the family home, and he lived with his grandparents, but he declined to give further details. I decided it wasn't important. You've met Gabriel. To quote—he's honest as the day is long. I've never met anyone else with the same confidence and integrity."

"I agree. After the meeting I attended with Gran I meant to ask more questions, but I got sidetracked. Stacey and her friend Darcy cornered me while I was getting cups of tea for Gran and her friends. They told me Gabriel was a liar and I shouldn't trust him."

Aidan blinked. "That's not the Gabriel we ken."

"Exactly. I asked Gran, but she told me I should talk to Gabriel. I meant to, but didn't get around to it."

Stacey yanked her gaze off Christina and Aidan and strode away toward the disembarking passengers. Oh. She was meeting Darcy. The other woman had a child with her—a boy with dark hair. Stacey hugged both mother and son, grabbed one bag and ushered them out to the carpark.

Christina watched until she could no longer see them. "Stacey made a point of telling me Darcy had a son. It was strange."

"Aye, well, if Gabriel doesn't speak with his sister and parents, something bad happened."

Christina lifted a hand and waved as her friends turned back for a final goodbye. "Gabriel's grandparents sided with Gabriel," she pointed out. "Whatever happened split the family."

"How about this for a suggestion? Let's not ask questions yet. Instead, just concentrate on us and enjoying each other."

"What if Stacey keeps bothering me?" Christina asked.

"That would be different, and if that proves to be the case, we'll talk to Gabriel together."

15

HEARTS ON THE LINE

WHILE CHRISTINA AND AIDAN delivered Christina's friends to the ferry terminal, Gabriel started on dinner. He'd taken a beef curry from the freezer and cooked a double pea curry plus rice to round out their meal. Christina's friends had irritated him—the way they'd commented about something private between the three of them.

This wouldn't be the first or the last time, friends, family, and strangers gossiped or judged on a relationship that didn't fit the social norm. A maverick, he was ready for this and had firsthand experience in being an outcast already. Aidan and Christina didn't possess the same armor as him, and he worried when it came to Christina and her bouts of depression.

Even when they were younger, he'd noticed sometimes

she was antisocial and plain grumpy. Back then, he'd enjoyed spending time with her, even if they'd not spoken much. Sometimes, he'd dragged her off for a walk on the beach, and other times, he'd picked up his drawing book or a comic and occupied himself while she'd knitted or done needlework. Usually, her mood had passed, and they'd gone for ice cream or swimming or raided Gran's biscuit tins.

Not that he didn't think she was strong because she was, but she looked at the world differently from him, reacted negatively to situations, and drew into herself.

Gabriel heard his vehicle pull up outside, and soon Aidan and Christina entered the kitchen.

"Something smells delicious," Christina said, moving to him and kissing him on the cheek.

"What's for dinner?" Aidan asked, hugging him and going in for a smooch too. "I'm starving."

"Gran's beef curry, a veg curry, and rice," Gabriel said. "I thought you were stopping to get Toby."

"He refused to leave his kennel. Ask Aidan. He came out to meet us and ate a little of his dinner, then he climbed back inside his kennel and declined to come out. Not even a treat stick tempted him. He seemed fine, so Aidan and I left him there. I've locked the gate, so he can't wander."

Gabriel nodded. "Probably for the best. Does he want to walk?"

"Short walks. I take my cues from him," Christina said.

"Bring him with you tomorrow. He enjoys playing with my dogs," Gabriel said.

"Do you need a hand?" Christina asked.

"Nope. You and Aidan relax in front of the telly. Make out. Put your mouth on her, Aidan. Get her hot. Decided I enjoy watching you both get off." His voice emerged low and husky. "I'll join you as soon as I'm done here."

Aidan quirked a brow at Christina. "Works for me. What about you?"

The frown lines on her forehead cleared, and Gabriel let his breath ease out. He worried about her. Too much stress wasn't good for Christina. Pushing her didn't work, but being there for her did, so he held back and tried to keep her occupied, again without sliding into too insistent.

He continued dinner preparations, his mind working as he twisted and mentally chewed on this problem. Keep Christina busy. Make her feel the love. Give her security. Let her talk. Listen. Aidan, he'd figured out. He needed to support him, ask for his help on the farm instead of shutting him out, and do things to foster Aidan's dreams. Plus the lovin' part. That was a given.

Fifteen minutes later, he had the curries both on low with the rice underway. He'd set the timer because the last thing he wanted was a burned dinner.

He sauntered into the lounge, uncertain of what he'd see or whether they'd followed his instructions at all because a rugby commentary had drifted to him in the kitchen.

Christina lay on the couch, naked from the waist down and with her T-shirt dragged up and her bra shoved to the side. Her thighs were spread wide, and Aidan was tending her with slow licks. He was teasing her rather than applying himself dutifully to make her come.

"Nice," Gabriel said and slid to the floor by Christina. He tugged up her T-shirt a fraction farther and worked his hand beneath her to unfasten her bra. When it loosened, he lowered his head and licked her nipple. Instead of taking it into his mouth, he traced his tongue around it, playful rather than intent while he caressed the mounds of her breasts.

"Let me taste her," Gabriel demanded.

Aidan moved aside, but instead of taking over, Gabriel grasped Aidan's head and kissed him, dancing their tongues together. The kiss tasted of Christina's sweet honey with the richer overlay of Aidan. Gabriel pulled back and pressed their foreheads together. Without looking, he reached for Christina, his finger colliding with her arm. He stroked the silky flesh, and his dick hardened even further as he pictured himself licking her soft skin.

"You are both perfection," he said. "I can't imagine being with anyone else."

Neither Christina nor Aidan commented, but this time, he didn't mind. They'd understand in time, and that, the three of them had. Six months for him to convince the pair they were perfect together.

"Aidan, loosen your jeans and give me room to play," Gabriel instructed. When Aidan hesitated, Gabriel said, "Please."

"What about Christina?" Aiden asked, his voice terse.

"Thinking you can multitask."

"I'd enjoy watching that," Christina whispered.

Gabriel smiled at Aidan, let his brows rise in question. "Can I unfasten your jeans?"

"Aye."

The tension that had crept into the room seeped away. Gabriel had no idea what it was or if he'd caused it, but he packed the topic away for later. With decisiveness, he unfastened Aidan's belt and lowered the zipper. He yanked the black jeans down Aidan's muscular thighs and maneuvered a pair of black boxer-briefs over Aidan's erection. Having both his lovers partially dressed and disheveled while he remained fully clothed was kind of hot. Yeah, he'd pay for this later with a hard-on and no satisfaction, but he wanted to give this to Christina and Aidan. Show them he appreciated them, wanted them, but didn't expect anything in return. He could wait.

"You carry on with Christina. I can reach if I lie on the floor." He cupped Aidan's hip and directed him back to Christina.

The instant Aidan's mouth made contact with Christina, she sighed. "Thank goodness. I thought you'd leave me hanging."

"Never," Aidan said.

"No," Gabriel agreed. "We're a team. Leave no man or woman behind."

Christina spluttered. "We have a team motto?"

"We do now," Gabriel said, amused as he ran his fingertips over Aidan's thighs and toward his groin.

Aidan licked and played with Christina—at least, Gabriel assumed he did. Gabriel touched Aidan's thighs and buttocks, exploring and pleasing his need for physical contact before he slid beneath Aidan and settled in to get him off.

One advantage of a male lover was that he knew what Aidan would enjoy because the same things pleased him. Accompanied by a soundtrack of Christina's mews and whimpers, her loud cries of *right there!* Gabriel applied himself and took Aidan's cock into his mouth. He let it sit on his tongue for a long moment, let Aidan experience the heat of his mouth before he tongued the crown.

Soon Aidan's groans and entreaties accompanied Christina's cries—a musical soundtrack Gabriel appreciated. Pre-come filled Gabriel's mouth, and judging by Christina's frantic groans, he figured he should hasten proceedings. He sucked Aidan deeper, thankful for his lack of a gag reflex. Aidan jerked, instinct driving him to thrust. Gabriel gripped his hips to hold him still and as a silent reminder to multitask.

"Yes," Christina cried. "Aidan!"

Aidan trembled, and Gabriel gave him what he wanted. Deep and hot. Attention to the delicate underside of his cock head. A massage of his balls. A faint twist.

Aidan bellowed, and an instant later, his orgasm struck him. He threw back his head and cried out again. Gabriel swallowed and held Aidan, letting the other man fuck his mouth as he needed.

A discordant sound pierced Gabriel's satisfaction. Christina's laugh filled the air too before he recognized the summons of the oven timer.

"Let me up, Aidan," Christina said. "I'll get the timer. Should I turn everything off?"

Gabriel released Aidan and rolled clear. "I'll get it. I will serve dinner in two minutes."

When Aidan and Christina appeared in the kitchen, they were fully dressed. Their cheeks were pink, and their eyes glowed with contentment. Gabriel's heart skipped a beat, and for a second, he experienced jealousy—an odd-man-out sensation. But Christina grabbed the plates, and Aidan collected cutlery, the pair setting the table.

"Gabriel, do you want a beer?" Aidan asked.

"No, I'll stick to water."

"Me too," Christina said.

Aidan poured three glasses of water while Gabriel placed the curries into separate serving dishes. He shredded coriander leaves and sprinkled them over as a garnish. Aidan transported the plates to the table.

"Christina, I think there is a jar of Gran's lime pickle in the fridge. Can you grab it, please?" Gabriel tipped the rice into another dish and fetched serving spoons.

"Gabriel," Aidan said.

Gabriel was studying the table. Yep, he had everything.

"Gabriel," Christina said.

Both stood by the table. Aidan pulled out a seat and waited.

Gabriel's brows rose. "For me?"

Christina shunted him toward the chair, and they both waited until he sat before taking a seat themselves.

"Thanks for dinner and before," Aidan said.

"No thanks necessary." Gabriel's voice emerged low and gruff, his emotions riding close to the surface at the thanks. He hadn't expected it. He cleared his throat. "Do anything for you." His gaze swept to Christina. "Both of you."

It was nothing less than the truth, and it scared him. If Aidan and Christina walked away from what they had, it would hurt. It'd hurt way more than when his parents had taken the side of his sister and turned their backs on him.

He'd known Christina and Aidan for years, and it hadn't taken much for him to see the possibilities, act on them, and topple into love with them both.

Yeah, this time his heart was on the line. If they walked away from this, it'd destroy him.

16

A Sad Death

THE NEXT MORNING, AIDAN rolled away from Christina, took care of business, and wandered out to the kitchen. Gabriel was already sitting at the breakfast bar with a mug of coffee cradled in his hands.

Gabriel smiled at him. "The coffee is hot. Is Christina awake?"

"Still asleep." Aidan poured coffee and took possession of the barstool next to Gabriel. "Nothing like excellent sex to relax a man."

Gabriel winked at him, giving Aidan a glimpse of his playfulness. "Know the feeling."

"I thought I'd head to town after milking, order paint, and start decorating the dining area. The kitchen needs a deep clean too before I can use it."

Gabriel's brow wrinkled. "I'd help, but I'm

cheese-making today."

"You have enough to do," Aidan said.

"Want to help," Gabriel replied. "Now that it's daylight saving time, it's lighter in the evening. What if we do a couple of hours after dinner?"

Aidan's chest tightened on hearing the suggestion. "You'd do that?"

"I want to support you. Can't speak for Christina, but I'm happy to give you an hour or two each day to get your place underway."

Christina ambled into the kitchen, her body dwarfed by Gabriel's robe. "What are you not speaking for me for?"

"Aidan wants to clean his kitchen and start painting the dining room. I volunteered my services."

"Me too," Christina said without hesitation. "Have you decided on colors yet?"

"Not yet. I thought I'd do that today," Aidan said. "You both want to help?"

"Yes," they replied at the same time.

"I can help this morning," Christina said. "I'll leave around midday since I need to design a sponsorship form for the zombie run before I open the cheese shop."

"Thanks." Aidan sipped his coffee, his heart full at the offers of help. Gabriel hadn't seemed enthusiastic at first, but now he was supporting him. He'd told Aidan he intended to go on his first assignment to the mainland. This was huge.

"Aidan, the photos you showed me are awesome. Have you thought of enlarging some of them and using them on the walls of the restaurant?" Christina poured coffee and leaned her hip against the counter. "Go with a Waiheke theme. You might even sell some of your photos as postcards."

"Great idea." Gabriel stood. "On that note, I'd better start the milking."

"Wait, I'll help," Aidan said.

"Finish your coffee first." Gabriel strode to Christina and kissed the top of her head. "Later." He kissed Aidan next and left the house, the notes of a whistled tune trailing in his wake.

Aidan turned to Christina. "He's happy. I've never seen him like this."

"When I first knew him, this was his norm."

"He offered to help me paint," Aidan said, his jumbled thoughts falling from his mouth. "He's never supported me in this way before."

"Maybe because you were always traveling, always leaving. This time, you're making plans that mean you'll stay. He's starting to believe you'll keep your word."

"Aye," Aidan said slowly. "I haven't been fair to Gabriel."

"You should tell him."

"I will. For the first time, I'm not getting restless. Usually, by now, I'd want to move on and enjoy new surroundings."

Christina rolled her eyes. "You've been here a week."

"Aye, but I've made life decisions and fallen for a beautiful woman. I have a job with the Tourist Board. This time is different. I'm happy," he decided in wonderment.

"Are you sure it's not the sublime sex?"

"That's part of it, but it's everything else. I have a purpose. A plan, and it makes me happy, you ken?"

"While we're painting, you can help me firm up my plan," Christina said. "Although I sold scarves at the market, most of them were Bernice's. Selling soap and scarves won't generate enough income to pay the rates and other cottage expenses."

"Aye, I hear you. I'll put my mind to thinking."

Christina grinned. "You do that. Thinking looks sexy on you."

"Really?" Aidan said, standing and stalking her until he'd corralled her against the kitchen cupboards. He grinned down at her wide eyes and the smudged lenses of her glasses. Her bracelets clattered as she gripped his shoulder, not to push him away, but to draw him closer.

He covered her lips with his and sank into the sweetness, thanking every instinct that had told him it was time to come home to Gabriel. Christina gave him different things. Softness. Gentleness. An urge to protect.

He eased back from the kiss. "I promised I'd help Gabriel. Better get a move on."

"Take my car when you're ready to go to Oneroa," Christina said. "The keys are in the fruit bowl. I'll catch a lift with Gabriel. Tell him to pick me up at the cottage."

Christina finished her coffee, cleaned the kitchen, and made the bed before she walked to her cottage. She was relieved to find Toby lying in the sun. He raised his head at her greeting, and she unlocked the rear door to the kitchen, considerably happier when he followed her inside.

"Ready for dinner, boy?"

She busied herself, and soon Toby was nudging his bowl. Not a big appetite, but he was eating. He came to her and licked her hand. Smiling, Christina crouched and ran her fingers along his spine. He nosed her then trotted to the door.

"Want to sit in the sun again? Okay, boy." Christina opened the door and let Toby out into the garden.

Deciding she was hungry, she made herself a piece of toast and a cup of tea. She sat at the kitchen table, a jotter pad and pen at her elbow while she tried to think of something else she could do to support herself. Scarves and soap-making, while fun, wasn't enough.

As often happened these days, her mind slid to Gabriel and Aidan. Gabriel should set up a website and an online shop for his cheese. And business cards to hand out at the market and in the shop. Business cards could nudge a person to remember the cheese they'd tasted and that they could order online. It wouldn't take much to grow an online business or to fill the orders and courier them around the Auckland area. He could also pick his favorite local vineyard and make reciprocal sales. Preferably, he should choose a vineyard with a restaurant that could offer cheeseboards alongside their wine.

She noted down bullet points to show Gabriel later. Her mind slid to Aidan and his restaurant. She got the sense that while he wanted to own and run a restaurant, he didn't want to do it full-time. What if he rented out the restaurant and allowed would-be chefs to do their stuff for one or two nights a week? Or let the Woman's Institute or another charity group do a roast dinner on a Sunday night? All he'd need to do would be to recover his costs—enough to pay for rent and power. Something to consider.

Christina wrote another list for Aidan.

"Excellent at organizing other people," she murmured, standing. A pity she couldn't plan her own way out of a paper bag.

She might as well do something she'd been putting off, which was to pack away Bernice's clothes. Gabriel would help her deliver them to the charity shop before they started painting.

Since she didn't have any suitable boxes for her packing, she grabbed a pile of rubbish bags and marched into Bernice's bedroom. Even before she'd started, tears stung her eyes. A little at a time, she promised herself. Just the wardrobe and the tallboy drawers.

Straightening her shoulders, she yanked open the wardrobe and started work. By the time she'd finished, and every drawer was empty—she'd decided not to stop at the tallboy—it was half eleven.

She dragged two of the four full black bags to the door. A glance into the garden showed her Toby lying in a patch of sun. She retrieved the last two bags and checked Toby's water before she searched for an old T-shirt to use while painting.

Outside, she washed out Toby's water bowl and refilled it with fresh water. "Toby, how come you're always sleeping? Toby?" Puzzled at his non-reaction, she wandered over to him. Foreboding slid into her—a swift, hard punch to the chest. "Toby. No, please. Please. *Please, wake up.*" She crouched beside him and slid her hand over his tan-and-white shoulder. When he didn't move, didn't react to her touch or voice, she shook him. She fell backward, her butt hitting the lawn. "*Toby!*"

None of her shaking or cries did a bit of good. She swallowed hard. Once. Twice. The painful lump in her throat refused to shift. She clutched herself and realized her tears were back, running down her cheeks and dripping off her chin.

Toby was dead.

Christina wasn't sure how long she sat next to Toby. Her

head throbbed. Her heart ached. And she couldn't seem to stop crying.

"Christina?"

Christina lifted her head and blinked, finding it difficult to focus against the light.

"Babe." Swift steps carried Gabriel to her side. He knelt and drew her against his hard chest. His show of comfort had her tears welling again, and she clung to him, sobbing because Bernice had died, and now Toby had gone.

A long while later, Gabriel stood and helped Christina to her feet.

"I-I can't leave Toby here." Her voice wobbled, and it was difficult forcing out her words.

"We're not going to leave him," Gabriel murmured. "We'll pick a spot in the garden and bury him. Did Bernice have a favorite shawl? We can wrap Toby in that. Later, we'll get a little plaque to mark his resting spot. Will that work?"

Christina nodded, tears welling again.

"How about over there in that patch of sun?"

Christina swiped the back of her hand over her nose. "Yes."

Gabriel hugged her close for an instant before setting her away. "I know where Bernice kept the garden tools. You find something special to wrap Toby in."

Gabriel took care of everything while Christina stood watching, her head bowed, and yet more tears rolling down her face. When it was all done, Gabriel set aside the shovel and strode to her. He pulled her into his arms and held her tight.

"Toby was old, sweetheart. He missed Bernice. Now they can walk together again. That's not a bad thing. Companionship with your best buddy."

"I-I tried to help him."

"You did. Bernice will know that too." He relaxed his grip on her and pushed her an arm's length away. "Now dry your face. Aidan will wonder what has happened to us."

"No, I can't go. I'll stay here."

"Not gonna happen. The last thing you need is to be alone. Come with me and help Aidan paint. You don't have to talk to us."

"No, I—"

"Not leaving without you, babe."

Gabriel bullied her into washing her face, and Christina found herself sitting inside Gabriel's SUV and on the way to Oneroa.

Once he'd parked outside Aidan's new place, Gabriel opened the door for Christina. On seeing them, Aidan opened his mouth to ask questions. He subsided at Gabriel's head shake.

"Christina is looking forward to painting," Gabriel said, shunting her farther into the room. "Where do you want her?"

"I'm still cleaning the kitchen area, but the paint is over there." He indicated two cans in the corner. "I have sheets to save the floors. Rollers and brushes. I intend to leave the ceiling white and paint the walls cream. The surface looks perfect, so I think it's fine to paint over the pale blue. Give me a shout if you need anything," Aidan finished.

Christina stood inside the door, her face blotchy from her crying. Gabriel frowned, not liking her behavior. She was upset and understandably. He'd start her painting and be there for her. That's all he could do at present. She'd talk—when she was ready.

Gabriel opened a paint can and organized an area for Christina to paint. She stared at him when he handed her a roller and gestured at the wall. Then, she blinked and took the roller. He watched, letting his breath ease out when she started painting.

Before he set to work, Gabriel sought Aidan.

"What happened?" Aidan murmured.

"Toby died."

"Crap. Is that why you're late? I was worried."

"Yeah, we buried him in the garden. Christina wanted to stay at the cottage, but I wouldn't let her. I don't think we should leave her on her own."

"Aye," Aidan said. "Is she blaming herself?"

"Yes."

"What are we going to do?"

"One of us will stay with her. I'll open the cheese shop. Gran might like to help, and if she can, I'll pop back. I wanted to start a new batch of cheese this afternoon."

"You take care of that," Aidan said. "I'll care for our girl."

17

SINKING, SINKING, PANIC

AIDAN FINISHED IN THE kitchen and moved on to painting after Gabriel left. Christina didn't speak, but she painted, so he let her stay inside her head. He'd give her a few hours before he began chattering at her and demanding responses.

Another hour passed, and Aidan set down his roller. Christina was working on the far wall, still silent, her shoulders curled inward. Her body language shouted *go away*. Aidan's belly rumbled even as worry had him frowning.

"I'm going to grab a coffee and sandwiches," he stated.

"Don't bother for me."

"I'll get you a coffee at least," he told her, and he meant to see she drank it.

"Whatever."

Aidan's eyes widened at her tone then he cut her some slack. At least she was speaking again. "I'll be back soon."

She never replied.

He paused a beat, the quiver in his stomach more than hunger. He glanced back at Christina. She ignored him and continued rolling paint over the wall. Slow and steady. Silent. Hell, it hurt watching her, the pain radiating from her a tangible thing.

Still worried, Aidan exited his place and strode toward the coffee shop. A five-minute walk. His nape prickled, and he glanced over his shoulder. A mother pushed a stroller along the sidewalk and held the hand of a second child, some distance behind him. The unease continued, and Aidan lengthened his stride. He'd settle once they were back at Gabriel's house with privacy. Aye. He'd wrap up the painting early and get Christina home. Get her to talk.

The coffee shop had a line. Aidan refrained from tapping his foot, but he scowled at the tourists who requested fancy coffee that wasn't the norm, and the local woman, standing two in front of him, who dithered over her selection of cakes for a work treat. She kept changing her mind. Resigned to waiting, he pulled out his phone and checked his email.

Christina concentrated on the painting and counted the strokes of her roller. Whenever she found her thoughts straying, she jerked them back. Half the time, her vision turned misty because of the tears wetting her eyes. But she controlled them, never let them free even when the sting became bad.

Footsteps behind her had her blinking. Once. Twice. She applied more paint to her roller and continued stroking it across the wall.

"You're alone. Good."

Christina started at the feminine voice. She ceased her painting, set the roller down, and turned. "What are you doing here?" she snapped, not even attempting politeness. Her mother and Bernice would be appalled.

Stacey Fletcher ignored Christina's attitude. "You need to learn the truth."

"Go away. I'm busy." Christina wasn't in the mood to fence words with this woman.

Another woman entered the restaurant, a young boy in tow. Darcy and the son Stacey had mentioned. He had dark hair. Brown eyes. Dressed in jeans and a tee advertising the Auckland Blues rugby team, the boy reminded her of Gabriel. A spear pierced Christina's heart, and the heaviness behind her eyes increased. She averted her gaze from Darcy and her boy to glare at Stacey.

"This isn't Grand Central Station," Christina snapped. "The door isn't open for you to walk through. It's there to disperse paint fumes." Yes, her mother would be aghast at her daughter's rudeness.

"You're a bitch," Stacey said. "I didn't want to tell you

this, but now I think you deserve to get hurt. Darcy, you'd better get Logan to sit outside and wait for us. I get the sense this won't be pretty."

Christina yawned and made a poor show of hiding it, but at least she'd locked down those tears. She peeked at the boy for a few seconds until he disappeared from sight.

Stacey's eyes narrowed. She glanced at her friend before directing her attention back to Christina. This time, determination etched into her features. The woman didn't intend to leave until she'd achieved her goal.

"Get on with it," Christina said, her tone belligerent. The anger tasted better on her tongue than her brooding rut. "I don't have much time."

Stacey's friend straightened her shoulders. "That was my son, Logan. Gabriel is his father. We were together and had an argument that blew apart our relationship. Now that I'm back on Waiheke, I'm positive Gabriel will want to meet Logan and have him in his life."

Gabriel truly had a son?

Shock struck Christina with a one-two punch even though the kid had reminded her of Gabriel. Hurt, because he hadn't told her. Pain that another woman had borne him a son. Along with that came unease. This behavior didn't seem like Gabriel—ignoring a woman who'd had his child.

"Why are you telling me?" Christina's voice emerged thickly, laden with emotion. If she could hear it, then so would the two women. They'd know they'd drawn blood. Wounded her. They'd suspect she cared for Gabriel, that they had her interest now, however unwillingly.

"Gabriel doesn't think sometimes. He acts, and in doing so, he hurts people who care for him," Stacey said. "Darcy has always loved Gabriel—since she was a teenager. They have a son together. Gabriel is single. Darcy is single. What do you think will happen when Gabriel sees his son?"

If the boy was his son, Gabriel would do the right thing, which might have repercussions for her and Aidan. Christina's thoughts spun until dizziness assailed her. She didn't want to think about this. Not now. Not today.

"Darcy and I are going now, but before we do, I'll give you advice. Gabriel rejected Darcy. He walked away from my friend, and the consequences are still rippling through our family. Why do you think my parents refuse to speak with Gabriel? He made a stupid mistake, and his silly pride impeded him from fixing his errors. I know Gabriel, know what he's like. When he sees Logan, he'll stand up, simply because he's matured and reined in his wild side. You should leave before you get hurt. Before you get in so deep you end up with nothing but pain.

"When Gabriel is faced with two choices—right and wrong—he'll pick right this time. He'll stop lying and apologize. If you're a sensible woman, you'll leave now and not look back." Stacey's expression softened for an instant before it blanked. "If you stay, don't say I didn't warn you.

Go on, Darcy. Let's get Logan settled."

The two women left, and Christina stared after them, numb and unable to move, much less think.

Gabriel had a son.

The minute Gabriel saw Logan... Well, Christina figured Stacey was right. Gabriel wouldn't turn his back on his child. Although she didn't know the details of the feud within his family, she'd guessed the reasons were major.

Anguish heaped over her, buried her.

Gabriel had a son.

A wave of heat engulfed her body, yet a chill settled in her bones. Soul-deep. Her ears rang while her thoughts tumbled over and over, round and round. The pressure behind her eyes became so fierce no amount of blinking barricaded her tears.

Something broke in Christina then. With tears rolling down her cheeks, she snatched up her handbag, plucked up the keys Aidan had returned to her, and ran from the restaurant. She jumped into her car and roared from the parking lot. Instinctively, she headed for the ferry terminal. She had to get away, had to think, had to make decisions for the future.

For an instant, she considered returning to Auckland and staying, but no. She owed it to Bernice to honor the conditions of the will. Right now, she needed space. Time to reassess.

In a few days, once she'd decompressed and gathered her

emotions together, she'd return to face Gabriel and Aidan. And bring a plaque for Toby.

A tear rolled down her cheek and dripped off her chin.

Somewhere in this situation, there must be something she could find to be grateful for. One tiny thing she could write in her journal, so the day her heart truly broke didn't suck so much.

It was thirty-five minutes before Aidan left the coffee shop. He'd purchased ham-and-salad sandwiches, two steak pies, and two pieces of ginger crunch slice. He'd also grabbed two bottles of water and carried two large coffees. With the concentration Christina had been using, she'd probably finished the painting.

He hastened his steps, not wanting to leave her alone for much longer. She'd seemed so fragile and broken when she'd arrived with Gabriel. He'd wanted to hug her, but she'd closed off, and all he'd done was offer his condolences. As soon as he returned, he'd make her put down her roller, and he'd give her that hug. He'd tell her with actions, he was there for her, ready for when she wished to talk.

When he arrived back at his restaurant, he bounded up the two steps and burst through the open door.

"Christina?"

He set down his bags and the two coffees in their holder and searched for her. It didn't take long to ascertain he was alone. Christina's coat still hung on the hook where he'd left it earlier, but there was no sign of her. Cursing under his breath, he ran outside to check the parking area behind his restaurant. Christina's vehicle had gone.

Aidan pulled out his phone and rang Gabriel.

"Yeah," Gabriel said.

"Is Christina there?" Aidan barked out.

"What the fuck?"

"Is Christina with you?"

"Haven't seen her since I left. Give me a sec. I'll check with Gran."

Equipment slammed. Doors banged.

"She's not here." Gabriel's words held worry. "She talk to you?"

"She concentrated on painting. I kenned she didn't wish to talk, so I didn't push. Thought it was time for a break, so I left her alone for around forty minutes while I bought us sandwiches and coffee. The coffee shop was busy, so it took longer than I thought. Crap, I shouldn't have left her alone."

"Not your fault. I'll check her cottage."

"I'll pack up here and come home."

"Later," Gabriel said.

There was a small patch left to paint on the wall Christina had been painting. Aidan finished that with rapid strokes of the roller and packed away the paint. He washed the rollers and cleared the floor of debris. Aye, his walls were painted and looked great. However, the progress meant nothing in the face of Christina's flit. She might think solitary sounded perfect, but she'd do better if she wallowed with them around. No words were necessary, but he'd come to like and admire her. Hell, he was halfway in love with the woman who made Gabriel so happy, so she should let them be there for her, care for her when she hovered too close to depression.

His phone rang. "Aye?"

"She's not at the cottage."

"Your Gran?"

"Gran hasn't seen her either. I'm coming to get you. We'll drive around. See if we can find her."

Aidan's throat tightened as he considered her mood. Her despair. Scenarios flashed through his mind. Horrid ideas he hesitated to state aloud. Finally, since this was Gabriel, he pushed out the words. "You don't think she'd do anything stupid?"

"Trying not to let my mind go in that direction," Gabriel confessed. "Be there in ten."

Aidan shut the restaurant windows, locked up, and hurried outside to wait for Gabriel. The bank was shut. The store next door—a secondhand clothes shop—was closing down for the day. On impulse, Aidan poked his head in the door to introduce himself.

"Hey, I'm Aidan. I've taken over the lease on the restaurant next door."

A buxom Maori lady stepped forward, a smile wreathing her lips. "Rena," she said in a musical voice. She wore faded jeans and a light green shirt that displayed her assets. "I'm pleased someone is moving in. What sort of food are you selling?"

"An emphasis on local produce and seafood," Aidan said.

Her dark brows rose as she grinned and fanned her face. "That sexy accent. You're not from around here."

Aidan smiled in return. "Half Scottish. Half Kiwi," he informed her.

"I noticed the activity this morning."

Aidan nodded. "Painting the walls. Lots of cleaning. I don't suppose you noticed a woman with glasses take off. Light brown hair."

"Sure, I saw her. She took off in a hurry after she had a visit from two women. Didn't see much after that because I had customers who needed my attention. Is there a problem?"

"No," Aidan assured her, even drumming up a faint smile. "I'm sure we'll see more of each other. Did you recognize the women?"

"No, but I haven't been here for long. Will be over to try out your restaurant," she informed him with another of her grins.

"Aye, I'll look forward to it. Ah, there's my ride. Nice to meet you, Rena." With a farewell wave, Aidan turned and jogged over to Gabriel's SUV. He yanked open the door and climbed in. "Any luck?"

"No."

Aidan clicked his seat belt into place. "I introduced myself to the woman next door. She said Christina left after a visit from two women. She didn't recognize them since she's new to Waiheke."

Gabriel cast him a glance as he drove down the main drag of Oneroa. "It could've been anyone."

"Aye." Aidan picked up his phone and dialed Christina. It clicked to voicemail. "Hey, Christina. Gabriel and I are worried about you. Please call us and let us ken you're okay."

"Left a message too," Gabriel said as he pulled up in the beach parking lot. They scanned the vehicles, but none of them were Christina's.

18

MAKING A RUN FOR IT

HALFWAY THROUGH THE FERRY crossing to Auckland, Christina switched off her phone. She sat huddled inside because she'd run from the restaurant without her coat. The wind whipped across the Hauraki Gulf, kicking up white caps and bringing bitter cold.

She stared at her hands, freezing to her bones and sadness a hefty burden, weighing down her shoulders. She saw Toby's still body and wetness pushed free, swamping her eyes. Fatigue crept over her, the heaviness sinking to her heart and encasing it with yet more grief.

Then there was Gabriel's son.

Her mind shied from the thought, a blast of pain making her curl in on herself. She slumped then winced at three rowdy kids who were demanding their parents purchase them ice cream. Gabriel's son had stood outside, obedient and somber. Hell's bells!

Her life had turned from crap to plain crappy. Where should she go?

She'd run to Auckland with no true destination in mind.

Her mind ran another circle.

Gabriel had a son.

A son.

When she was younger, she'd wanted kids. Still did, but now, she hesitated. Who wanted a broken mother? A depressed one. What if she hurt her child or worse, she passed on her faulty genes?

A surge of self-pity had her blubbering again, and she sprang to her feet and headed for the restroom. Her foot skidded on a wet patch on the deck. Someone had vomited. Christina groaned. The noxious stench had her gorge rising. She croaked and drew her next shuddering breath through her mouth. She grabbed a fistful of toilet tissue and retreated to wipe her face and clean her boot. When she returned, someone had taken her seat. She found an empty corner, leaned against an internal pillar, and closed her eyes. Tried to tell herself she wasn't cold, wasn't upset to hell, wasn't coming unglued and hovering close to a tipping point.

She forced her mind to blankness. A momentary distraction since Gabriel, Aidan, Toby, Bernice, Gabriel's kid—they swirled around, making her giddy. Pushing her closer to breaking. She stared at her boots. Concentrated on whatever it was that she'd missed and had stuck to one toe. The crossing seemed longer than usual. No doubt, the wind, and the rain had slowed the ferry.

When the ferry berthed, she trailed the other passengers and shivered at the polar blast. Christina still had no idea of where to go. She tossed up between Susan and Maggie and Julia and settled on Julia.

If Julia and Ryan weren't at home, maybe Caleb would be around.

She could ring. Her steps slowed. No. She didn't want to speak via phone. Not to Julia. Not to Aidan. Not to Gabriel.

Not right now.

The cool temperature and her lack of a coat sent Christina on a cab-hunt. Everyone else had the same idea, and it took her ages before she gave an Indian driver the address and sat her backside in the rear of a taxi. Focusing on the driver's pale blue turban distracted her for mere seconds. Rain splattered the windows. Darkness fell despite the early hour. The polar front lashing Auckland was making a statement.

When she arrived at Julia's house, lights showed at least someone was at home. Christina paid the driver, swallowed hard, shoved at her negativity, and exited the cab. Julia had told her to call if she wanted to talk. She did. Desperately.

After a deep breath, Christina knocked and wrapped her arms around her torso to keep warm. Luckily, she didn't have to wait long.

"Christina," Ryan said in surprise. "Come in."

Ryan was Julia's husband, and he ushered her toward the kitchen. Christina paused to remove her boots before she trailed him.

"Look who I found on our doorstep," he said.

Julia wiped her hands on a towel and came to greet Christina. She hugged her, and the kindness, the welcome, the weight of her friend's arms squeezing her in a hug had tears forming in her eyes.

Christina blinked again, wondering if she even had any tears left because she'd cried so much today. When she'd found Toby. When Gabriel had arrived at the cottage to help her. When she'd been waiting for the ferry. And now, it appeared she'd cry while hugging Julia.

Julia pulled back from the hug, her huge smile fading on seeing Christina's face. "Christina? What's wrong?"

"I'm sorry. I shouldn't have come."

Ryan walked up behind her and wrapped his arm around Christina's shoulders. "Sweetheart, you having a bad day?"

"The worst," Christina managed between sobs.

"Why don't I take over dinner prep, and you and Julia sit down with a glass of wine? Caleb should arrive soon, so he can help me in the kitchen. The kids are in the family room. Settle in the lounge, and I'll bring in two glasses of wine and snacks to hold you until dinner."

Julia urged Christina toward the lounge. She took a seat at the end of a three-seater couch and gestured for Christina to join her. No sooner had they sat than Ryan arrived with drinks plus a tray of eats. A hummus dip, fresh bread and olive oil, and a dish of sliced vegetables. Ryan had also brought two small plates and napkins.

Once Ryan left, Julia watched her over the rim of her wineglass. "Did something happen with Aidan and Gabriel?"

Christina's fingers tightened on her glass then forcibly relaxed in case she broke it. "Yes and no." She stared into the wine, trying to assemble her scattered thoughts. But they refused any order, zapping around like an action figure in a gaming machine, instead of marching in a straight line.

Julia reached for a carrot stick and dragged it through the hummus. She crunched down, her gaze on Christina. Sympathy shone in her eyes.

Christina swallowed and set her drink on the chrome-and-glass coffee table. "Everything is going wrong. I...I've never told any of you this, but I suffer from depression. When I worked with you, my depression was reasonably mild, and I dealt by keeping busy and doing things. I didn't know it was depression. I...I thought I was overtired or stressed.

"After Susan married Tyler, it was like I was left alone. You all had someone else in your lives, other commitments. I get it. I do. But it was hard because whenever we made plans, you'd cancel. When you came to Waiheke, it was the first time I've seen the three of you for six months."

"And we tried to tell you there is no future with your two men," Julia said in a soft voice, apology in her expression.

"Yeah."

"What else happened? Why aren't you with your guys?"

"Bernice died, and today, Toby died." Another bout of tears rolled down her cheeks, and Christina fumbled in her bag for her packet of travel tissues. It was empty, so she used her hand to swipe away the moisture.

Julia leaned forward to cover Christina's hand with her own. "Toby?"

"Bernice's dog. He was old, and the vet told me animals get depressed too. I tried my best, but he died. Gabriel came, and we buried Toby in the g-garden." A sob escaped.

"Oh, Christina. I'm so sorry. What about Gabriel and Aidan? Why aren't you with them?"

"I-I tried to feel happier, and I helped Aidan to paint the interior walls of his new restaurant. I was keeping busy, doing something, even if I didn't want to talk. Aidan left to get coffee, and that...that's when I saw the boy. Gabriel's son."

Julia's brows shot upward. "Gabriel has a son? He's

been married before?"

"No, he's not married, but I saw his son. He's around ten. I think. I never talked to him. Everything crashed over my head. I couldn't process or use any of my coping strategies. All I could do was cry. I've cried all day."

"Did you speak with Gabriel?"

Christina gave her head a hard shake. "No," she whispered, ashamed of her actions.

Even when depression dug in its claws, running away was stupid. Dumb. Dangerous. But a frank discussion and the possible blowout had seemed like an insurmountable challenge. She hadn't had it in her—the mental fortitude—which was why she'd fled.

"Does he know where you are?"

Another shake of her head.

"Christina, he'll be worried." Julia frowned at her. "Aidan?"

Christina gulped, shame heating her face. "No."

"You should call them, so they know you're here."

Julia was right. She plucked her phone from her handbag and stared at it, images flashing through her head again. Faster and faster until the dizziness became even worse. A croak emerged. Panic.

Julia rescued Christina's phone from her trembling hand. She opened the address book and put through a call to Gabriel. "Gabriel, it's Julia. Christina is in Auckland with me." She paused. "Not tonight.

Tomorrow morning." Her tone was decisive.

Christina cringed and stared at her golden bracelets. They gave a faint jingle, and she realized she was trembling.

"No. I do now. She told me. No, talk to her about that tomorrow." Julia listened for a moment. "I'll ask." She looked at Christina. "Gabriel wants to know if you intend to return."

"Yes," Christina whispered, only able to hold Julia's gaze for seconds. "I just needed some time."

"Yes," Julia reported. "I think she's overwhelmed by everything." She paused again. "I get it. Have you heard of patience?"

This time, her friend's voice held a snap.

"I promise Christina will ring you tomorrow." Julia wrinkled her nose. "Yes, I will. I'll tell her." She hung up and handed the phone back to Christina. "Gabriel told me to tell you he loves you. Aidan loves you, and no matter what's going on, you'll work it out because you're meant to be together. He says you're stronger collectively." Julia stood and crouched in front of her. "He meant it, Christina. I thought he might shout or issue orders, but he didn't. He and Aidan clearly wish you'd hung around to talk through your problems instead of running away. I like him. I admit your situation worried me, but I like him. You trust him if you told him you're having problems. I mean, you didn't tell us."

"I wanted to, but you were busy with your new families.

Your work. Different friends."

"You could have rung one of us," Julia chided. "If you'd explained, I would've understood. After I lost the baby, things were hard for me. Ryan had gone, and with the miscarriage, my life was in turmoil. I'm not saying my situation is the same as what you're coping with, but I've stood close."

"You were pregnant," Christina said. "You were settling into your new role as a wife and mother. Then there was Maxwell's."

"Perhaps, but we'll never know because you didn't contact me or the others."

"I tried—"

"Never mind. Going forward, this is what you'll do. If Gabriel or Aidan aren't available, or you can't talk to them, you'll ring Ryan or me."

"I couldn't talk to Ryan."

"Caleb then. I'll brief him," Julia said.

Christina swallowed hard.

"Christina?"

Hesitant, she lifted her head and studied Julia. Her friend's expression told her Julia meant every word. "Are you sure?"

"I'm positive. If you need a face-to-face, call and come to stay with us. I'll put you to work at Maxwell's in payment and to keep you busy. You're welcome here anytime, Christina, but promise me one thing. If you leave

Waiheke, I want you to tell Gabriel and Aidan you're leaving. Running away solves nothing."

"I'll try," she murmured. "I'll try hard, but sometimes my thought processes aren't rational. It takes me time to work through."

Julia nodded, her face full of sympathy instead of judgment. "Before you get to the stage where you disappear and hide, that's when you ring me. If you can't get me, ring Caleb or Ryan."

"I'll try," Christina whispered. "There's the helpline at depression dot org too. I hadn't thought of it before, but they're always helpful. They have an online journal I find useful. They push positivity, lifestyle, and problem-solving."

"Right. So along with Gabriel and Aidan, you have three other options in us plus the helpline. Tell me about this journal. Have you been filling it out?"

"No, I stopped."

"Why?"

"I was better."

"Can you show me?"

"I will," Christina promised. "I'll work through my journal tonight after dinner and show you tomorrow."

The next morning, an empty spot, a hungry, emotional gap resided in Christina's chest. Tears prickled at her sore, dry eyes, and she blinked hard. Sleep had been elusive, and her reflection in the mirror showed that.

One thing was clear, however.

She had to return to Waiheke and ask Gabriel about his son. Running away had been stupid. Fruitless.

Her stomach gave an anxious buck at the thought of facing Gabriel. He'd be angry. At her. A shiver tap-danced along her spine, and she scowled into the mirror. Julia was right. Burying pain never worked with the fallout multiplying tenfold. Better to suck up her fears. Better to return and rip off the plaster. Better to talk even if the end result wasn't what she wanted.

The fear of what-ifs was ten times worse than action. *Ten times.*

Christina splashed cold water over her face.

A tap at her bedroom door had her starting. She spun around to stare at the carved wooden door, her pulse racing.

"Christina? Are you awake? I've brought you a change of clothes."

Christina opened the door to let Julia enter.

Julia frowned. "You didn't sleep."

"Not well."

"Would you like some makeup? I can help you cover the damage."

"Yes, please." Christina didn't hesitate. Julia held mad skills with makeup, and since Christina intended to return to Waiheke, she required armor. Which was all kinds of stupid, but if she could reduce her blotchy face to something resembling normal, her confidence might make an appearance.

"Then that's what we'll do. Caleb is here. I hope you don't mind, but I filled him in a little. He volunteered to do the school run for me, so I'll have plenty of time to check out your journal and help you with whatever else you need."

Christina cringed. "Caleb knows?"

Julia stilled. "Shouldn't I have told him?"

"No. That's fine." Her stomach did a tumble. "Ah, would you mind not sharing with Susan and Maggie? I... This is hard for me. I've told Gabriel and Aidan and now you. Ryan and Caleb know. I don't want to worry about what you think about me on top of everything else."

Julia reached for her and grasped both of Christina's hands, forcing Christina to meet her gaze. "I don't think of you any differently than I did last week. You're my friend, and I'd help you no matter what. Ryan or Caleb will treat you the same as usual..." She trailed off, her expression thoughtful. "Actually, we will amend our interactions. Ryan, Caleb, and I will ask about your journal. We'll ask if you need to talk or if we can do anything to help." Her face cleared. "So really, it's not that different from usual."

"I need to take small steps. That way, I feel as if I'm in control."

"Anything you need," Julia assured her.

The morning passed way too quickly, and soon Julia

dropped Christina on Quay Street near the ferry terminal.

"I'll check in with you every day," Julia said before Christina climbed out of the car. "You can tell me about your journal, or we can talk about anything else you need. If you need a male perspective, talk to Caleb. Confidential information for your ears only. Caleb was the other man with Ryan and me. Just once. If you need advice or just want to talk, I'm here for you. Christina." Julia's voice turned sharper. "I mean it. I will discuss anything you want." An impish grin took her face from pretty to gorgeous. "Even sex."

A snort escaped Christina. "That's the only part that doesn't worry me."

"I imagine juggling two men will be difficult."

Christina nodded. "That's why I have to improve my communication instead of processing everything internally."

"If you understand that, you're doing great. Call me after you speak with Gabriel and Aidan. I have experience in surprise children that pop out of the woodwork." She spoke of her oldest son who wasn't Julia's biological child.

"Thanks, Julia. I'll call you later."

The ferry motored at double-speed to Waiheke. At least that's how it seemed to Christina. The unease in her mind and the turmoil churning inside her stomach increased the closer she came to Waiheke. She hadn't contacted Gabriel or Aidan this morning, but her car was in the parking lot, so she'd drive back to her cottage, bolster her bravery, and go to face her men.

Aidan was working in the kitchen, preparing chili for dinner. A light tap sounded on the exterior door before it opened, and Christina stood at the entrance.

"Hi," she said, uncertainty etched into her features.

"Christina." Aidan dropped the vegetables he was peeling, wiped his hands on a nearby towel, and flew across the space between them. An instant later, he wrapped his arms around her shoulders and crushed her against his chest. Her delicate floral scent swept over him, and he pressed a kiss to her cheek. Now didn't seem the time to give in to his impulse to kiss the hell out of her.

"I'm so glad you're back," he murmured against her hair. He pushed her away but kept physical contact. "Are you all right?"

"I..." She cleared her throat. "Is Gabriel around?"

"He's fixing a fence. He told me he'd be two hours." Aidan checked his watch. "An hour and a half now. Would you like tea or coffee? I made a batch of cookies."

"I'm not an invalid," Christina snapped.

"Aye, but if you don't talk to me, I'll never ken what you're thinking. I'll never ken if you have a problem."

Christina sighed. "You're right." Her shoulders slumped before she straightened. "Yes, I'd like a cuppa and a cookie. Meantime, did you know Gabriel had a son?"

"He what?" Aidan didn't have to pretend surprise. It struck him over the head and had him gaping at Christina. "Are you sure? He would've told me."

"I've known Gabriel for even longer than you, and it was a shock to me."

"Wait. When did you learn this? How do you ken Gabriel has a son?"

"His sister Stacey popped in while you were buying us lunch yesterday. I saw the kid. He is about ten."

Aidan stared at Christina. "His sister? Are you certain she was telling the truth?"

"The kid looks like Gabriel. He has dark hair and brown eyes."

"We'll ask Gabriel," Aidan declared. "I can't believe he wouldn't say something. Gabriel is an upfront guy, and given what happened to him with his family, I can't see him walking away from a son. You look tired."

"I didn't sleep much last night."

Aidan poured boiling water into the teapot. "Have a nap after you drink your tea."

"I might."

Aidan sent Christina off to the bedroom, finished making the chili, and cleaned up the kitchen. Gabriel sent a text to say he had to repair a broken cupboard for his grandmother. Aidan texted back to say Christina was home. That done, he checked on Christina. She appeared fragile and uncertain. Nervous. Every part of him wanted to reassure her, and he moved toward the bedroom. She was lying on her side, facing the bedroom door. Her eyes were wide open.

"Can't sleep?"

"My mind is too busy."

Aidan hesitated because the image that popped into his head wasn't exactly PC. But it might take her mind off her problems. He strode the remaining distance to the bed and lay beside her. He curled his arms around her body and drew her against him. She rested, pliant, and accepting. Time to raise the stakes. He cupped her face and kissed her. Slow and deep and hot, leaving her under no illusions as to his intentions.

For long seconds she remained still, not participating then, to his relief, she wrapped her arms around him and kissed him back.

"Take your clothes off for me," he ordered once their lips parted.

"But Gabriel—"

"We have to tell him what we've done. Remember?"

"Gabriel gets off on bossing us around," she retorted.

"He does. It never worries me because the end result is always spectacular."

"There is that," Christina said. With a nod, she rolled to her feet. "This would be much easier if I had my burlesque clothes. I could flick buttons, and my clothes would melt off."

"I need to see this some time," Aidan said.

"Maxwell's, Julia's club, is amazing. It was run down and sleazy when she took it over, but it's pure class now." As she spoke, she unbuttoned her cream blouse and shrugged it off her shoulders. Her black wide-legged trousers fell down her legs and pooled on the floor. She stepped out of them, bending to pick up her clothes and fold them. Her lingerie was a champagne-color with lace trim—comfortable and one of her favorite sets.

"You're gorgeous." Aidan inched nearer and roved his hands across her bare shoulders and down her arms. His fingers chased the shiver of anticipation as it raced through her body. Aidan drew her against him and kissed her. He nibbled her mouth, swept his tongue across her bottom lip. He stroked and nipped. Tasted and seduced. Aidan took his time, each caress sweet and decadent. As if he had all the time in the world.

Long moments later, Aidan scooped her into his arms and set her on the bed. After a second to admire the sexy picture she made, he kissed her mouth, her neck, her chest. He stroked her upper arms and traced the cups of her bra before delving his fingers beneath to touch her aching flesh. Throughout this all, Christina gripped his shoulders. She caressed his back and explored his muscled chest, making Aidan suck in a quick breath. When she pushed their lower bodies together and deliberately brushed against his erection, he couldn't contain his urgent groan of need.

"So sweet," Aidan whispered. "Let's take these glasses off." He set her glasses aside, and she slowly blinked, her soft smile sending a bolt of lust through him. "I'm not sure where to touch and kiss next."

Christina's smile widened to a grin, and the last of his residual tension faded.

"Any requests?"

"My neck first," she said.

"I can do that." Aidan pressed his lips to the delicate skin beneath her ear, then sucked lightly.

"No hickeys," she said primly.

He smiled against her neck and trailed his kisses lower. Her sexy moan thrilled him, and Aidan continued to tease her with tiny kisses and delicate nibbles. His fingers wandered across the slopes of her breasts, and he palmed one. With his other hand, he tormented her nipple. He used the lace on her bra to add a layer of torture.

"Aidan," Christina murmured, his name a seductive groan.

"What do you need?"

"I want skin on skin. Take off my bra."

"Soon," he promised, and he proceeded to tease her further with his hands and mouth until she writhed and pleaded.

"You're so pretty."

"What I am is desperate."

Aidan chuckled and continued with his kisses, his sensual caresses until finally, finally, he removed her bra.

"Should I take off my panties too?"

"Not yet. There's no hurry," he murmured against her throat.

"Can I take off your clothes? Then I won't feel as vulnerable."

"Anything you want," he whispered, his breath warm against her nipple.

An instant later, he drew hard, and her body bowed upward.

"So good. Perfect," she murmured.

Unhurried, his big hands roamed her body, slipped between her thighs for a brief teasing foray.

A stroke.

A lightning-fast skim across her clit.

Aidan's fingers were damp as they trailed back over her leg, the faint drag of his calluses reminding her of Gabriel. Her mind darted forward, imagination taking over. Instead of books and movies to help her imagine, she had previous encounters and experience of the different ways the two men handled her. Gabriel was bossy while Aidan sought her permission more, but both knew their way around her body. No road maps required.

Aidan's hands tangled in her curls. He tugged to give her a faint sting while his mouth sought her breasts.

"Aidan," she murmured. "More. Give me more. Not fragile."

"Want to have you crazy for me."

"You've already done an excellent job," she murmured. "My pussy is wet. Now and then, when you suck on my nipples, my clit pulses." She glided her fingers over his pectoral muscles, paused to pinch one of his nipples. He flinched, and she lowered her head to lave away the pain. He groaned.

"Aye, that is fantastic. Do it again."

"The pinching part?"

"Maybe not so hard."

She obliged, drawing another deep groan from Aidan.

She tested his muscles and caressed his hard body. Tasted his cock and sucked it into her mouth for a quick taste.

He stroked and murmured about her sexy curves.

When he donned a condom, his thrusts were slow and deep. Unhurried, but hitting the perfect spot. She clenched around his shaft, and he groaned. Their lips met, their kiss taking on an urgency that paralleled their rising passion.

"Faster," she whispered.

"I wanted to make this last. Wait, you get on top."

"Next time. Second round."

Aidan laughed—the sound joyous. He increased the pace of his strokes, and Christina was with him every step of the way. Her climax crashed over her, and she swept Aidan with her. Pleasure—stark and real. A sense of belonging. Christina cuddled with Aidan as their heartbeats returned to a normal speed.

A magical moment in time, she thought drowsily. Special. The thrill and charm and excitement was as good with Gabriel, and their sexual encounters when they were together—dynamite. She never wanted to lose this connection with her two men, and she intended to work hard to keep her mind straight and her eye on the prize.

Her future.

19

THE DIRECT APPROACH FROM THE PAST

CHRISTINA AND AIDAN WERE sitting in the kitchen, having an afternoon snack/late lunch when someone knocked on the door.

Aidan answered the summons while Christina finished her tea.

"You. What are you doing here?" Aidan demanded.

Christina rose and joined Aidan at the door. Stacey Fletcher and Darcy stood there.

Panic roared through Christina. She gasped, focused on her four-second breathing exercises. Julia had told her a child wasn't the end of a relationship. It was the secrets and the reasons behind that hurt and broke trust. Julia had suggested she listen and ask questions before jumping to conclusions. "What do you want?"

Stacey jerked up her chin. "It's time for Gabriel to take responsibility for his son."

"Don't you think you should discuss this with Gabriel?" Aidan demanded. "It's nothing to do with Christina or me. Approaching Christina at my restaurant was mean."

"How are we meant to do that?" Darcy demanded. "He refused to—"

Anger flared through Christina. "Stop, dammit. You will leave now. This is Gabriel's phone number." She rattled off his cell number. "Ring him to arrange a suitable time." Another thought occurred. "And don't drag your son with you. He shouldn't be part of the discussion," Christina snapped, recalling everything Julia had told her about her and Ryan's oldest child.

"This is none of your business," Stacey informed Christina, her chin rising as she began a stare-down.

Aidan walked to Christina and slipped his arm around her waist. Christina leaned into him, taking his shared strength and controlling her shivers.

"You've gone out of your way to place us front and center. Firstly, by confronting Christina at the restaurant, and now by turning up here when you must have known Gabriel is busy on the farm," Aidan accused. "Leave us out of this. You have Gabriel's number. Call him and arrange a convenient time to discuss this."

Aidan withdrew from Christina and glared at the two

women. "Leave."

"You're treating us like criminals," Darcy complained.

"No," Christina denied. "You're misbehaving. You know the obvious thing is to contact Gabriel, so do that instead of trying to drag us into your plan."

Darcy's gaze swung from Christina to Aidan and back. "Why are you here without Gabriel?"

"He invited us, you ken," Aidan said.

"We need to open the shop for business," Christina said. "We're busy."

Finally, the two women left. Christina started shaking.

"Hey, Gabriel will be here soon," Aidan said. "Aw, sweetheart. Come here." Aidan wrapped his arms around her. He held her close and ran his hands up and down her back, offering her comfort.

Christina sighed and cuddled close. She should've stayed yesterday instead of running for cover. Yet Julia hadn't told her she was stupid. Aidan hadn't shouted at her. It was vital for her to use her communication skills instead of letting her head take over.

"Okay, aye?"

"Yes."

"Then let's sell cheese and wait for Gabriel's return."

Christina followed Aidan to the shop. "Will we tell Gabriel about his sister's visit?"

"Aye, he needs a heads-up. We need an explanation."

"I panicked," Christina blurted. "Toby... I let Bernice

down by not looking after Toby properly."

Aidan placed a hand on each of Christina's shoulders. "Recall what you just told me. Do you think Bernice would blame you? You fed Toby. You walked him and spent time with him. You took him to the vet. What more could you have done?"

"Kept him alive," Christina said with a hard swallow.

"Toby was old." Aidan pushed his face closer to hers until the tips of their noses touched. He smiled at her, the outer edge of his eyes crinkling. "Besides, now he and Bernice are together again. I never met Bernice, but from what Gabriel has told me, she's looking down and shaking her finger at your silliness."

Christina jerked away from him, and her eyes widened. "Can dead people see everything?"

"You mean sex?" Aidan barked out a laugh. "I'll let you know once I get to that stage."

A car pulled up outside the shop.

"I'll top up the cheese in the chiller. Give me a shout if you need anything in a hurry."

Christina expected Gabriel to arrive at any time. He didn't. Instead, she and Aidan sold cheese together and had fun collecting possible names for Gabriel's newest blue cheese. One precocious kid suggested Escapee because he wanted to flee from his taste buds. According to him, blue cheese was akin to smelly socks. His mother rolled her eyes and suggested Fantastico or Magician because that cheese was pure magic.

She was sitting at the breakfast bar while Aidan was whipping up an apple pie for dessert when Gabriel strode inside.

"You're back," he said, and he headed straight for her and wrapped her in a tight embrace. He planted a kiss at her neck before pulling back to stare at her. "Missed you. Don't ever scare us like that again."

"I can't promise, but I'll try," Christina whispered.

"Good enough," Gabriel declared. "But you need to talk, pick one of us or ring one of your girls. We'll try to help."

Christina nodded. "Julia is checking in on me most days. Ryan and Caleb told me if I need to talk they're available."

A growl rumbled through Gabriel. "Hate that idea."

"Sweetheart, Ryan is Julia's husband. Caleb is his best friend. Mine too. Caleb and I have never been lovers. I told you that."

"Sometimes, it's easier to talk to someone outside the situation," Aidan remarked. "Cease your growling, mate. If Christina needs their help, she'll take it with our blessing. We want our girl happy."

Gabriel scowled but gave a clipped nod.

"What took you so long?" Aidan asked.

"Gran had a list of jobs, and she wanted me to take her grocery shopping. Told me she wanted to stock up on the basics and needed me to tote that shit."

A snicker burst from Christina. "I bet she didn't say it in those words."

"Nope. I simplified." Gabriel's eyes gleamed with humor. "That's what she meant."

Christina stared at Gabriel, the issue of a child filling her mind again. "Do you have a son?" she blurted.

From the corner of her eye, she witnessed Aidan's wince then Gabriel filled her attention.

"What the fuck? Why would you ask me that? If I had a kid, I'd be with him."

"Your sister came by for a visit," Aidan said into the charged atmosphere.

"I don't have a sister." Gabriel's voice was harsh and decisive. "Not talking about this crap now. Spoil my mood," he muttered, sharing his glare with both of them.

Christina's pulse raced. Gabriel denied a child. She'd seen the kid. She swallowed and glanced at Aidan. He gave a faint shake of his head.

"This pie is almost ready to go into the oven. While I finish here, ask Christina to tell you what happened in our bedroom."

Gabriel's dark brows rose, and a tiny smile flirted with his lips. "Afternoon nookie?"

"Aye."

Both men turned to her: Aidan with a grin and Gabriel with speculation.

"Babe, want a beer or a glass of wine?"

Christina nodded, her stomach doing a strange flutter of anticipation.

Aidan grabbed a glass from the cupboard while Gabriel pulled a bottle of white wine from the fridge along with two bottles of beer.

Aidan handed over the glass of wine. Gabriel picked up one bottle of beer and held out his other hand to her.

"We'll be chilling in the lounge," he told Aidan.

"Aye."

With her stomach still doing those crazy tumbles, she allowed Gabriel to tug her into the lounge. He released her hand and took her glass of wine from her, then he set it and his beer aside before dropping onto the leather couch.

He patted his lap. "Take a seat, babe."

Christina hesitated.

"Want to hold you."

Christina still hesitated.

"Not gonna ask again."

Christina took a stumbling step forward and planted herself on Gabriel's knee. He grasped her upper arms and situated her to his liking.

Christina relaxed, savoring his familiar scent and his touch.

"Tell me what you and Aidan did," he murmured.

She froze. "Ah." *Really?*

"Serious about this, babe. You do this, I won't feel left

out. Avoids jealousy. That sort of shit."

While Christina could see his point, it didn't make a confession any easier. In fact, it was embarrassing. At that conclusion, a whoosh of heat converged in her cheeks.

"Help you out by telling you Aidan, and I fucked last night. Made love this morning. Missed you in the mix. Wanted you there, but we understood you needed time. Won't say it didn't piss me off, but I get it. Aidan gets it too."

Christina stared at him—a common occurrence since his honesty, the way he laid things out made her feel bad for containing her emotions, for letting them take her over. For thinking the worst and allowing fear to rule her actions. "I...ah..."

Gabriel pressed her against his hard chest. He ran his hand through her hair and tugged off the band she'd used to contain her mass of curls while she worked in the cheese shop. He played with a lock of hair and wound it around his finger.

"Aidan and I wanted rough last night. So that's what we gave. Surrendered to need. Passion. First, though, I sucked him off. Love the taste of him, the growls he makes in the back of his throat when I lick away the first drops of pre-come. They make me crazy. Go right to my dick. Make me harder. Desperate to fill him. Experience the heat of him surrounding my cock."

"He tastes delicious."

"The man does," Gabriel agreed. "Another reason I enjoy taking him in my mouth. Did you swallow?"

"No. I stopped before I got that far. Aidan took off my clothes. He said I was pretty, and he likes my boobs."

"Our man has taste," Gabriel confirmed and kissed her temple. "Your curves are seriously sexy."

"I should stop eating so much."

"Nah. Don't, babe. Love those curves of yours. Had other lovers in the past. Prefer padding. Some cushioning. The soft against the hard. My dick," he added with a trace of teasing.

Christina snorted and found herself giggling.

"Just have to think of you or Aidan. My cock gets hard," he confessed. He pulled back and studied her. A frown creased his brow. "You saw my sister yesterday?"

She searched his gaze. Nodded. Averted her eyes to study his chest.

"She say something to you? Wait. Never mind. I'll deal with Stacey tomorrow. Rather talk about what you did with Aidan. You sucked him, yeah?"

"I did," Christina whispered. "We stopped for him to undress me, and once I was almost naked, we fell on the bed."

"Were you in a hurry?" A smile twitched at his lips. "I get that."

"I think Aidan wanted to distract me and fill up my head with other things. Better things."

"Get that too, babe. You deserve happiness. Had a bad run lately."

"Not everything has been bad," Christina whispered. "I found you then Aidan. I reconnected with my friends."

"Your friends stuck their noses in."

"They did, but they care for me."

"Funny way of showing it. They upset you," he reminded her.

"I talked to Julia, and she helped me a lot. She got me on track with my journal."

"You can tell Aidan and me about your journal over dinner. Still want to hear about you and Aidan. You stopped at the part where you fell on the bed."

Christina inhaled. Exhaled. She cuddled against Gabriel. "Aidan touched me. Teased me. He cupped my face and kissed me. Slow and deep. He's a great kisser. Like you," she added. "We made love twice."

"Excellent to know," Gabriel said.

"Aidan sucked on my neck. Not hard enough to leave marks but enough to make me wriggle and want more. I thought he'd go for my breasts next, but he surprised me. He nibbled his way down my ribs and teased my bellybutton with his tongue. Then, he nipped the underside of my breasts. He cupped them with his hands and pushed them closer together. He tongued both of my nipples until I was begging him to do more. That was the second time."

"Love hearing you beg, babe. You do it so pretty. Makes a man feel powerful and important. Like you can't get enough of him, and only he can do the job." He tugged on a lock of hair, the small sting bringing a wash of pleasure.

She wriggled, pushing closer to Gabriel. While she imagined telling Gabriel everything might embarrass her, she hadn't realized it would bring this arousal. A need to repeat the same actions with Gabriel.

"He-he played with my breasts for a long time. My nipples were hard, and every time Aidan sucked on them, I experienced it down here." She let her hand drift down her belly.

Gabriel grinned. "Where's down here?"

Christina twisted to meet his gaze, confirming the fact she was right. He was grinning. "A corresponding tug in my vagina."

"Huh?"

"My pussy," she said.

Gabriel's grin widened. "Nice. What happened next, babe?"

"Aidan pulled me on top of him. He told me he wanted a visual. One he could describe later to you."

"Carry on. Don't worry. I intend to ask for Aidan's input later."

"I straddled his body and guided his cock into me."

"How was it?"

A shiver of remembrance worked through her.

"Amazing. Aidan's cock stretched me."

"You liked it?"

She issued a sigh and attempted to ignore the heat in her cheeks. "Very much."

"What next?"

"I rode Aidan, and when I couldn't get the right angle, Aidan told me to finger my clit."

Gabriel nodded. "Did you?"

"Yes. I came fast after that. Aidan turned me and thrust hard several times until he came too."

"Excellent job, babe. I can picture that."

"Dinner is ready," Aidan called.

Decadent scents wafted from the kitchen. Aidan had set the table with three bowls of chili. A large yellow-and-blue serving bowl contained rice while a smaller matching one held sour cream. Aidan had also heated a pile of tortilla, chopped cilantro, and lastly, he produced a bowl of grated cheese.

Gabriel pulled out a chair for Christina and seated her. He seated Aidan too before taking possession of a third seat.

"Thanks for cooking, Aidan," Gabriel said. "How did the sales go this afternoon?"

"Reasonable," Aidan said. "We had fun with the customers, asking them to name your new blue cheese."

Christina laughed. "I doubt whether any of the names are suitable, but we had a laugh. Aidan, I had an idea for your restaurant. On the nights you don't intend to open, you could rent it out to charities. They could have a restaurant for an evening or lunch and raise funds. Just get them to pay for your fixed costs like power, a day's rent. That sort of thing."

"That's brilliant," Aidan said with enthusiasm. "I love that idea. It'd bring a community feel to the business. If I work it right, I might attract celebrity chefs or talented amateurs who want to experiment with a special menu or style of food. I'd have to work on the advertising."

"You might have to offer guidelines or set rules or perhaps charge a deposit to cover breakages, but I thought it would be a way to involve the community," Christina said.

Gabriel paused with his fork in the air. "Your main concern regarding Bernice's will was you wouldn't fit into the community. You're blitzing this. Gran conned me into sponsoring her for the zombie run. You've given Aidan a fantastic idea for his restaurant, which means the place won't be sitting idle while he's doing his travel gig, and you've increased my cheese business. You underestimate yourself, babe."

"Aye, I agree. Perhaps marketing is more your thing because you have fantastic ideas."

Chatter turned general while they ate, and Christina mentioned Gabriel working in conjunction with the local vineyards.

"Not a bad idea. Can you organize it?"

"Me?"

"Your idea. Aidan, Christina told me what you did together. Your turn," Gabriel stated.

Christina glimpsed Aidan's face, caught his splutter. While she understood his trepidation, it was funny too.

Aidan straightened his shoulders and met Gabriel's challenge with an upward jerk of his chin. "I stripped off Christina's clothes—apart from her bra and panties—almost first thing because I enjoy her curves. She's soft, and she smells better than you." With this, he added a glare, but it didn't make the slightest difference to Gabriel.

"Details," Gabriel demanded as he set his cutlery across his empty plate. "Anyone want more?"

"No, thanks," Christina said.

Aidan shook his head. "I'm good."

Gabriel stood and scooped up empty plates and bowls. When Aidan tried to stand, Gabriel stayed him with a hand curved around his shoulder.

"Thanks for cooking dinner. Your hard work does not go unnoticed," Gabriel stated. "Since you and Christina arrived, you've both made my life easier by pitching in and helping whenever and wherever I need you. This is appreciated, and it's why I'm looking forward to returning the favor. Grandad tells me he's up for the milking, and he intends to rouse his two cronies to help him. Gran and her friends promised to turn my cheese for me. She's done it before and likes to poke her nose into my cheese room."

Aidan's eyes grew wide. "Seriously?"

"Yeah," Gabriel said, his voice gentle. "See, that expression of wonder on your face tells me I haven't worked hard enough for you. In the past, I've made this relationship about my needs, and that's wrong." He turned to Christina. "Thinking that a break will help you too. We'll try a few different things and have time together, where it's the three of us with no outside influence. Bonus, we get to understand more of Aidan's job."

"I've never visited Muriwai or the vineyards up that way," Christina said. "What else will we see?"

She and Gabriel cleared the dishes, stacked the dishwasher, and wiped counters. It wasn't a massive job because Aidan cleaned as he prepared and cooked his meals. Meanwhile, Aidan told them of his planned itinerary. Matakana. Goat Island. Puhoi with its historical pub.

"Will we get a chance to visit Puhoi Cheese?" Gabriel asked.

"Aye, we can do that."

Gabriel nodded and continued to wipe the final counter.

"The next day, we'll hit the West Coast beaches, check out the Muriwai Gannet colony and some vineyards, the Waitakere Visitor's Center before we head back to Auckland to drop off the rental car and return to Waiheke," Aidan said.

"Where are we staying?" Christina asked.

"The accommodation is a secret," Aidan said. "It's not my usual backpacker place."

"Looking forward to it," Gabriel said. "Anyone object to an early night? I'm thinking instead of Aidan telling me what you guys did together, he can show me. What do you say, Christina?"

A quiver worked through her. A blast of excitement, followed by her nipples prickling to hard points. She nodded instead of speaking because her throat and mouth were so dry.

"Did some online shopping," Gabriel said. "Parcel arrived today. Think we might have fun tonight."

20

HOT LOVING

THE EXPRESSION IN GABRIEL'S eyes had Aidan's blood pumping and sinking to his groin. Not for the first time, peace settled in his heart, despite his excitement. This thing he had with Gabriel and Christina felt right on so many levels. Each day had the bonds between them tightening. Strengthening.

"I can do that," Aidan agreed. "In fact, it'd be my pleasure." He held out his hand to Christina, and his pulse jumped when she curled her fingers around his. Another of those sharp jolts rocked him, and this time, he savored the way his body behaved. A part of him had resented Christina's presence when he first arrived.

But he'd been wrong.

Christina added an extra element to them. Somehow, she'd made them tighter, and Gabriel had shared more of himself than he ever had in the past. He'd taken them to dinner with his grandparents. Made no secret of his feelings and intentions. The strong, usually silent Gabriel had made himself vulnerable.

He got the sense Gabriel would soon reveal what had happened to blow apart his family, which was huge.

"Let's go." Aidan tugged Christina from the kitchen and down the passage. Gabriel prowled after them.

"Suggestion," Gabriel stated. "I fuck Christina, and you fuck me."

Aidan turned around and stared, realized he was gaping, and pressed his lips together. "I...you..."

"I want this," Gabriel said. "I want to claim and be claimed. Above all, I want you to understand I'm all in."

Aidan licked his lips, nodded. "I'd enjoy that."

"Christina, have you done anal before?" Gabriel demanded.

"No."

Gabriel strode to his nightstand, pulled out a bottle of lube, and what looked like a toy. No, two toys.

Gabriel straightened. "Show me how you undressed Christina." His big hand drifted to the buttons on his shirt, and he absently unfastened them while his gaze rested expectantly on them.

Aidan winked at Christina, who hovered in the doorway. "Walk to me, love."

Her brown eyes rounded when she heard the

endearment.

"I mean it," Aidan whispered. "We haven't kenned each other for long, but you've crept into my heart. You're special. Gabriel thinks so. I agree." He widened his smile and beckoned to her. "Come here, love. I get the pleasure of undressing you."

She crossed the bedroom, her hips swaying, her gaze on Gabriel, and then him. When she reached him, she halted. Aidan leaned closer and pressed a soft kiss to her mouth. It felt sweet. Tasted sweet. Aidan glanced in Gabriel's direction, and more warmth bloomed in his chest when Aidan witnessed his approval.

Aidan ran his fingers over the softness of Christina's cheek before taking a step back. "Shirt and jeans off. Show Gabriel the pretty bra and panties you put on after our shower. You have to see them, Gabriel. They're a pale blue with sheer lace insets. The bra is so delicate, it's a wonder the silky fabric holds her breasts."

"Is that right, babe? Do you have sexy underwear?"

Christina cleared her throat. "Bernice always loved pretty lingerie. She started my love affair with lace and satin."

"Show us," Gabriel whispered. "You listen to Aidan and follow his instructions."

"Christina," Aidan prompted, gratified when she smiled—a slow curl of her lips. Her bracelets collided musically as she removed her shirt and jeans. Her feet were bare, so soon, all she wore was the delicate blue bra and lacy panties.

Aidan closed the distance between them. He wet the tip of one finger and ran it along the right cup of her bra. She shivered, and he smiled at the way her brown eyes widened behind her glasses. Aidan plucked them off her nose, folded the arms, and set the glasses in a safe place on the dressing table. When he returned, he strummed her nipples, glorying in her soft gasp. Aidan stepped behind her and unfastened her bra, sliding the straps down her arms before tossing the garment aside. He tugged her panties down her legs and held her arm to keep her balanced when she stepped out of them.

"So beautiful," Aidan whispered.

"I'm underdressed compared to the two of you," she retorted.

"We're going to pet and play with you, babe. Then I'll insert a plug. It's a small one. Help you prepare for when one of us fucks your arse. Want us to take you and feel each other while we make love."

"Aye," Aidan breathed, loving the idea of total sharing and togetherness. Two lovers sounded better and better.

"What did you do after undressing Christina?"

"I kissed and teased her until she was ready to take my cock."

"I'll help," Gabriel stated.

Aidan nodded and ran his fingers over her breasts.

Creamy and full with nipples that tempted him to taste. He directed her to lie on the bed. "Spread your legs for us, love."

She followed his instructions to reveal beautiful pink flesh and her glistening juices.

"I can't wait to get inside you again," Aidan said.

"My turn this time," Gabriel said.

"Same words apply to both of you. I'm eager to enjoy your heat and the way you flex around my cock."

Gabriel moved between Christina's legs and didn't muck around. He touched her with fingers and mouth, Gabriel's dark head against the creaminess of her thighs making a gorgeous picture. For long seconds, Aidan took in the image, committed it to mind. This was not only beautiful but something perfect. He pinched himself, the sharp pain reassuring him none of this was his imagination. He sat on the bed then stretched out so he could touch both of his lovers at once. But first, to speed up the process. He stood again and ripped off his clothes before reclining beside Christina. Giving in to temptation, he allowed his fingers to trace over the underside of one breast. He'd already learned she enjoyed having her nipples caressed, and he gave her that while Gabriel feasted on her. Aidan tugged a nipple and tongued the other one. He drew on it, giving her suction.

"Yes." Christina arched her torso.

"Not too much, Aidan," Gabriel warned. "Let me

prepare her for the plug."

Aidan settled in to kiss Christina. Hot and wet and deep. Passionate.

Gabriel climbed off the bed to retrieve the lube. In seconds, he was back. "This will be cold," he warned Christina. Carefully and patiently, he prepared Christina.

Aidan returned to kissing Christina and playing with her breasts. "Okay, love?"

"Yes," she whispered. "Oh! That is strange."

"Ready." Gabriel moved up Christina's body. He kissed Aidan on the lips before he guided his cock to Christina's opening. "Gonna take it slow, babe. Condom."

Aidan handed him a condom, and Gabriel rolled it onto his shaft. Once again, Aidan watched the pair together, and instead of isolation, he experienced a sense of belonging.

"Ooh," Christina muttered as Gabriel pushed into her. He took it slow, and Aidan's mind took him on the same journey Christina was experiencing. The stretching. The aching fullness. The beauty of giving and receiving pleasure.

"Your turn, Aidan."

Aidan reached for the lube and got down to business. He figured it'd been a while for Gabriel, so he took his time while Gabriel remained still, balls deep inside Christina.

"Okay?" he asked Gabriel.

"Yup."

The first careful stroke into the heat of Gabriel was so perfect. As he pushed forward, Gabriel waited a bit before he withdrew from Christina. Together, they surged forward, merging into a sequence of slow, gliding strokes. So good. *So perfect.*

A groan sounded, and Aidan wasn't certain if it came from Christina or Gabriel. All he knew was that he wanted this to keep going. He pulled back, increasing his speed in increments until he was plunging into Gabriel. In turn, Gabriel was doing the same to Christina.

"Christina is close," Gabriel warned. "Her channel is pulsing around my dick."

Gabriel flexed around Aidan's cock, Gabriel's buttocks tensing as Christina exploded into her climax. The pressure around Aidan's cock intensified, and seconds later, he was flying. Gasping. Shouting encouragement for Gabriel. In front of him, Gabriel's broad shoulders shuddered, his body tensed. Aidan pressed himself against Gabriel's back and kissed his shoulder. He inhaled Gabriel's scent and the heady sexual aromas in the bedroom. A few moments later, once his breathing had evened out, he pulled out of Gabriel and rose to clean up. He returned with warm cloths and tended to Gabriel. He removed the plug for Christina and cared for her, too, murmuring praise and sweet nothings the entire time. Heat and lightness filled him. Happiness, he realized. A sense of security. He wasn't considering running away, for the first time content and settled even though he wasn't flitting from place to exciting place.

With Gabriel and Christina, he had enough challenges right here.

Yeah, joy bubbled inside him.

They crawled into bed with Gabriel in the middle. Smiling and satisfied, Aidan cuddled against him and closed his eyes. That had been amazing, and it could only get better.

21

VACATION TIME

SUNDAY, THREE DAYS LATER.

WHILE CHRISTINA HAD VISITED North Auckland, she'd never stopped at Matakana or visited the areas Aidan took them to. Her family holidays in the Bay of Islands had meant a long drive from Auckland with brief relaxation stops before her father had hustled her and her mother back into the car and continued to their destination.

Gabriel parked in the small hamlet of Matakana. They climbed out, and Christina noted the town was bustling with drivers attempting to locate parking and pedestrians heading in the same direction as them. The weather had cooperated, despite Aidan fretting it might rain, and the sun shone overhead with a strong promise of summer.

Aidan grabbed several shopping bags and thrust them at

Gabriel. "You carry these." He scooped up his camera bag next. "Your mission is to buy us food for a picnic lunch."

Gabriel turned to her. "Aidan has turned bossy."

"This is important," Aidan snapped.

Gabriel reached out to squeeze Aidan's shoulder. "Christina and I know that. We'll do exactly as you tell us."

"I'm wearing my red bikini, aren't I?" Christina piped up with a wink at Gabriel.

"You are," Gabriel purred, his eyes glowing, and he stared at her breasts as if he could see through the green blouse and black shorts she wore over her bikini.

"Focus," Aidan said, relaxing his tense shoulders and grinning. "Let's move. I want to take photos of you shopping at the market. Buy coffee or wine or whatever else you want to drink. Try the samples at each of the stalls and buy us a delicious lunch."

Christina had fun, and she thought Gabriel enjoyed weaving through the crowd and stopping for a glass of apple juice, a morsel of salami, and sampling the tart olives. She purchased filled rolls and a beautiful fruit flan. Gabriel hoofed it to the cheese stall and interrogated the owner before tasting samples. There, they bought a wedge of creamy blue cheese and walnut crackers.

Aidan snapped photos of them and stall owners. He took pictures of food.

"We have enough food to last us for days," Gabriel grumbled.

"Fresh air makes me hungry," Christina chirped.

"I have enough here if you're ready to leave," Aidan said.

They returned to the vehicle and headed to Goat Island, which was a fifteen-minute drive. The marine reserve was busy, but Aidan grabbed a bag of snorkels and flippers while Christina planted a hat on her head and toted towels, sunscreen, and a bottle of water. Gabriel carried their lunch.

The tide was on its way in, the sun sparkling on the water. A small island thrust from the seabed, near to the shore, but Christina suspected it was farther than it looked. Swimmers floated on the sea surface, their faces pointing downward to take in the marine life. Around the edge of the island, a boat bobbed, and several divers wearing wetsuits disappeared beneath the water.

"Is that a dive boat?" Christina asked.

"No, a glass-bottom boat," Aidan said.

Gabriel scanned the sand and people. "I didn't realize the beach would be so busy."

Several families had claimed shady spots beneath a gnarled pohutukawa tree. Young toddlers raced across the sand while others dug and filled their tiny plastic buckets. Aidan pulled out his camera and started taking photos.

"This is brilliant," he said. "Normally, I'm on my own and have to talk bystanders into posing for my photos. Then, I need to get releases before I can publish the photos. With you, it's so much easier."

Christina spread a towel on the sand and stripped to her bikini. Aidan's camera whirred. "You'll be showing me the photos before you publish them," she stated. "I'm not sure I want to appear in my skimpy bikini."

Aidan lowered his camera and grinned. "I need a photo for my wallet. Gabriel, strip and cuddle up to our Christina."

Our Christina.

Christina stilled, her mind going mushy inside. Aidan meant it, and she loved the solid bonds that were forming between them. It helped she'd known Gabriel for so long, but she'd never experienced this sense of rightness.

Gabriel's bare arm slipped around her shoulders. His gaze was warm and intense as he turned her into his arms. He kissed the tip of her nose. "Going to try snorkeling?"

"Yes! Aidan hired a prescription mask for me. I should be able to see without my glasses." Another element of thoughtfulness, and something she'd never considered.

"Have you snorkeled before?"

"When I was a kid. I love swimming, but I haven't snorkeled for years," she said.

"I'm not hungry," Aidan said. "Anyone want to snorkel now?" He swapped cameras. "Our stuff should be fine here."

"I'll ask the family over there if they're hanging around for a while," Gabriel said.

They were and agreed to watch over their possessions.

"Let's go." Gabriel grabbed her hand and started running.

Laughing, she ran with him. They hit the sea, and it was freezing. "Gabriel!"

"Best way," Gabriel said. "Cold turkey." He dipped his mask into the water before pulling it on. He thrust his feet into flippers with an expertise that made her blink.

"How did you manage that?"

"Practice," he said. "Here, let me help."

In no time, they were ready to go.

Christina floated beside Gabriel. When she started, Aidan was busy taking photos, but soon she forgot about him. Huge silver fish darted past her nose in a school. Over to her right, a colorful orange starfish clung to a rock. She kicked her flippers and followed Gabriel. Six bright blue fish—mau mau—flitted into a rocky outcrop, and mesmerized by their color, she floated after them.

It seemed like barely any time had passed when someone tapped her on the shoulder.

"Time to go back to shore, babe," Gabriel said when she lifted her head and trod water. "It's been an hour."

"Wow. It's awesome. The fish are huge!"

Christina followed Gabriel to shore and removed her flippers in the shallows. Even in the thigh-deep water, large snapper glided around their legs.

"Look this way!" Aidan shouted, and he snapped a photo of her and Gabriel.

They ambled up the sand to their possessions and called thanks to the family who was now eating.

"My father told me when he used to come here as a kid," Aidan said. "The visitors would feed the snapper frozen peas. A few people lost fingers and suffered bites on their legs."

"I'm not surprised," Christina said. "Some of those fish were enormous, and their teeth looked razor-sharp."

"They've grown big because they're protected," Aidan said. "There's talk of the government instating new marine reserves to protect fish stocks."

"They should." Christina plopped down on her towel. Now that she'd stopped, her legs trembled from overexertion. "I'm starving." She reached into the food bag and pulled out filled rolls. She handed one to Aidan and another to Gabriel before taking one for herself.

Aidan put his aside to snap another photo.

"Did you get enough photos?" Gabriel asked.

"I have heaps. I stopped snorkeling before you two and used the time to photograph the beach, the island, and the glass-bottom boat. Are you both okay to head off to Puhoi after we've eaten?"

"Sure," Christina said. "I'm enjoying this. It's like a magical mystery tour."

Aidan chuckled. "I love traveling and visiting new places, but I'm having more fun with both of you along. I've arranged a visit to the cheese factory first, then we'll have a one-drink stop at the pub before we head off to our evening's accommodation."

The rest of the afternoon was fun. Gabriel took the cheese factory visit very seriously and grilled the girl giving the tour. She disappeared and came back with a reinforcement to help her answer his technical questions. A serious discussion ensued.

Christina giggled and tugged on Aidan's elbow as Gabriel followed the man from the visitor center.

Aidan grinned at her and clasped her hand in his. "Come on. We'll take photos. I need you to pose for me near the shop sign."

Aidan still had her posing and was taking photos half an hour later when Gabriel reappeared. His guide offered Gabriel a business card before disappearing.

"Are you finished?" Christina asked.

"He refused to give up his secrets," Gabriel said with a grin. "But he gave me contact details for a group of cheese-makers. He said they have regular meetings and share knowledge and tips."

"You can tell us more during our stop at the pub," Aidan said.

"I'll keep driving," Gabriel said. "I'll have a low alcohol beer."

The day continued with the surprises growing as Gabriel, following Aidan's instructions, turned off the main highway and drove up a long, winding tree-lined road to arrive at a private hotel. Extensive gardens, full of flowers, were visible on each side of the main building.

"We're staying here?" Christina asked, her eyes growing wide.

"We are," Aidan said. "Wait here while I check-in and get the room key."

He trotted back after ten minutes and climbed back into the car. "Drive down here and around the side of the hotel."

Gabriel did as instructed, and that's when Christina realized they were near the coast. A few trees were planted in front of them, and she suspected their purpose was to direct the gaze toward the Tasman sea.

"Drive to the second chalet," Aidan said. "We have three hours before dinner. We're booked in at the restaurant to try out their award-winning menu. Pacific fusion," he said. "Lots of seafood and local produce."

"Is that why you told me to bring one dressy outfit?" Christina asked.

"Sort of. No. I wanted to see you glammed up," Aidan confessed. "I already ken you have gorgeous legs. I dream of seeing them while you're wearing a dress."

"Yeah." Gabriel jerked up his chin, his gaze intense. "Wanna see that."

"Meantime, I thought we might try out the private hot tub on the deck of the chalet. It overlooks the sea. From what I understand, it's the perfect place to chill with a drink or two," Aidan said.

As soon as Gabriel parked the car, Aidan jumped out and strode to the door of the chalet. He opened the door and disappeared inside.

"You enjoying today?" Gabriel asked.

"Very much. Aidan is so excited."

"Yeah. Makes my heart ache. Shows me I didn't support him enough in the past. Took him for granted."

"We're both here now. Are you enjoying this?"

"Hell, yeah."

"Then that's enough. Will you say yes if Aidan asks again?"

"Yeah. Do my best to help Aidan with his travel gig. I can't go for some reason, perhaps you could go. At least one of us goes with him. Deal?"

She nodded. "We need to support each other."

"My point," Gabriel said.

"Deal," Christina agreed with a grin. "Let's go." She climbed from the front passenger seat. "Should we take our bags?"

"No, we'll grab them later." Gabriel jogged around the hood to join her. He slipped his arm around her waist and hugged her to his side. Together, they ambled toward the chalet and entered.

"What took you so long?" Aidan snapped several photos. "Come out to the deck. It's awesome. I need a photo of you in your red bikini, lounging back in the hot tub with a glass of wine."

She glanced at Gabriel and caught his wink. His quick grin.

"For you." Christina blew him a kiss. "I'll pose in my red bikini, and once you're done with photos, I'll take it off."

Gabriel's grin widened to toothy, and his eyes sparkled. Christina sucked in a quick breath, her pulse jumping. The man did it for her when he smiled with such genuine humor.

Aidan pursed his lips in a silent whistle. "I dare you."

That set the tone for the rest of the afternoon with touching and caressing and her breasts naked to anyone with a boat and binoculars. Luckily, they saw no one or nothing except birds since they were all very naked. Christina hadn't had so much fun for ages.

She showered for dinner, put on a delicate mauve bra and panty set with a dab of perfume between her breasts, and donned a little black dress that clung to her curves. At the last moment, she smoothed on thigh-high stockings before she fastened a pair of black and silver shoes on her feet. When she stood, she'd acquired three extra inches.

"Wow," Aidan said, halting in the middle of the en suite door. "You're breathtaking."

Christina beamed, his compliment bringing a wealth of pure happiness. A tiny voice at the back of her mind stepped forward to ask how long this would last, but remembering Julia's words, she shoved away the interloper.

Bernice had always said, *don't borrow trouble*, and she'd work hard to keep to that motto.

Gabriel stepped into the main bedroom. In the interest of speed, he'd used the second shower to prepare for their evening. He made a slow scan of Aidan before grasping her shoulders and turning her to face him. "My lovers scrub up well. Babe, the rear view, your arse in that dress did it for me. The front. You're stunning." His gaze lifted to Aidan. "You always do it for me. Tonight..." He trailed off with a low growl of appreciation.

Aidan flushed, but Christina could tell Gabriel's words meant a lot to him. Both men wore black trousers and long-sleeved button-down shirts. They'd tamed their hair and used aftershave. Christina caught hints of citrus and a touch of sandalwood.

"We should walk over to the main building," Aidan said.

Christina picked up her black-and-silver clutch bag and moved with her men. Outside, Aidan cocked an elbow for her, and she curled her arm through his. He did the same to Gabriel, and laughing, Gabriel took hold.

"My dates," Aidan said with a trace of pride. "I'm a lucky man."

The meal was exquisite. Christina ate seafood, Gabriel tried venison while Aidan decided on the rack of lamb. Dessert was a difficult choice, but she narrowed it down to lemon meringue pie and stole a spoonful of Gabriel's chocolate brownie and Aidan's apple pie.

"Getting to try two extra meals is a definite benefit," she declared.

Aidan chuckled while Gabriel shook his head, a grin etched into place as the waitress served coffee.

Back in their room, Aidan turned to Christina. "Dress off," he ordered, sounding more like Gabriel. "I've been driving myself crazy wondering which set of underwear you wore tonight. If it's one I've seen before or a new set."

She jumped at the warm hands that cupped her shoulders. Her zipper eased down.

"Guess what color," Gabriel said.

Aidan stared hard, as if he'd developed superhero powers and could see right through the fabric of her dress. "Our girl loves color. I'm guessing it's a pretty color. Blue."

"Purple," Gabriel announced.

"Mauve," Christina corrected.

"Nice. Take off her dress so I can see."

Gabriel whisked off her dress, leaving her standing in her lingerie, stockings, and shoes.

"Beautiful," Aidan breathed.

"On the bed, babe."

"Aren't you going to strip? At least take off your shirts and give me some prime chests to perv."

The two men shared a glance, communicated silently, and stripped off footwear then their shirts and trousers.

"Ah, an even playing field," Christina said.

"No, babe. Lie on the bed and spread your legs as wide as you can."

Aidan offered her a reassuring nod, and she strutted to the bed. Might as well tease her men. *Her men.*

Once she reclined, she beamed up at them. They both crawled on to the end of the king-size bed, and with no audible communication, they each kissed one of her knees.

Unexpected.

Her breath caught as she waited for their next move, and neither man kept her waiting long. A kiss on the inside of her knee. The drag of a tongue traveling from her knee upward. The tension released from her body and her eyes fluttered closed. She sank into a world of sensations. Soft mouths. Slow licks. Decadent caresses.

Gradually, they worked their way up her legs, every delicate kiss, lick, and nibble zapping pleasure through her. Her sex ached, yet neither touched her there. She wanted—needed—one of them to stroke her clit.

They were moving so slowly, their warm breath misting across her inner thighs and lighting signal fires on her flesh. A moan escaped her, drawing a chuckle from Gabriel.

"Tonight, I have a yearning for wet, hot pussy," he whispered.

"Yes." The sound hovered close to a groan.

"Aye, that works for me," Aidan agreed.

"You first," Gabriel ordered. "Grab the condoms while I have a taste."

The mattress moved a fraction, although Christina kept her eyes closed.

"Lift your hips for me, babe."

She followed Gabriel's instructions, and he tugged her panties down her legs. An instant later, his mouth was between her legs, his breath washing against her swollen flesh. The tip of his tongue slid over her clit and made a return pass that had her arousal ramping up another notch.

"More," she demanded.

"Take off your bra for me, babe. It's too pretty to damage. You do that while I get Aidan ready for you."

Her eyes opened, and she watched him roll away. As she removed her bra, Gabriel yanked on Aidan's boxer-briefs and tugged them downward, maneuvering the fabric over his erection. Once Aidan kicked his underwear free of his legs, Gabriel fell to his knees, licked Aidan's cock and took him in his mouth. His cheeks hollowed before he withdrew and winked at Aidan.

"You're ready. Can taste your pre-come." He held out his hand. "Condom."

Aidan handed over a foil package, and Gabriel had it open in seconds. He rolled it onto Aidan's cock before standing.

"Never realized how much I'd get off on watching the two of you together. It's beautiful. Knowing I can join in and touch either of you. A real turn-on." He sat on the bed and watched Aidan maneuver into position. Then Gabriel guided Aidan's cock to her entrance.

"Go in slow," Gabriel ordered. "Want to see your dick disappear inside her. Yeah. Like that. Perfect."

Gabriel kissed Aidan, and as always, watching them together brought a rush of enjoyment. A blast of arousal because their interactions were honest. They didn't care that their love for one another was untraditional. They didn't care if others might look down their noses at them. They didn't care she was watching.

All they wanted was each other. Even better, they wanted her too.

When their lips parted, both men glanced at her and grinned. Aidan pulled back before gliding into her again, hitting the right spots on the way. Meantime, Gabriel slid close to her, his big hands and his talented mouth playing with her breasts and nipples. With the twin sensations, her mind hazed, desire becoming a primitive throb through her veins.

Aidan slid his hands beneath her buttocks while keeping up his even, rhythmic strokes. These sensations married with the slow slide of Gabriel's tongue around her nipple. Gabriel ended this with a hard draw of his mouth that echoed in Christina's pussy.

The pleasuring caress of his fingers added more layers, and Christina gave a soft cry, her hips rising with desperate need.

Aidan drove into her again, and the beginnings of sweet spasms flooded her. One more hard plunge pushed her off the cliff, and she came with a cry, her channel contracting around Aidan's shaft.

So decadent.

She gasped, trying to catch her breath as sensation bombarded her.

"Hell," Aidan muttered, his mouth seeking hers while his climax broke over him.

He shuddered, his eyes closed, his head thrown back, and every muscle taut.

"He's gorgeous too," Gabriel murmured against her ear.

"Yeah."

Aidan's eyes flicked open, and a slow smile spread across his handsome face. "Thanks, love."

Gabriel ran his fingers over Aidan's jaw, the faint stubble on his jaw rasping loudly enough for Christina to hear. They kissed again before Aidan pulled out of her. Aidan stood and discarded the condom. He tossed it before grabbing another condom and handing it to Gabriel.

"Babe, round two," Gabriel said.

She rolled toward Gabriel and offered her mouth for a kiss. The hard ridge of his cock thrust into her stomach, his kiss intoxicating as he invaded her mouth. A moan fell from her lips as she savored the heat of Aidan at her back. The sleek thrust of his tongue against hers, and his hot intent look told her this would be fast.

Aidan kissed a trail down her spine. He nipped one buttock, making her jump, then licked away the sting.

"He licked my backside," she told Gabriel.

"Yeah, babe. He does that."

"Hey, I licked part of your butt cheek. Nothing too kinky with that," Aidan shot back.

Christina grinned and leaned forward to run her hands over Gabriel's chest. "Bulging pectoral," she whispered and let her hands drift lower. "Ridged abs. Flat stomach. Magnificent cock."

"Hey," Aidan protested.

"I'm lucky to have two such well-endowed men to play with." She tried not to laugh. "Men who know their way around a woman's body."

"Aye," Aidan said. "And a man's, you ken."

Christina laughed then, and that was nice too. Shared laughter along with the fulfilling sex.

"Hands and knees, babe. Give Aidan room to work his magic."

While Christina scrambled into position, Gabriel reached for a condom. Aidan got busy, using the gentle suction of his mouth. His hands skimmed her curves, all purpose and skill.

A nip on her backside had her starting and turning her head to eye Gabriel in reproach.

His eyes were full of laughter as he murmured, "Thought I'd make it even. Now you have marks on both cheeks."

Christina snorted and turned back to face the headboard, her lips quivering in silent amusement. Her men were coming out of their shells, as was she. They were relaxing and growing into the possibilities.

A tongue strummed her clit, and sensual energy redirected her mind.

Gabriel settled behind her and guided his cock inside her. He issued a growling sound of approval as her flesh clamped down on his shaft. His cock invaded and retreated. Aidan sought her sensitive places—the spots that had her growing wetter, her flesh clenching and aching and fluttering.

Primitive hunger grew until the erotic promise exploded over her. She was vaguely aware of Gabriel coming. Steeped in satisfaction, she wilted. Male voices murmured, bodies resettled, and her eyes closed, exhaustion drawing her into sleep. Her last thought was that if this was happiness, she wanted to keep it close. She'd bonded with Gabriel and Aidan. They were her future. The two men accepted her weaknesses along with her strengths and were actively trying to help her keep her head above depression. She'd even showed them her journal and explained how it helped her maintain a more even balance.

Yeah, they were tight now.

In sync, and she didn't think anyone could break their bond.

22

A SHOCK ELEMENT

MONDAY EVENING

CHRISTINA YAWNED AS THEY disembarked from a late ferry and headed to the parking lot where Gabriel had left his vehicle.

"I'm exhausted," she said. "But I had a great time. Thank you for taking us with you."

Aidan piled the bags he carried into the rear then reached for the one she was carrying. Gabriel followed in the back, toting a box of wine. A smaller box balanced on top of this, and it contained two jars of marinated olives, a packet of savory walnut biscuits Aidan wanted to recreate to serve with Gabriel's cheese, and a T-shirt from one of the vineyards. Its pithy wine quote had made Christina laugh, and she'd wanted it as a souvenir of their wonderful two days. That and as a reminder to design T-shirts for Gabriel's cheese shop. Once they decided on a design, she'd sell them and wear them behind the counter.

They piled into the vehicle, and Gabriel headed for home. He slowed as he neared her cottage.

"Stay with us tonight, babe. Don't want our vacation to finish."

"All right." She hated their break to end, as well.

Gabriel continued past her cottage and let out a vicious curse when he turned onto his driveway. He parked, and they climbed out of the vehicle to stare at the carnage, highlighted when the external lights switched on automatically.

Someone had upended trash over the customer parking area. Something stinky that made Christina gasp a breath and hold it before commencing inhalations through her mouth. She stared at the walls of the shop and Gabriel's house. Several pithy slogans were spray-painted on the walls in pumpkin orange.

Arsehole.

Take responsibility.

Liar. Liar.

Something she thought might be dried egg smeared the windows, given the number of eggshells underfoot.

"Did you speak to your sister?" Aidan asked.

"Not yet," Gabriel snapped. "Fuckin' can't believe this. If Stacey is the culprit, she's gone too far this time." He pulled out his phone.

"Who are you ringing?" Christina asked, the turmoil in her stomach making her nauseous. Had his sister done this? She moved closer to Aidan, relieved when he placed his arm around her shoulders in silent comfort.

"The cops. This is vandalism, and if my sister is responsible, I intend to charge her. It'll take hours to clean this mess." He stopped speaking to her and informed the person on the other end of the line of the property damage and vandalism they'd found on arriving home. "Half an hour," he acknowledged and ended the call.

"You think someone else did this?" Aidan asked.

Gabriel's mouth twisted. "Given the wording—no."

Christina swallowed hard. "They mentioned you have a son."

Gabriel whirled to Christina, his anger apparent. "They?"

"Stacey and Darcy," Christina whispered, the fury in Gabriel's face sending her to seek even closer contact with Aidan.

"When?" Gabriel's voice was scarily quiet.

"The day I helped Aidan paint his restaurant," she whispered.

"The day you ran away." Gabriel turned from her, but not before his expression imprinted on her mind. His nostrils flared, and his face tightened to a scary mask. "Go inside. Both of you. I'll wait for the cops to arrive."

"We can help you clean up," Aidan said.

"Why didn't you tell me? I could've stopped this. Saved you some anguish."

"They had a child with them," Christina whispered. "He resembled you."

"Fuck it. *Fuck it!*" Gabriel roared.

Christina winced, and even Aidan tensed at Gabriel's fury.

"You should've told me," Gabriel bit out. "Aidan, take Christina inside. I'll deal with this."

"Don't be angry with Christina. I kenned about the child. Christina told me."

"Fuck. It," Gabriel bit out, and a vein twitched in his jaw. "I'm pissed you mentioned it, and I blew you off. Things were going so well with us that I didn't want to discuss the past. Wanted to look forward instead. Go. We'll talk later."

Aidan nodded at Gabriel. He collected two of their bags from the back, Christina grabbed the other, and after fishing the keys from her pocket, they entered the house.

"Wait," Aidan said. "We'd better check to see if they've broken in and damaged the interior."

Christina flicked on the hall light. To her relief, the house appeared untouched.

"Go to bed, Christina. I'll grab the last of our stuff before I come to join you."

Christina nodded, picked up her bag, and trudged

down the passage. After a fantastic two days, this was a horrid way to end their sojourn.

Gabriel was leaning against a portion of clean wall when Aidan emerged from the house. His temper still simmered, his pulse racing as he thought of his sister and her bitch of a friend. He ground his molars together and waited for Aidan to spill what he needed to say.

"You should've rung your sister when we mentioned this," Aidan said, accusation clear.

"I know that now." Gabriel grunted, bitterness tightening his chest. He'd tried to get past this fuckin' farce, but his bloody sister wouldn't leave it alone. Her and her friend. He sucked in a breath, struggled to contain his temper and project calmness. "Thought about it, but I knew she'd jerk my chain. I didn't want to take that with us on our break."

The truth.

Every time his sister got in Gabriel's face, she screwed with his life. He should've left Waiheke, but he loved living on the island, and he'd wanted to stay close to his grandparents. He'd wanted to offer his support for what they'd done for him.

"Maybe Christina and I should leave. Go to her cottage tomorrow while you sort out your problems with your sister."

"Running away," Gabriel taunted. "Isn't that your

thing? When things get tough, you leave instead of facing them."

Aidan froze, a flash of hurt in his face. Then, he surprised Gabriel. He met Gabriel's gaze straight on. "You're right. That is my usual MO. We'll stay, but we want explanations."

Gabriel gave a grim nod, understanding the trust and honesty between them had to be total. "You'll get them."

A cop car pulled into the driveway. Gabriel straightened while Aidan squeezed Gabriel's biceps then left to grab the last of their things from the rear of the vehicle.

"George," Gabriel greeted the tall, lean cop who climbed out of the driver's seat.

"Gabriel." George jerked his head toward the graffiti emblazoned across the walls, his boyish face set in a frown. "That looks personal."

"Yeah," Gabriel agreed. "Christina, Aidan, and I have been away for two days. We arrived home to this." He gestured at the graffiti, the egg-smeared windows, and the trash littering the area in front of them.

"Had problems with anyone?" George asked.

"My sister is hassling me," Gabriel said.

George looked startled. "I thought you didn't speak to your family."

"I don't," Gabriel snapped. "But she confronted Christina at Aidan's store, then she came here looking for me. I wasn't here, but Aidan and Christina were. They told Stacey they'd pass on her message."

"Did you contact her?"

"No." Gabriel left it at that. Inside, he seethed.

"I'll take photos and go to see your sister," George said.

"If Stacey did this, I want her charged," Gabriel stated. "You tell her to stay the hell away from me, or I won't be responsible for my actions."

Even as he stated this, he knew his sister. If she wanted a confrontation, she'd bring it. He met George's even gaze.

"Are you sure charging your sister is the right thing?" The cop's tone was cautious.

"Seriously?" Gabriel gestured at the damage. "This is more than a prank. It's malicious."

"Unless someone witnessed the culprits, it'll be hard to prove."

Gabriel dragged a hand through his hair. Did fuck all to stomp on his frustration, the anger with the lies that had dogged him since he was a teenager. "Right. Do your best. I'll be at the station tomorrow to take out a restraining order. Stacey's beef is with me, not with Aidan and Christina. Flip me a text once you've done with your photographs. Too angry to sleep. I'll get a start on the cleaning once you're done."

Gabriel strode inside, leaving George to his work. He found Aidan and Christina in the kitchen, both nursing a cup of soup. The scent of toasted sandwiches and tomato soup drifted on the air, bringing to mind his childhood. A punch in the chest, it stole his breath for a long moment. Fuck.

"Soup and a sandwich?" Aidan asked.

"Please." He planted his butt on the stool beside Christina. "You okay?"

"You're the one who resembles a storm cloud," she countered.

"Yeah. I'll contact Stacey tomorrow. After that, I'm taking out a restraining order to keep her away from me, the two of you, my place, and your cottage."

"Is that kid yours?" Aidan asked, his gaze intense.

It hurt. The question. The doubt. The lack of faith.

"No," he snapped, unable to look at either of his lovers. "If I had a son, I'd *never* toss him away. Reject him. Refuse to love him."

Tight pressure formed in his chest, but he swallowed, pushing back the emotion that threatened to sever old wounds. His parents had turned their backs on him. Thrown him from their house without a backward glance. If it hadn't been for his grandparents, his life would've sucked even worse.

His phone beeped, and he checked the incoming text. Perfect timing. He stood. "Don't worry about the sandwich. George has given me the all-clear to clear the mess."

"We'll help," Christina said.

"Stay here. I'm too fuckin' angry for company right

now." He stomped away, that pressure in his chest increasing until he had to rub it with his fist. The churn of his stomach faded, but the ball of anger remained. This situation fuckin' sucked and knowing he had to deal with it and the fallout that was sure to occur did nothing to calm his turmoil.

"We hurt him," Christina said. "Wanting the answer to that question."

"Aye. I saw his face. I've no idea what's at play here, but I've never seen Gabriel so furious. What could've caused such a huge breach within his family? My family loves me. They'd support me through any drama."

"My parents too, although there would be lectures."

"What should we do?"

Christina pulled a face. "I hate to say it, but we need to take a leaf from my depression journal. Don't let him push us away. Be there for him and not question him about a son again. We have to trust him and wait for Gabriel to tell us his side. We could ask his grandparents, but I think it'd be better to proceed at Gabriel's pace."

"Right. If his sister approaches us, we turn our backs and walk away."

"I have an Institute meeting tomorrow night. Chances are his sister will be there."

"Stick by Gabriel's grandmother."

"Easier said than done. She hangs out with her particular

friends. If things go the same way as the last meeting, I'll ferry tea and food to them before joining the younger women."

"Aye, I get it. Your best bet is to pick a friend and cling without looking needy, or if it's someone you know, tell them Stacey is hassling you. They might support you." He winked at her. "You'll get something to write in your journal for tomorrow—something you're grateful for."

Christina snorted. "That's not the way it should work, but I *am* grateful for friends. Did you take enough photos for your blog post?"

"Aye. Plenty. I've decided to write an article or two and try to sell them to newspapers and magazines. And, I'll post to my social media pages."

"Leave my red bikini out of it," Christina said.

"Love, I don't think you understand how gorgeous you look in that bikini, but I'll run the photos I pick to use past you and Gabriel first. I'll give you veto rights."

"Thanks."

"No problem. Let's clean up here and go to bed."

Christina frowned. "Are you sure we shouldn't help Gabriel?"

"Let's give him space. Hopefully, tomorrow will provide answers so we can move on."

She issued a harsh sigh as she met Aidan's gaze. "Between the three of us, we're a hot mess. Are we sure we can work this relationship with none of us getting hurt?"

"No," Aidan said, giving her open honesty. "I'm not certain of anything. But the last two days have solidified what I want. You and Gabriel. For once, I'm not running from something that's difficult. I intend to fight, and if my best isn't enough, so be it."

Christina lifted her chin. "Right there with you," she declared. "No running away for me, either."

"Okay, love. Work on your journal. Julia will call expecting a report, and Gabriel and I want details too."

Hope bubbled in Christina at Aidan's words. "I love you, Aidan."

Aidan's face turned soft, his eyes full of emotion. "Love you too, Christina. It's happened fast, but I can't imagine my life without you in it."

"So, we're united to support Gabriel?"

"We are, love. Gabriel acts tough, but he experiences things deeply. He needs us."

23

CONFRONTATION

GABRIEL ROLLED OUT OF bed at six the next morning.
Hadn't slept worth shit. Aidan and Christina had been
asleep by the time he joined them. They'd lay tangled
together, making him the odd one out. Fuckin' stupid,
he should let this get to him, but if his sister wrecked
his relationship with Aidan and Christina, he'd lose it big
time.

He pulled on his jeans and grabbed a T-shirt from the
drawer. Neither Aidan nor Christina stirred. After pulling
on a pair of socks, he padded to the kitchen to put on the
coffeemaker.

Bloody Stacey and that bitch of a friend of hers.

They had the power to make his life difficult if he didn't
handle this right.

While he'd scrubbed the graffiti on his walls, he'd

planned his approach. No way did he want to risk meeting either of his parents, which meant visiting their house and catching Stacey there was out of bounds. First, he'd speak with Stacey and Darcy, and if they persisted with their assertions, he'd demand a DNA test. That would prove his position, then he'd go to the cops and organize the restraining order against Stacey and Darcy.

Yeah. Plan.

He poured a cup of black coffee and hustled outside to check on his property.

The spray paint was still discernable, but another scrub and a tub of graffiti cleaner from the hardware store should do the trick. By this afternoon, when his cheese shop opened, not one customer would note the damage.

With another cup of coffee inside him, Gabriel headed off to start the milking.

Later that morning, on the way home after a hardware store visit, Gabriel stopped at the vet's surgery. His sister stood behind the counter, and a snarl appeared on her lips the instant she saw him. Although they both possessed dark brown hair—hers jaw-length with blonde highlights—brown eyes, and height, his sister's constant lousy mood had left frown marks etched into her olive skin.

"Bastard. You set the cops on me. Mum and Dad are pissed."

"Not my problem," Gabriel snapped. "Consequences."

"You're a fine one to speak of consequences," Stacey snapped back.

"You wanted to speak with me."

"Not here at my place of work. At the beach where it's private."

Gabriel didn't trust her an inch. "At a café in a public place."

"This situation requires delicacy."

Gabriel snorted. "You're the one waging a private war against me. We meet in a café or not at all."

"Fine. Eight-thirty tonight at the café on the corner."

"I'll be there." Gabriel walked away and swore her eyes bore holes in his back. He prayed she didn't have a handy knife because, given the ferocity between them, a sneak attack might happen.

He arrived at the house to find only Aidan, who was working at the table with his laptop, a notebook at his side.

"Where's Christina?"

"She walked to her cottage to check on things. Said she had a few job ideas and thought she'd ponder them while she made a batch of soap to sell at the market on Sunday."

"She okay?"

"Aye. She showed me her journal and seemed happy enough. Julia called her as she left."

"You?"

Aidan stood and closed the distance between them. "We're both here if you need us."

"Could do with a wingman when I meet Stacey at the café tonight. What's Christina doing?"

"She has an institute meeting tonight. Tell her what you're doing and that I'm going with you. She'll be fine with that."

Gabriel nodded. "Sorry."

Aidan stepped even closer and wrapped his arms around Gabriel. "We all have tempers and spots that hurt if someone pokes them. Nothing to apologize for."

Gabriel jerked his head in acknowledgment. "Be in the cheese room."

"Do you want help?"

"Not great company today," Gabriel said.

"I'll be here working."

"Right. Later," Gabriel said.

He lost himself in making cheese, and the day passed fast enough. Between tasks, he stocked the fridge, and he greeted Christina and Aidan with a wave when they opened for business.

It was after five when he finished sterilizing his equipment, and he strode into his kitchen. Christina was peeling potatoes. Aidan had gone up to the gate to remove the open sign for the shop.

"Aidan mentioned you're meeting your sister tonight."

"Yeah."

"At least she won't be at the meeting to hassle me. Do you want me to go with you too?"

"Babe, thanks for the offer." Gabriel kissed her cheek. "My gut tells me it's not gonna be pretty. I'll tell you everything afterward. Promise."

Voices outside had them both turning toward the door off the kitchen. A raised voice—a familiar one—pushed Gabriel to action. He stormed outside to find Aidan facing off with Stacey and Darcy.

"Thought we were meeting at the café at eight-thirty."

"Told you I wanted a private meeting," Stacey snapped.

Not gonna happen. He refused to deal with her without witnesses.

He stood aside and gestured. "Come inside." This'd be the first and the last time he faced his sister. No matter what she told him, he was done.

"Lounge," he said to Aidan.

Aidan nodded, not asking questions but leading the way through the door. At least this way, Christina could attend their *meeting* and Gabriel wouldn't need to go through everything again.

Gabriel gestured to Stacey and Darcy, indicating they should enter. They followed Aidan, both women taking covert glances of his house and belongings. He snarled—a silent burst of anger.

Once they seated their butts on his furniture, he strode to the kitchen. "Christina, can you join us? It will save me explaining everything and I want witnesses. I don't trust Stacey."

Christina gave him a nod and walked toward him. She caught his hand and tangled their fingers together.

"Anything you need," she whispered. "Same goes for Aidan."

They walked into the lounge holding hands. Gabriel didn't bother taking a seat. "What do you want?"

"A *private* word." Stacey stressed the word private.

"You've invaded my home. You don't get to make the rules," Gabriel said. "This is your last chance to speak with me before I organize a restraining order with the cops."

"You bastard," Stacey seethed.

"Stacey." Darcy spoke for the first time. "It's okay." She met his gaze, her expression determined. "I have a son. Your son. It's time for you to take responsibility instead of leaving my son and me with no help. Gabriel, you should see him. He looks like you. He *is* your son."

"Darcy lost her job through no fault of her own. As a result, the bank foreclosed on her mortgage. It's why she returned home and is staying with me. You need to step up instead of ignoring your son."

Anger pumped through Gabriel until Christina squeezed his hand in a silent show of support. He caught her gaze, and she offered him a faint smile. Aidan edged closer until he stood on Gabriel's other side.

"Your boy is not my son," Gabriel said firmly. "We'll do a DNA test to prove it. My lawyer will conduct the test. That way, you can't accuse me of tampering with the results. Or we can do it at the local police station. Your choice. If you'd stuck around on Waiheke, I would've insisted on a DNA test, anyway. It wasn't an issue until now."

Stacey stared at him. "If the DNA tests prove what we say, you'll accept responsibility for Darcy and her son?"

"I won't need to," Gabriel stated. "I'm not lying and have never lied. The kid isn't mine. We done now? This is an end to it?"

Stacey and Darcy shared a glance, and Darcy nibbled her lip.

"Yes," Darcy said.

"I'll contact Henry Wainscoat tomorrow and let him know you'll be by for the same test," Gabriel said.

"I'll show them out," Aidan said.

Gabriel nailed the women with a glare. "One more thing. I intend to go ahead with the restraining order. If I see you on or near my property or Christina's cottage, I will press charges. Aidan will see you out."

"You can't do that to your son," Stacey snapped.

"As I keep telling you, he's not mine."

"You were in bed with Darcy. I saw you," Stacey said.

"Yeah," Gabriel drawled. "Leave before I lose my temper." He kissed the back of Christina's hand and released it. "I'm gonna take a shower."

"I'd better keep on with dinner," Christina said.

"Thanks, babe." Without a backward glance, he left a

fuming Stacey and a pale Darcy, trusting Aidan to deal with them.

"Are you okay?" Christina asked when Gabriel wandered into the kitchen to help with dinner.

"Yeah."

"Beer?" Aidan asked.

"Thanks." Gabriel planted his butt on a counter stool. Once he had the beer in hand, he started to talk. "I was seventeen, almost eighteen. Whenever I had the opportunity, I partied with my mates, and I had lots of girlfriends, a couple I slept with. Darcy and Stacey were tight, and I knew Darcy had a crush on me. I stayed away from her and didn't say more than a polite hello if we ran into one another. One, she was young. Too young for me, and I had a thing for Christina. I was hoping I could look you up in person once I started university instead of exchanging emails, texts, and the odd phone call."

"I wish I'd known that then," Christina said.

Gabriel shrugged, his mouth twisting at the lost opportunities. He could drop a lot of bitter words about injustice. He didn't. Instead, he continued with his story. "While I partied, I also worked hard. It was the school holidays, and I was helping my grandfather during lambing and working at the local fish and chip shop every night. I was dog-tired since it was a Saturday night, and we were busy. I worked later than normal, and it was midnight by the time I arrived home.

"Mum and Dad were away for the weekend, and they'd left me in charge. While I was at work, Stacey and Darcy decided to have a party with their friends. Things had got out of control. Word had spread. Loud music, alcohol everywhere, and naked people in our swimming pool greeted me. I hadn't a hope of getting everyone to leave, so I called the cops. Told them what had happened—that I'd arrived home to find a drunken party with underage drinkers and needed help to get rid of everyone.

"I waited in my bedroom until the cops came, but I was exhausted and fell asleep.

"It was a few hours later when I woke, to find a naked Darcy wrapped around me and my room stunk of alcohol. Before I was fully awake, my bedroom door flew open, and Stacey appeared. She shouted at me. Something along the lines of she knew it. I sprang off the bed, still fully clothed. Stacey disappeared then reappeared with my parents in tow. Unbeknown to me, the cops had called my parents, and after speaking with the police, they came home early.

"Everyone started shouting at me for sleeping with Darcy and taking advantage of her. My parents were furious about the party and blamed me. A drunken partygoer bumped into me when I arrived home, and alcohol had spilled all over my shirt, which made my parents assume I'd been drinking. Darcy wasn't much help since she was out of it. All she did was grin and say she loved me."

Aidan frowned. "But you weren't naked."

Gabriel snorted. "A fact I tried to point out, but my parents wouldn't listen. Stacey backed up Darcy. I got the blame for the party and the alcohol. Everything was my fault. My parents grounded me. I tried to tell them I hadn't done any of what they accused me of, but they were more worried about their reputation. They worried Darcy's parents might charge me with underage sex. Fuck, I've never kissed Darcy, flirted with her, or led her on. And I didn't fuck her.

"Two months later, the shit hit the fan again when Darcy turned up pregnant. I knew the baby wasn't mine, but Stacey, Darcy, and my parents told me I needed to man-up. I reiterated I was innocent, and this aggravated the situation. Finally, my father lost it and told me if I refused to take responsibility, I should pack my bag and get the fuck out of his house. He hadn't brought me up to be a lying good-for-nothing, and he refused to support me any further. The money they'd put aside for my education would support Darcy and their grandchild."

Christina reached for Gabriel's hand and squeezed it in silent commiseration. She'd never known Gabriel to lie to her. The man was refreshingly honest. "What did you do?"

"I went to my grandparents' place and told them the full story. They believed me and tried to talk to my parents. My father told them he refused to listen to my lies, and as far as he was concerned, I was dead to them."

"Holy hell," Aidan muttered. "I don't get why your parents refused to believe you."

Gabriel's lips twisted. "My sister liked to drop me in it with my parents. Growing up, I was often in trouble. I was mischievous rather than malicious. My penchant for trouble didn't help me. And my sister was a spoiled brat. She liked to get her way and wasn't above subterfuge to direct matters in the way she wanted them to go. She loved Darcy like a sister and wanted them to be related. Truly, it was a whole lot of small things that collided and turned into a tsunami that crashed over my head. All I know is that Darcy's son isn't mine."

"Why didn't you have a DNA test years ago?" Aidan asked.

"That's what I was wondering," Christina said.

"Darcy's parents sent her to live with an aunt on the mainland. I didn't ask after her because I wasn't interested. Not my kid. Not my problem." He dragged a hand over his face. "Fuck. That sounds heartless. I try not to be bitter, but Darcy and her kid changed the direction of my life. I'd wanted to study engineering. After my parents withdrew their support, I had to change direction and earn my own way. Back to the DNA test, this is the first time Darcy and her son have returned to the island. I hadn't seen Darcy for years and never discuss her."

"Who do you think the father is?" Christina asked.

"No idea. All I know is that it's not me."

Aidan tapped his finger on his chin. "I watched your sister when you told them you'd do the DNA test. She looked pleased. Does she truly believe you're the father?"

"Fuck if I know," Gabriel muttered. "But we're doing this through a lawyer. I refuse to allow any wiggle-room for Stacey or Darcy to fix the results. I'd better ring my grandparents and let them know what's happening."

"Is there an outside chance you're the father?" Christina asked. "No, don't get pissed at me. You told us you were tired. What if you don't remember?"

"Had sex earlier in the day. Tried to," Gabriel muttered, glancing down at his hands. "I couldn't get it up. Ended up needing to use my mouth to get my girl off. I was so embarrassed, I broke up with her. Told her there was someone else, and I didn't think I should string her along when there was no hope for us. I'm certain I didn't have sex with Darcy."

"Me?" Christina whispered. "I was the someone else?"

He gave a hard nod. "Yeah. I truly had intended to contact you once I got to Auckland."

"I would've said yes," she whispered, and pleasure at his words shimmered through her.

"My life didn't go the way I originally planned, but I love what I'm doing now. Enjoy working on the land and making cheese. Maybe it wasn't the smartest thing to do staying here where I can run into my parents or sister, but I wanted to support my grandparents. They helped me so much. Sustained me. Encouraged me. Gran told me I might miss out on university, but I should try an online course and get qualifications that way. Grandpa listened to Gran and informed me he'd always wanted to make cheese. Would I be interested in doing the course with him? He's dyslexic, so it was a way for me to help him learn. That's how my interest in cheese started. I'd always enjoyed eating it, and the process fascinated me."

"I love your grandparents," Aidan said.

"Me too," Christina chirped.

"Let's finish dinner and have an early night."

"Aye," Aidan said. "Christina and I are on your side one hundred percent."

Gabriel's eyes went soft. "Means a lot. As a reward, you both get to choose our sexual positions tonight."

Aidan winked at Christina. "What do you say?"

"Works for me. I'll ring Gran and make my excuses."

And it did. When they fell into bed after dinner, the sex was stupendous, and they did it their way.

24

RESOLUTION AND LOVE

TWO WEEKS LATER

GABRIEL SAT IN THE lawyer's office with Aidan and Christina. He was thankful for their support. Stacey and Darcy sat in the remaining two chairs.

Henry Wainscoat, his longtime lawyer, glanced over his horn-rim glasses and peered at them. "Do you want me to read the results?"

"Please," Gabriel said.

"This is private," Stacey snapped. "I don't think they should hear the results."

"Aidan and Christina are my support." Gabriel worked to keep his tone even.

Henry glanced at Darcy. "Shall I continue?"

Darcy dipped her head and gripped her hands together

in her lap. "Yes, please."

"Gabriel is not Logan's father, however, he is related to the child," Henry stated.

Gabriel felt his jaw drop. "What?" He'd known the truth, but this was a bombshell.

"What do you mean?" Stacey demanded. "That can't be right."

"Logan and Gabriel have DNA in common, but it's a minor amount. Gabriel isn't Logan's biological father," Henry repeated.

"Can you explain what that means?" Aidan asked, and Gabriel sent him a grateful glance.

"It means someone related to Gabriel is the child's father."

Stacey gave a bitter laugh. "That's not possible. You've rigged the results."

"I assure you these are the results you will receive if you repeat the DNA test. You're welcome to do that, but it won't change the facts."

"Thank you, Henry." Gabriel stood. "I believe the police have notified you of the restraining order. You've made my life hell for something I didn't do. All I want is to get on with my life and not see either of you again."

"Wait. Please," Darcy said. "I don't understand. If you're not the father, who is?"

"You were there," Gabriel snapped. "I wasn't, so how should I know?"

"Gabriel." Christina squeezed his hand in warning.

Christina was right, damn it. Just because this situation frustrated him, he shouldn't act with cruelness.

"Sorry," he muttered, finally glancing at Darcy and comprehending her open shock—her pale face and open mouth. Her tremulous breaths on hearing the outcome of the DNA test. She'd truly believed he was the father of her child. Even though she and Stacey had given him hell, Darcy was a victim here too. "I'm sorry the test has posed more questions rather than given you answers."

"Well, Dad wasn't there. He and Mum came home after the police arrived," Stacey said.

Aidan coughed. "I hate to point this out, but how do you know you got pregnant on the night of the party?"

Good point, Gabriel thought, although he bit back his snide comment this time.

"If that will be all, I have cheese to make," Gabriel said. "Thank you, Henry."

Christina and Aidan followed Gabriel out of the lawyer's office.

"Anyone want a donut and coffee?" Aidan asked. "We can get them to go."

"Yes," Christina declared. "I feel sorry for Darcy, but at least your innocence is established."

Gabriel frowned. "The whole situation is a mess."

During the drive back to the farm, Gabriel pondered the identity of the child's father. Surely his father...

"So who's the daddy?" Aidan asked.

Gabriel snorted. "The obvious conclusion is my father, but I can't see that." He shook his head. "Hell. What do I know?"

"Darcy looked shell-shocked," Christina said. "How drunk was she?"

"Did she take drugs? Or had someone drugged her drink?" Aidan added.

"Not our business," Gabriel stated. "My name is cleared, and that's all I need."

Gabriel's hands tightened on the wheel because he sounded like an uncaring bastard. The news he wasn't her son's father had stunned her. She'd truly thought he'd had sex with her and walked away, despite her pregnancy. She'd suffered from his denial. But Darcy and his sister had turned his life to hell with their accusations of him lying. His parents. None of the things that had happened were easy to forget since he'd known he'd been innocent.

Gabriel didn't know what had happened on that night so long ago, but the repercussions were long-lasting and still held power to create havoc with his life.

It was a silent ride back to the farm. Aidan worked on his blog, Christina informed them she had phone calls to make, and Gabriel wandered out to his happy place—the cheese production room.

The entire time he was making cheese and later, turning wheels of cheddar, he tried to make sense of the DNA results. It was apparent Darcy had been so out of it, so hadn't known who she'd had sex with. His mouth tightened. Perhaps more than one man.

When he'd arrived at the party, some of his friends had been there and others he hadn't known. The situation had been out of control, which was why he'd called the cops. No other option with that many people crammed into his parents' house.

His mind slid to his father. It seemed logical—given Darcy's state—she'd become pregnant that night. His father hadn't been there until after the cops had cleared the house.

Gabriel kept turning the problem over and over in his mind. Nothing made sense. He kinda felt sorry for Darcy now.

By the time he'd finished, it was six. He was ready for food and the company of his two favorite people. As he toed off his work boots at the door, it occurred to him his grandparents might provide answers.

"Hey," he said on entering the kitchen. A meaty aroma drifted from a pan as Christina and Aidan prepared dinner. He paused, his heart full as he studied them.

"What?" Aidan asked.

Christina's brow crinkled. "Are you all right?"

"Mightn't always say or show my feelings, but having you around makes my house feel like a home. It always seemed empty before, but now it's full of laughter and delicious food and hot, sexy loving. Wanted to say again, I appreciate the way you pitch in with my work and the way you cook meals." Gabriel paused, registering the loaded silence that'd fallen. He pushed on anyway, wanting to get this out while he could.

"Thought I had an okay life before. Having you with me through good and bad makes me realize I was cruising on a half-tank." He rounded the counter and reached Christina first. He cupped her face and kissed her—soft and sweet. Trying to pack in every emotion and communicate it to her. "I love you, babe." Gripping her hips, he brushed past her to stand in front of Aidan. He took Aidan's face between his hands, skimmed a finger over Aidan's cheek before leaning in and stealing a sweet kiss from him too. "I love you, Aidan."

Aidan moved into Gabriel, and without warning, Christina pressed against Gabriel's back, her soft heat bringing a rush of arousal underscored by a bone-deep, soul-deep satisfaction that this was right. So right, and he'd be a fool to let either Aidan or Christina slip through his fingers.

He was no fool.

Something had changed in Gabriel. Aye, Christina sensed it too, since several times, Aidan caught her studying Gabriel with her brow furrowed. Gabriel didn't seem as angry. No. That wasn't right. He'd let go of his bitterness toward his family.

"Can I do anything to help with dinner?" Gabriel asked.

Christina wiped her hands on a towel. "We're done. I was gonna break out the wine. Do you guys want a wine or beer?"

"Beer," Gabriel said. "I'll get the drinks. Grab a seat. I need to make a phone call."

"I'll get them." Aidan shouldered him away. "You make your call."

"I'm phoning my grandparents. I'll put it on speaker, so you can both listen." Gabriel grinned. "Go. Sit."

"He's different," Christina murmured, staring after him. "Happier."

"Aye. Irresistible."

Gabriel brought out drinks and glasses on a tray along with a bowl of mixed nuts—the luxurious kind that excluded peanuts. He grinned when Aidan and Christina gaped at him.

"Thought I'd break into my stash for my special people."

"Yum." Christina helped herself to nuts. "My favorite."

"I remember from when we were teenagers. Crunch quietly while I call Gran," Gabriel ordered.

Aidan grabbed a handful of nuts, curious about this call.

"Gran, it's Gabriel. I've got you on speakerphone so Aidan and Christina can hear. I'd like Grandpa to listen too. Do you remember how to put the phone on speaker?"

"Of course I do," Gran scoffed. She promptly cut them

off.

"I'll let them squabble and work it out for a few minutes before I ring back," Gabriel said.

"Are you all right with the results of the DNA test?" Aidan asked.

"Relieved as hell I have proof I never lied. I never touched Darcy. She tried to kiss me once, but I was too fast for her, and she kissed my cheek."

"Will you speak to your parents?" Christina asked.

"No, they refused to let me explain. If they ever see me in town, they stare straight through me," Gabriel said. "It's hard to forget or forgive their lack of support."

The phone rang as Aidan mulled over Gabriel's words. He got it. He did. He was luckier with his parents, and when they came to understand Aidan's relationship with Christina and Gabriel, they'd welcome the additions to the family. Gabriel's parents didn't understand the depth of their loss. Gabriel was an amazing man and a credit to his grandparents.

"Gran, have you found the right button?"

"We're both here," Grandpa said.

"Aidan and Christina are here with me," Gabriel said. "We visited Henry Wainscoat this morning for the results of the DNA test I took. I'm not the father of Darcy's kid—which I knew anyway—but the test shows he is related to me. Any ideas?"

"Oh, James." Gran cleared her throat. "Gabriel, your

father?"

"I was thinking about that, but it doesn't seem likely. He and Mum were with friends and came home after the cops had dispersed everyone. It's possible the baby was conceived on another day, but Dad was furious with me. Told me I'd wrecked her life and I owed her my support."

"There is one other possibility," Grandpa said slowly.

"What?" Gabriel demanded.

"Before your parents married, they had a huge blowup. They didn't see each other for three months, and during that time, your father dated an older woman. Don't know if it's true or not, the rumor was the woman wanted a child. She left the island, and as far as I know, has never returned. That is a possible explanation. Or your father had an affair and has another child," Gran stated.

Aidan's gaze connected with Gabriel's. Gabriel's eyes widened then he blinked, his posture stiffening at his grandmother's words. Christina reached for Gabriel's hand, and Aidan was relieved when Gabriel relaxed a fraction and drew Christina against his side.

Gabriel sipped his beer before speaking. "Dad was brutal with me. If this is true, he's a hypocrite."

"Gabriel, you need to let this go and move on," Gran said, her voice gentle. Caring.

"Part of the reason I called," Gabriel stated. "The DNA test cleared me of blame. Everything else is just curiosity. I wanted to tell you I love Aidan and Christina. If it was legal, I'd marry them both. That's not possible, but we're together, anyway. I did tell you I liked both of them, so it's probably not a surprise."

"One of those threesomes? Like in the romance I showed you, Christina?" Gran asked.

Aidan watched a flush move over Christina's cheeks, and he winked at Gabriel.

"Christina?" Gran prompted.

"Yes," Christina whispered.

"My. My," Gran murmured.

"Is a threesome what it sounds like?" Grandpa asked.

"I'll read the romance to you tonight when we're in bed," Gran said. "Gabriel, if you're happy, then so are we, although some of the locals will have kittens. They'll gossip. You won't have an easy road."

Gabriel chuckled. "When have I ever done easy, Gran?"

Aidan cleared his throat to enter the conversation. "So, we have your support?"

"As long as I finally get my great-grandchildren," Gran said. "Hmm, how will you work that?"

"Gran, that part is private," Gabriel said. "When we get that far, you'll be the first to know."

"We love you, boy." Grandpa's voice trembled full of emotion. "Come for dinner tomorrow night. I'll buy champagne."

"We'll be there," Gabriel said. "Goodnight."

"Sweet dreams, Gabriel," Gran said.

The phone clicked, and Gabriel ended the call.

"I hope that's okay. Gran and Grandpa are the most important people in my life. They've been worried about me. Wanted them to know I'm doing great."

"My parents will be cool," Aidan said. "Once they see I'm happy and settled, the rest will be easy."

Christina pulled a face. "My parents won't be as calm. We'll need to move at a snail's pace with them. A grandchild might help."

"You do *want* to have kids?" Aidan asked. "I know we've discussed it before, but I'm doublechecking."

"Yes, my answer is the same as earlier. But not straight away. I'd like to enjoy us first."

"And you still don't mind which one of us is the biological father?" Gabriel asked.

Christina smiled, her eyes soft and glowing. A faint blush colored her cheeks. "No, I figure once we get to that stage, we let nature take its course. It won't matter in the slightest. Besides, both of you have similar coloring. Our child will have dark hair and brown eyes."

"Works for me," Aidan said.

"And me," Gabriel seconded.

Christina jumped up, her curls bouncing. "We should celebrate." She cocked her head. "Perhaps leave dinner until later. It won't spoil."

Aidan looked to Gabriel. Gabriel's grin was broad and happy as he nodded.

"I'll turn off the elements." Christina skipped toward the kitchen, her curls bouncing as she left.

Joy spread through Aidan, and with it came a desire to be with Gabriel and Christina, and never, never leave them. "I'm so happy," Aidan whispered.

Gabriel embraced him in a hard, rib-cracking hug, and Aidan hugged him in return, rejoicing in the energy and exhilaration that radiated back to him. The wanderer had found his home.

"Hurry," Christina called from outside the bedroom. She'd spied her men hugging and decided to get a head start. "Last one naked is a rotten egg." Giggling, she hurried into the bedroom, ripping off her clothes and letting them fall where they may.

Aidan and Gabriel arrived in the bedroom with their T-shirts in hand, their broad chests on display.

"Pretty," she murmured and licked her lips. "Mine."

"Yours," Aidan agreed. "I'm glad I stayed instead of fleeing when I discovered the two of you together in bed. Would've been the biggest mistake I ever made."

"We've all made mistakes," Christina said. "I have to keep managing mine, but we're better together."

"While you two have been gabbing, I'm naked," Gabriel stated.

"Looks like *you're* the rotten egg," Christina said to Aidan. "You get to go on the bottom."

Gabriel got it straight away. "You ready to take both of us?"

"Yes." She never hesitated.

Gabriel stalked to the bedside cabinet and removed lube and condoms. He slapped them on top within easy grabbing distance. "Aidan, on the bed."

The instant a naked Aidan reclined on the bed, she jumped him, laughing as she claimed a kiss. Gabriel must've headed farther down Aidan's body because Aidan gasped into her kiss, his big body jerking. Curious, Christina parted their lips. Gabriel had his mouth on Aidan's cock and was teasing him with slow strokes.

Smiling, Christina returned to kissing. She loved kissing—the intimate stroke of tongues, the suction of mouths, the nipping of teeth. She groaned into Aidan's mouth as he stopped her teasing and took control of the kiss. He kissed her jaw and curved his hand around her neck, holding her in position.

A hand—Gabriel's hand—smoothed over her backside and between her legs.

"Yes," she whispered.

Aidan sucked on her neck, drawing her attention from Gabriel. Her nipples puckered, and when Aidan stroked one, then pinched lightly, heat flowed from his touch and settled between her legs. A purring sound of approval escaped her, and Gabriel's touch had heat and pleasure flushing her skin.

Aidan's deliciously sinful mouth moved lower to replace his fingers. She sucked in air on experiencing the dual ministrations of Aidan's mouth and Gabriel's fingers. So, so good. Another curl of heat pooled low, and she shivered, the sensual energy exploding on and in her, scorching her body, her mind.

"You're so pretty, love," Aidan whispered.

"Babe, you're soaking wet." Gabriel's voice held approval. His fingers lifted, and her swollen flesh prickled. He retreated to grab a condom and rolled it onto Aidan's cock.

"Love, take me inside you."

Christina clambered over Aidan's leg and situated herself. Slowly, she eased down, taking Aidan's cock. She rose up, and Gabriel slapped her on the arse.

"Neither of you move. No thrusting or rocking," Gabriel ordered. "Kissing and touching only."

"We can do that," Christina said to Aidan. "Right?"

"We can try." His face was lost in pleasure.

Christina's stomach had gone all fluttery, and the urge to move was strong. Instead, she kissed Aidan's strong jawline then took his mouth long and slow.

Gabriel played with her, his fingers coated with lube as he invaded and retreated, stretching her for his possession. Although he worked fast, he teased her clit while her sex pulsated around Aidan's cock. Excitement filled her—a sense of anticipation.

"Ready for me, babe?"

"I'm ready," Aidan said, his snippy impatience making her laugh.

"Ready," she said with breathless agreement.

Gabriel added more lube, the cool, thick gel making her writhe and pant. "Easy, babe. If it's too much for you, just say. We have loads of time." He worked his cock, his breath striking her shoulder blade as he curled over her.

Meantime, Aidan used his thumb to make suggestive circles around her nipple. The other, he took deep into his mouth and sucked hard.

"Sweet mercy," she murmured. Her pulse did a bump and grind as Gabriel's rigid flesh invaded her body. So tight. So unbelievably fantastic.

"Ready to move?" Gabriel asked.

"Yes," Aidan snapped.

Christina giggled and squirmed while her body hummed. "I'm ready."

Following Gabriel's directions, they moved with even strokes, one cock entered her while the other retreated. Muscles surrounded her. They rippled while she writhed and attempted to catch her breath. She twisted as decadent warmth filled her, starting as a spark, the sensation kept growing until it consumed her. Christina bucked and moaned while Aidan thumbed her nipples.

Aidan's next kiss inflamed her further, and she burned while he plundered her mouth. Her vaginal walls clamped down. The hot fire between her legs exploded, and she was gone, ecstasy tumbling over her body, her mind.

Aidan cursed softly, his face contorting with desperation. Christina nipped the strong column of his neck, and he groaned, his release powerful enough for her to experience too.

"Perfect," Gabriel murmured, his lips roving across her back. He rocked into her three times and stilled. He gave her his full weight for a few seconds before parting their bodies.

Christina kissed Aidan, this time a languid one that spoke of her emotions. Her contentment. Fully pleasured. In love.

"I love you, Aidan."

"I ken. It's amazing, isn't it? Making love instead of just having sex."

"Yeah."

The shower started, and Gabriel returned to the bedroom. "Come on." He picked her up without so much as a grunt and carried her to the en suite. Aidan dealt with the condom and followed.

"Lucky, we have a large shower," Aidan said.

"Gut instinct when I redid the bathroom."

"I love you both so much," Christina cried. She relaxed against Gabriel and let him bathe her. Laughter and kisses punctuated their shower, each of them stress-free and exuberant.

After she dressed in lacy panties and a robe, and her men pulled on sweats and T-shirts, they wandered to the kitchen to ease a different hunger.

"First, a toast." Christina poured glasses of wine for them and raised her glass in salute. "To the two wonderful men who burst into my life and seduced me with promises of forever, despite my fears and emotional warts. I love you both."

"My toast," Aidan said. "To the man and the woman who gave me a reason to grow roots and helped me to flourish. I love you." He lifted his glass to her and repeated the action with Gabriel.

"I've already told you having the two of you here in my house has made it into a home. But even more, you've supported me when others have walked away. That means the world. Love you, Aidan. Love you, Christina."

Christina drank before grinning at her men. Then she thought of something Bernice used to say to her—life is defined by moments and their repercussions. They'd had their moments. They'd weathered the effects to get to the happy.

Three mavericks together.

25

EPILOGUE—FAMILY CHRISTMAS

CHRISTMAS DAY, JULIA'S HOUSE, AUCKLAND

"ARE YOU CERTAIN YOUR friends won't mind us arriving for Christmas dinner?" Gran fretted for the tenth time.

"I spoke to Julia," Christina said as they pulled into the driveway of Julia's and Ryan's home. "The entire b-bunch...ah...several of Ryan's friends will be there, and my friends who are still in Auckland are popping in before they head off to their family gatherings. Elise, Julia's mother, is visiting with her friend, Janet. Remember, I told you about Maxwell's?"

"You promised to take me to visit," Gran said promptly.

Gabriel groaned as did his grandfather.

"I did, and I will." Christina grinned. "Tomorrow night. Remember? That's why Gabriel arranged for someone to watch over his farm, and we're staying at a hotel."

"This house is huge," Aidan said.

"It needed to be," Christina said. "Long story, but Julia and Ryan have a lot of friends staying over, which is why I know our presence isn't a burden. Besides, we brought desserts."

Gabriel parked the car with several others, and they piled out. Julia's oldest son ran outside in front of his mother.

"You're here." Julia beamed. "Christina, you look amazing. I knew from our talks you were doing well, but your men must be doing something very right." She turned to Gabriel's grandparents. "You must be Beth and James. I feel as if I know you since Christina talks about you all the time."

After the welcomes, Christina, Aidan, and Gabriel carried in desserts and presents. Julia ushered Gabriel's grandparents inside and took them on a quick tour. She arrived back in the kitchen a few minutes later.

"My mother took charge of your grandparents. She's doing the tour for me. The desserts will fit in the fridge," Julia said. "That pavlova is incredible. Is it chocolate? And those strawberry tarts are way too pretty to eat."

Christina nodded. "I know, right? Aidan made them. He's a whiz in the kitchen. I was the sous chef."

"This box is cheese. If you want to eat cheese today, leave

it out to go to room temperature, or if you save it for later, it will need refrigeration," Gabriel said.

"Thank you!" Julia gave Gabriel a quick hug. "A little bird told me you'd bring cheese, so I didn't buy any. We'll have this later this evening."

The entire time music had drifted on the air. Something unfamiliar, but a catchy tune. Christina figured *French Letters* had another hit on their hands. The music stopped before a current hot tune—a Christmas song—blasted out.

"You have excellent taste in music," Aidan said. "Christina is always playing this band's songs. She says they're her favorite. Gabriel and I didn't have any choice but to give in and agree with her."

Julia winked at Christina. "I'm a fan too. Follow the music over to the studio and tell Ryan I said it was time to finish and act sociable."

"Studio? What does Ryan do?" Gabriel asked. "I don't think Christina has ever mentioned it. We hear about Maxwell's a lot."

"Speaking of Maxwell's," Julia said, "how are your fitness levels? Maggie, Susan, and I thought we'd hit the stage for old time's sake. I know you're fitter than you have been since you've been doing the routines for exercise. Do you want to join us?"

Aidan and Gabriel halted and turned to stare at Julia and Christina.

"I'd enjoy seeing that," Gabriel murmured, his brown eyes on her.

"Seconded," Aidan said.

"I'm out of practice. I'll probably flash my boobs," Christina protested.

"We have a rehearsal tomorrow morning." Julia's smugness aroused Christina's suspicions.

"It was you who suggested I get fit by doing the routines."

"Method in my madness. We're doing the dance of the Susans," Julia told Gabriel and Aidan. "It's a Maxwell's favorite. The minute the music starts, the regulars yell, which one is Susan? These days, I don't even have to organize people to shout from the audience."

"She'll do it," Gabriel said. "We want to share this part of your life, babe."

Aidan nodded. "Please, love. We've shared everything with you."

"But none of it involved taking off your clothes," Christina said.

"You'll do it?" Julia asked.

"I suppose," Christina said grudgingly.

"Excellent." Julia flapped her hands at Gabriel and Aidan. "Go and pry Ryan free from his studio."

Once the men left, Julia grasped both of Christina's hands. "You're glowing. You've put on the weight you've lost, and you look amazing." Her eyes widened. "You have a tattoo." She held up Christina's left hand to study her wrist. "It looks like a Celtic knot. What does it mean?"

"It's a triquetra," Christina said. "It's a symbol for three. Our relationship isn't a normal one, and we can't marry legally. Instead of rings, we decided to get the same tattoo. It has meaning for us. Commitment."

"You're happy?"

"Julia, I've never been so happy. By pure luck, I've found my niche in marketing. I love working with small businesses on Waiheke. I've helped Aidan with his restaurant, Gabriel with his cheese, and I'm working with several of the vineyards now. The work is varied, and I was thinking I might try a school holiday program for teenage girls with makeup and clothes to keep my hand in."

"You could bring them over for a shopping day. You still have your contacts here, right? I'd be willing to help," Julia said.

"We're here!" Ryan shouted.

Thumps and shouts sounded from the hallway.

"Where are our women?" Ryan yelled.

Julia rolled her eyes. "The man thinks he's funny. Grab that tray of glasses, will you? I'll bring the champagne." She opened the fridge and pulled out two bottles.

When they entered the lounge, it was full of laughter and teasing. Gabriel was introducing Ryan and the others to his grandparents. Julia's two children were playing, supervised by their nanny.

A massive, live pine sat in the corner, decorated with baubles of many colors. Some decorations were homemade while others were store-bought. Colored lights flashed on and off, and dozens of presents surrounded the tree's pot. Christmas cards covered the mantle.

A black leather couch sat at a right angle to two matching two-seaters. All were arranged to take advantage of the view of manicured lawn and gardens and the city and the harbor beyond. A vase of apricot roses lent a faintly floral scent that married with the pine. To the right, Christina glimpsed the dining room, the large table set ready for lunch with gleaming crystal glasses, plates, and silverware. Bright red Christmas crackers lay across the plates.

"Sweetheart."

The familiar voice had Christina spinning around. "Caleb!"

He wrapped his arms around her in a tight embrace. "I like your men, sweetheart, but I thought you were waiting for me."

She patted his cheek and smiled. "I fell in love."

"They treat you well?"

"They do," she whispered.

"I can see that," he said. "You're sparkling with happiness."

"You?"

"Been too busy," Caleb said. "We have an eight-stop

tour starting early in the New Year."

"I thought you'd agreed to stop touring."

"We talked about it and decided we'd do a short one. Julia and the kids are joining us for a few of the stops. You guys should come too. Maybe Sydney?"

"I'd like that. I'll talk to Aidan and Gabriel."

"Talk about what?" Gabriel murmured, carefully extracting her from Caleb's arms.

Aidan slotted into a gap on her other side.

"Caleb suggested we try to take a break and hit one of their upcoming concerts in Sydney. We could do a weekend, right?"

"You didn't tell us you knew the band members," Aidan said in faint accusation.

"Only our close friends know," Caleb said, grinning at Christina in a way that informed he was amused at Gabriel and Aidan and their possessiveness. "You're in the club now."

"Where else are you touring?" Gabriel asked.

"London. New York. Berlin. Los Angeles. I can get you a list. Edinburgh, too, I think."

"Maybe it's time to look into hiring a full-time employee," Aidan said to Gabriel.

Gabriel nodded. "I was thinking that."

"My younger brother is looking for a new job," Caleb said. "He's working in the Hawkes Bay area at present, but he wants a change. He's young, but he's responsible. I could give you his phone number if you're interested."

"Actually, that might work. My grandparents still have a farm. They raise beef cattle. I milk cows and goats and make cheese. Accommodations would be with my grandparents. Do you think he'd be tempted?"

"From what John told me yesterday, yes."

"Gabriel?" Aidan asked.

"I was thinking if we can sort out a reliable worker, we might swing two weeks in Edinburgh. We could visit your family," Gabriel said. "Perhaps take in a *French Letter's* concert."

"Really?" Christina squeaked. While she'd been to Australia and several of the Pacific Islands for holidays, she'd never traveled to Europe.

"Seriously?" Aidan asked, sounding equally stunned.

Gabriel grinned. "We work hard. We deserve a treat now and then."

Christina glanced at Aidan, and almost as one, they threw themselves at Gabriel. They embraced in a tight huddle.

"Christina?" a feminine voice said.

Christina pulled back enough to see more friends had arrived. "Maggie! Susan! Connor!"

With much chatter and laughter, the new arrivals mingled with those who'd been there for a while. Christina introduced her friends to Gran and Grandpa.

"Quiet, everyone," Julia shouted. "I'm passing around

the champagne and glasses. It's time for a Christmas toast."

Ryan and Caleb acted as waiters, dispersing glasses of champagne.

"Does everyone have a glass?" Julia asked. "Right, before I make the Christmas toast, I want to welcome Gabriel and Aidan to our extended family, and of course Beth and James. I have never seen Christina look so happy and healthy, and it's thanks to you."

"They know our secret now," Ryan said. "They're stuck with us."

Christina squeezed between Gabriel and Aidan, so happy she could burst. Their arms came around her, and she beamed with delight.

"To Christina, Gabriel, and Aidan," Connor said firmly, his approval shining in his eyes.

Maggie offered her a thumbs-up and raised her glass while Susan and Tyler both did the same.

Tears filled Christina's eyes, but they were happy ones. She missed Bernice and the *click-click* of Toby's claws on the wooden floors. While working in the cottage, which she'd set up as her office, she thought of them often. Because of Bernice, she'd found her happy place.

Although she had two more months to go of her six-month trial, Henry Wainscoat had told her only yesterday, that as far as he was concerned, she'd aced Bernice's requirement to integrate into the Waiheke community activities.

"To Bernice," she whispered, but Gabriel and Aidan heard and understood what she meant, as they so often did.

"To Bernice," Aidan whispered back.

"To Bernice," Gabriel repeated.

"Merry Christmas, everyone!" Julia shouted.

"Merry Christmas," Christina repeated the toast. With her men at her side, she had everything she wanted. She had friends. Family.

She had everything her heart desired.

26

EXTENDED EPILOGUE HAPPINESS

SIX MONTHS LATER

"I'VE BEEN THINKING," CHRISTINA said as she stacked the last of the dinner plates into the dishwasher.

"What?" Aidan asked, his attention on the paper planner spread open before him.

Gabriel smiled, the corners of his eyes crinkling. "What, babe?"

"We should have a commitment ceremony. I'd like to wear a fancy dress and invite our friends and families to see us promise each other we're all-in with this relationship. A party."

Gabriel's smile faded. "Is this because you overheard those women gossiping and talking trash about you at the book club meeting?"

"No, I told you I laughed at them and informed those women they had no idea what they were missing. I mean, two are divorced. One had been married three times. Bottom line, they're jealous of my adept handling of two men." Christina hugged the real reason close. "I want a party and a commitment ceremony so I can wear a sexy dress and so our friends and families witness our determination and love. I'd like to wear a commitment ring."

Aidan glanced at Gabriel, and the two men communicated silently. "Aye, love. We could do that. When would you like to hold this celebration?"

"Next month," Christina said. "On the third of July at Richardson's vineyard."

Gabriel's eyes narrowed. "That's a little under three weeks. Does this have anything to do with the Richardsons going into the wedding venue business?"

"While it might have played into my thought processes, and Gerard was saying they'd like a practice run, the truth is I want everyone to understand we're committed to each other. I'd like to make it as formal as we can, and I've always dreamed of wearing a sexy wedding dress."

"Mum and Dad are talking about a visit," Aidan mused.

"Yes," Gabriel stated. "If we can make one of your dreams come true, we're doing it."

Christina's chest grew tight, but it was with happy

emotion. She crossed the kitchen floor to Gabriel and wrapped her arms around him. An instant later, the heat at her back told her Aidan had joined their huddle.

"Who do you want to invite?" Aidan asked, pulling back.

"Our families. Our friends. The people who are important to us," Christina said. "Let's make a list. I'll ring Gerard and ask him if we can book in, then we'll divvy up the list and make phone calls to invite everyone. Julia will help me with my dress, and I'll talk to Gerard about the food. Sorted."

"Who will commit us?" Aidan asked.

Gabriel grunted out a laugh while Christina giggled.

"You know what I mean," Aidan said, his lips twitching. "Who will conduct the ceremony?"

"Justine Wainscoat is a celebrant," Christina informed them. She and Justine had become close, cementing their friendship over torrid romances. "Justine will conduct the ceremony."

Gabriel studied Christina. "You've been thinking about this for a while."

"I had plenty of time to think when I caught the flu last month and had two days of puking," Christina said drily.

"It's a fantastic idea," Aidan said.

"I agree." Gabriel opened a drawer and pulled out a notepad. "Let's get our list done."

Commitment day

Christina had stayed at the cottage the previous evening, and Julia arrived on the early ferry to help Christina get ready.

"I've brought my makeup bag," Julia said after they unpacked Christina's car.

"Great. I was thinking—" Christina clapped a hand to her mouth and fled to the bathroom. After barfing up her breakfast, she washed her face and rinsed out her mouth. Sighing, she returned to the kitchen. During her absence, Julia had set out her makeup supplies.

"I recognize that dash," Julia said. "Are you pregnant?"

"Yes," Christina said.

"Wow! Congratulations. Are Gabriel and Aidan happy?"

"I intend to tell them tonight. They'll be beside themselves with excitement," Christina said, every part of her convinced of this fact.

Julia tilted her head. "I thought you were on the pill."

"Flu plus pill," Christina said, wrinkling her nose. "I'd hoped for more time. That's what we'd planned, but I'm excited. I've known for just over three weeks, which is how I came up with the idea of a commitment ceremony. I figured we should do it before I started showing. It was difficult keeping this secret, but I wanted to be certain."

"Christina, I'm so happy for you." Julia hugged her before stepping back. "Gabriel and Aidan have been good for you. You're glowing."

"Thanks. Shall we get started with the makeup? I promised my men I'd be on time."

"We can, but I have an idea," Julia said with an impish grin. "What do you think about this?"

RICHARDSON'S VINEYARD

"Your parents have sold their property," Gran said. "They're moving to Tauranga."

Gabriel stood with Aidan in the flower-and-ribbon bedecked pagoda. Guests milled around, chatting with each other while Caleb played background music on his guitar. Gabriel gaped at his grandmother, shocked by this turn of events. "Stacey?"

"Your mother told me Stacey and Darcy are moving to Australia. They want a fresh start and decided to pool their resources," Gran said.

"Mum talked to you?" Gabriel asked, his brows rising as he tried to get his head around this.

"Your parents came to see us. They apologized and gave me a letter to give to you."

"I'm not sure I want to read it," Gabriel confessed.

"Who says you have to read it now?" Aidan had been listening to the conversation. "Save it until you're ready."

"Aidan's right," Gran said. "Your parents told me it was an apology. I'll keep the letter safe until you ask for it. But one thing I can tell you is the mystery of Darcy's son is solved. You have a half-brother who is a year older than you. He's Logan's father. Your father tracked him down, and Christopher took a DNA test as did your father."

"An older brother? I'm not sure I want to meet him," Gabriel said. So much lousy history because of this mystery brother.

"According to your mother, he was shocked. Christopher told your father he remembered attending the party with a friend, but he'd drunk a lot, and the details were hazy," Gran said.

"Which is a piss poor excuse," Gabriel snapped.

Aidan squeezed Gabriel's arm. "Is he going to help Darcy and her son?"

"Your mother, who isn't happy at learning about Christopher, told me your father is arranging a meeting. It helps that your father didn't know either, but from what I understand, he's busy mending fences with your mother." Gran shook her head. "Whenever you're ready, come and get that letter."

"Thanks, Gran. I love you," Gabriel said.

Gran's face went soft. "James and I are proud of you, Gabriel. So proud. You've turned into a wonderful man, and we love you."

The background music changed to bridal music. The chatter ceased. The guests found their seats, and expectancy filled the air.

"I'm nervous," Aidan whispered as they shifted into position.

Gabriel tested his emotions. "Me too, but excited. I'll settle once I see our girl."

"Do you have the rings?"

Gabriel leaned closer and kissed Aidan's mouth. "I have the rings."

"Ready, boys?" Justine asked.

"Aye, we're ready," Aidan said.

"Turn around then, and check out your girl. She is stunning."

Gabriel spun with Aidan, his throat tightening as emotion grabbed him. The last six months had been magical and full of contentment and laughter. A few arguments and some excellent make-up sex. With Aidan and Christina at his side, each day was an adventure.

Now, Christina walked toward them, her brown curls loose around her shoulders, her golden bracelets jingling with every step. Her white dress was long, and patches of it sparkled. There was lace and sexy cleavage and a bunch of perfumed cream-and-pink-tinged roses.

She was gorgeous.

The music ceased once she stepped into the gap they'd

left between them. A wide grin spread across her face as she kissed first Aidan and then him before turning to Justine.

Justine beamed as she spoke about togetherness and commitment.

Gabriel handed over the rings at the appropriate time, every part of him full of certainty and love.

Justine smiled. "You may now claim your kisses."

"Wait," Christina murmured and turned toward Julia, who sat in the front row.

Mystified, Gabriel watched Julia pull two small parcels from her handbag. She stood and hustled over to Christina.

"What's happening?" Aidan whispered.

"No idea," Gabriel replied.

"Thanks," Christina said to Julia.

"Wait, let me get my camera," Julia said.

Christina nodded, and in seconds, Julia was back with her phone.

"I have a present for each of you." Beaming, Christina handed them each a small package. "Please open them now."

Gabriel exchanged a glance with Aidan, who seemed equally mystified. He opened his parcel and frowned at the tiny pink bootee. Aidan held up a blue one.

"What?" Gabriel began then his brain clicked into gear. He gawked at Christina.

"We're pregnant," she whispered.

"Pregnant?" Aidan gripped Gabriel's arm.

"Pregnant," Gabriel said in a louder voice. "How?"

"If you don't know how, boy, you need to read some of Beth's romance books," his grandfather declared from behind them.

Laughter ensued.

"We're gonna have a baby," Aidan said.

"Yep," Christina agreed. "Isn't that something?"

"Yes," Gabriel whispered.

He wrapped one arm around Christina and the other around Aidan and the kissing began. Cheers rang out. Applause. Gabriel clutched the baby bootee in his hand, his heart full to bursting. His father had accused him of being a maverick, and maybe he was, but he'd found his posse—his fellow mavericks—and they had built a solid foundation for happy-ever-after.

He loved and was loved, and stepping out to his own beat was the best thing he'd ever done.

Thank you for reading **Maverick Lovers**. Did you enjoy Christina's story? I'd love to learn what you thought so please consider leaving a review at your favorite online bookstore, Goodreads, or Bookbub. A review would make my day!

Christina, my heroine, suffers from depression.

Depression can be caused by the past or a change in your life circumstances. Christina sought help online and with her family doctor. In New Zealand, one great online resource is https://depression.org.nz/. This is an excellent starting point, and the place where Christina found her helpful journal. If you live elsewhere in the world, you'll probably find a similar resource in your own country. Don't be afraid to ask for help from medical professionals—the sooner, the better.

The next book in the *Friendship Chronicles* series is Sports Lovers

(www.shelleymunro.com/books/sports-lovers)

Check it out!